Valley of Dragons Book 3:

The Daughters of Scyth
Fanny Garstang

To my daughter, may she grow up as strong and independent minded as the Daughters of Scyth.

One

The population of the walled town of Linyee, heard the roars first and dread filled many of their hearts. Linyee was a town that had survived every hiccup that Keytel had ever had. It still had the scars from when Titan's mercenaries had attacked. It could be described as the capital of Keytel due to the presence of their Nejus but it wasn't a sprawling city. It happily lived within the confines of its double walls apart from on market days. The walled town covered a large rocky outcrop that had been added to with layers of human habitation, in an otherwise flat plain surrounded by farmland and little farmsteads.

The fortress itself was a large square keep on one side of a walled courtyard. The crenelated wall had two large towers on it, one of which had been converted previously for dragons to nest and now the other had as well as Joli and Ozi didn't always get along. They had a tempestuous relationship. Ozi had absorbed and magnified some of her Nejus' pain and anger and had become, at times, a quite vicious dragon with scars from the fights she had gotten into. Few dared approach her apart from Diego and Ozanus.

Though they liked the fact their Nejus had re-occupied the fortress they didn't like the others who lived with him as unruly mercenaries. Though there were some older Suwars who held on to their honour the younger ones could be unruly with no Kittal to tame them. They missed their old Nejus, Ozanus' father, for it had been a time of peace for Keytel but not now.

As the dragons were spotted the citizens of Linyee hid their sons and daughters, and brothers and sisters indoors, out of sight. The younger undisciplined Suwars tended to start fights in the taverns when they ventured out from the fortress and occasionally violated some of the women whether willing or not.

Thankfully they were quiet on their return, tired from the two-day journey back and Diego tended to be a cause for sobering heightened emotions as well. They slipped off their dragons and removed saddles. Only two dragons remained at the fortress nesting in an adapted tower; Ozi, a dirty red scaled dragon with her front claws on her wings, and Joli, a throwback to a seacliff dragon with a sea green blue colouring. The rest had to return to the Valley where they nested on the cliffs outside like outcasts trying to stay close to home.

A few hours later they had recovered, and their mood was once again jubilant. They sat on the two long tables in the hall laughing and joking as they were served dinner of stew, roasted meat, bread and cheese. To accompany it there were plenty of jugs of small beer. They occasionally glanced across at their young Nejus as normally he joined them but tonight, he was more likely to snap their heads off if they approached.

Ozanus sat apart from his men, his short golden brown hair damp from a wash, staring moodily through brown eyes into the fire. His hands gripped the carved arms of the wooden chair. They had just come back from acting as deterrents for some cross border raiders in the next country over to the southwest of Keytel. It had been another successful job, but he didn't feel fulfilled like he use to. Even after all these years he still felt angry with the world and it didn't help that Diego had given him a message from Ioan when he had got back demanding he return to the Valley as soon as possible. He considered ignoring it but knew Diego wouldn't let him.

He didn't want to go to the Valley as it held too many bad memories. It was there that as a six-year-old he had watched his mother get eaten by a God and where the father, he had adored, had killed himself rather than live without his wife. Canaan and Tania had brought the four of them up a long with their own daughter but as soon as he was old enough he had left with his father's armour and weapons.

He'd rather have been further away than Linyee but his dead uncle's castle above the River Nytel felt haunted by its past and he hadn't liked the atmosphere. His great uncle's in Keytelia hadn't attracted him either. It was a pleasure palace falling into ruin where the last two concubines clung desperately to their lost youth in four habitable rooms. Nature from the untended gardens was already starting to reclaim it. Before long the women would die and their bodies likely eaten by scavengers while the city continued to thrive around the palace, oblivious to the abandoned people inside.

That had left him with the fortress of Linyee. Once there he had created a band of Suwars with him as their leader who hired themselves out as mercenaries using the honed fighting skills he had learnt and inherited from Da'ud and his father. He may be Nejus by title but Ioan was it in everything else, and was better at it then Ozanus would ever be. He always laughed bitterly when he remembered the prophecy revealed by the Dragon Lord at Ioan's naming. Ioan certainly did support him.

With a growl of frustration he threw his empty beaker into the fire where the screwed up message already smouldered and stood up. Silence descended on the thirty men and five women at the tables. His second in command, a veteran of the group who was warily respected by the others, cautiously asked, "are you alright?"

Ozanus looked at the older man who was a few years younger than Diego. He had poxed skin and a talent for getting out of scraps uninjured. He replied, "I'm going to bed. Tomorrow we go to the Valley."

"You sure?"

"Are you questioning me?" Ozanus snarled, hand on his father's dragon headed knife which had his parents' blood engrained into the wood grain.

The man threw his hands up in defence, "no."

"Good." Ozanus stalked out of the dining hall and slowly conversations started back up.

Sat in his own corner Diego, away from the rest, watched the scene with his normal observant quietness. He had once been like them but then he had gained responsibilities. He had found himself taking over Ozanus' training when Da'ud couldn't cope with the adolescent's unpredictable rage. He had followed his Nejus wherever the young man went, watching over him like his father would have wanted.

He hadn't escaped unscathed in that time. One hand had lost two fingers, thankfully not the ones needed to pull back a bowstring. His own brown hair was turning grey but his brown eyes were still alert and had become more scrutinising. His round face had become more gaunt from the new stresses of life. Age had also begun to affect his limp again and there were times when it ached. He now spent most of his time in Linyee acting as the go between for Ioan and Ozanus. He dealt with most of the communications without Ozanus ever realising. He only went out if it was a big job or Kenene wouldn't be enough to keep the pack disciplined.

He frowned to himself as he saw Ozanus march from the hall. Recently Ozanus had started to become distracted and Ioan's message hadn't helped his mood. It hadn't been one that he could keep away from Ozanus. There was trouble brewing on a distant border of Keytel.

He hoped that the change in Ozanus might mean he was finally ready to take on the full responsibilities of being Nejus. Then his mercenaries could be disbanded and the unruly ones brought back under control by the main dragon knight force.

There was a part of Diego that wanted to permanently return to the Valley. He would love a wife and have some children before he died since the fortress was no place for a family. He missed the loving happy family atmosphere that there use to be before the deaths of Lulizan and Kittal. It had been tense for a few years after their deaths while Canaan, Harim and Ifor grappled with looking after Keytel, Jukirla and ensuring five young children all reached adulthood without too many traumas.

One of the few maids in the fortress hurried through the keep to warn Salli that Ozanus was heading to his rooms. She had heard he was in an odd mood and hoped that Salli might cheer him up to ensure the atmosphere in the fortress didn't get too tense.

Salli had been rescued from a slave train which Ozanus and his men had attacked on their way back from one of their paid jobs. They hadn't planned to attack but they were all still high on adrenalin and with a blood lust that was still up. He had lost control of his men as they urged their dragons down on the four heavily guarded wagons filled with chained men, women and children. It hadn't taken long for the guards to die as they were ill-

8

prepared to deal with arrow firing Suwars.

Neither Kenene nor Ozanus had been able to stop the group of Suwars gathering the women together and arguing over who they would have. Finally Ozanus had been able to get their attention as they started to split the women up. Sword in hand he had shouted, "enough!" They all stopped. The tone of voice was enough to warn them off doing anything more until he let them. They knew to obey that tone. Kenene was the only one to recognise the tone as Kittal's. Sternly Ozanus said, "we are not brutes. We have saved them and that is enough."
The women remained tense but some took a few cautious steps backwards ready to flee like the men and children had already done. He turned to them, "go. I can't stop them forever."
The women ran.

Only one had remained, standing tall in her ripped dress, chin up, daring them. Her dark brown hair hung lank down her back and under the dirt was smooth mulatto skin. Ozanus had smirked, "not afraid?"
"No."
"Do I get thanks then?"
"Why? Your men were about to rape the best looking of us." She glared at him.
The smirk became a smile, he liked her boldness, "why have you not gone with the rest of them then?"
She shrugged.
"You're coming with me then." He grabbed her and dragged her to Ozi.

It wasn't the best start to a relationship but it was a relationship that had grown on them over two years but was now on the decline though neither of them would admit it. She had nowhere else to go and no money to be able to look after herself. He had never been one to bestow many gifts on her. He probably wouldn't let her go as she was the only one who could distract him from his angry thoughts most of the time. Sometimes he was gentle and loving during their lovemaking, other times he was rough, almost brutal, before sending her on her way. It was like there was a fight between two different versions of himself happening within him.

She got to his rooms with a few minutes to spare. She lay on the large bed ready for him. She sat up and smiled as he entered the room. It faltered as she realised he wasn't in the mood for pleasantries. She shifted to the edge of the bed and quietly suggested, "I can go."

"Stay." He growled as he crossed the bedroom. She stayed where she was, trying not to shake. The expression on his face looked as dark as the mood he was in.

He twisted her over on to her front and lifted her skirt out of the way. He stuck two fingers inside her and roughly rubbed at her. She squealed in surprise then covered her mouth to stop herself from making any more noise as he unbuttoned his trousers. His fingers came out wet and he replaced them with his erection.

She allowed herself to release her breath as he came with a groan. He stood, pressed against her buttocks for a moment before withdrawing. He slapped her bare bum, his signet ring stinging her skin and leaving a red mark, "get lost."

She rolled over, slipped off the bed and adjusted herself before scurrying out of the room and to her own bedroom to nurse her pride.

As for Ozanus he wiped himself clean with a folded cloth beside the large bowl of water left from cleaning himself earlier. He stripped off his clothes before climbing into his bed feeling neither satisfied nor calm. He hadn't had any desire for sex but as she had come he thought it might as well use her and hope it might distract him away from his mood. Ioan irritated him so much, more than it should do.

A few hours later he sat up, sweating and gasping, trying to shake off the nightmare that had never quite gone away. The image of himself hitting the Thunder God with a wooden sword while the dark purple dragon devoured his parents slowly faded. He swung his legs out of bed and sat on the edge of it with his head in his hands as he tried to calm his rapidly beating heart.

Reluctant to go back to sleep he pulled on his bed robe and wandered through to his antechamber where there was a jug of small beer. With beaker in hand he crossed to where his father's armour and weapons lay on racks on display with pride. On his free hand he twisted the signet ring on his ring finger. He had found it in his father's belongings but couldn't recall him ever wearing it. However, it felt right when he first put it on and so he had continued to wear it and play with it as a distraction ever since. Though he often thought of them as his father's he used them all. He ran his hands over the sword and bow and tears silently fell.

Even though his memories of his father had faded with time he still missed him. None of the men that had looked after him had matched up to the six year old's idolisation of a father. The sorrow had turned to anger quickly enough, why had his father abandoned him? How dare he love his mother more? Damn the Gods!

That was why he would never be able to measure up against his father or marry. He didn't want to love someone so much that he would die for them. He had no faith in the Gods considering they had allowed his parents to be taken away from him. And damn Ioan who had an unwavering belief in them and felt he could make demands on his older brother.

Before he lost his temper and broke something he would regret he downed the beer and retreated back to bed. He would need his strength to deal with Ioan and his silly demands though he knew it was a serious reason since Diego had told him about it. He knew that Diego dealt with a lot of the correspondence that never reached him and was grateful though he never showed it.

Returning to bed he shrugged off his robe making it look like the large dragon tattoo outlined on his back was flapping its wings. He may dislike the Gods but he had huge respect for the dragons. Without them he would be no one. The fact they could turn on every man, woman and child but chose not to. They were better at controlling their violent urges than he was and that was why he went through the pain of the tattoo.

Two

    The sky was clear as Diego and Ozanus, on their dragons, flew over the green plains. A few Suwars flew a respectful distance behind them led by Kenene. They were all in padded coats and head scarves that matched the colouring of their dragons that they had all ridden since childhood. The padded silk coats were tight chested with a knee length gathered skirt attached at the waist. The sleeves were loose to the elbow and then became skin tight so that they could use their bows. Kenene tended to have a leather strap wrapped round the looser part of his left sleeve where he pulled the string back. Trousers were tucked into boots.

    Ahead of them the grey cliffs of the Valley of Dragons rose up on the outside of the huge crater that was like a scar on the land stretching out for several miles. Inside the ground level was lower creating higher cliffs. They flew over the dragon statues that guarded the entrance to the Valley for anyone travelling by foot, horse or cart. They towered above anyone passing through, one claw resting on an egg. Only one of them was complete, the other had lost its snarling head long ago.

    They circled his childhood home where Ioan lived with their two sisters and cousin, before descending on to the lawn. It hadn't changed much from its rebuilding by Kittal apart from a climbing rose taking over a quarter of the roof. The veranda still surrounded the two storey building with its dragon ridge tiles. Within the wild gardens the pavilion was still used, claimed by Lylya.

Ioan had been alerted to their arrival and stood on the veranda, hands clasped behind his back looking solemn dressed in a shirt with an embroidered collar and a sleeveless robe over trousers and currently bare feet. He may only just be in his twenties but he acted older. Currently he frowned disapprovingly at his older brother. He didn't like how his brother ran from life. He felt that Ozanus should give up the title completely and let himself be Nejus but Ozanus stoically would not give it up. Ioan felt sure he would make a better one. There were times in the middle of the night when everyone else was asleep and he would pull on their father's red robe embroidered with its spiralling gold dragon and pretended he was Nejus and not his brother's support.

Ozanus approached the house and stiffly acknowledged his black-haired brother, "frowning does not suit you brother."

"What else can I do when you aren't behaving like a Nejus should?" Ioan retorted and narrowed grey eyes that he had inherited from their father. There was no love loss between them. They got on under a mutual agreement. Ozanus scowled and demanded, "what do you want anyway?"

They were interrupted then as Lylya ran barefoot out of the house in a long flounced skirt and a loose collarless blouse with embroidered edging. She flung herself at her brother and gleefully announced, "Ozanus."

His face softened as he hugged his dark brown-haired sister, "it's good to see you."

"You don't come often enough." She pouted at him but held tight to his hand as she stepped back.

After their parents' death they had grown close as

14

the only two old enough to understand what had happened and to remember. She relied on him to tell her what he remembered of their parents. Shuang had had nightmares for a few weeks but they had passed as she cleaved to Tania as her surrogate mother.

He pulled his hand free, "I've got to talk to Ioan."

"Oh." She was disappointed. She had hoped it was a rare social call.

"Maybe before I go back to Linyee." He suggested with a tight smile.

"Promise?"

"Promise." He left her standing on the lawn and joined Ioan on the veranda and demanded, "what do you want?"

"Come with me." Ioan beckoned him into the study which had been re-arranged by Ioan when he had taken it over. A large table dominated the room with paperwork piled up at one end while a large map covered most of the surface. Gaerwn, Ifor's son and now leader of the Suwars was studying it and the oldest of the three men and a distant cousin of the brothers. He was a broad chested man dressed in the clothes of an off duty knight, tunic trousers and knife tucked into his belt. He was tugging at his brown beard as he studied the spot on the map marked with a chess piece.

He briefly looked up and acknowledged Ozanus and Diego with a nod.

"What's going on?" Ozanus asked, becoming concerned. He stopped at the table and stood opposite Gaerwn. He looked down at the map where Keytel was placed in the centre of it. Small pebbles with blue, black or red dots marked where various groups of Suwars were on the borders. The plains of Keytel were in front of him. At the top was Gloabtona, their mother's home country which curved round to meet Keytel close to the coast. Separating the majority of Gloabtona from Keytel was the high plains of Moronland. Between Moronland and themselves were the lower mountains, a no man's land of wilderness where the borders didn't really exist.

A blue line cut through them, a river linking Keytel to the high plains of Northeast Moronland. The river had its own natural defences with several cataracts before travelling through Keytel and meeting the sea east of Senspanta. The egg-shaped pawn was on the river where it dropped down through the mountains close to the trading town of Drukgang that like Senspanta paid taxes to Keytel but otherwise ran themselves.

Ozanus asked again, "what is going on? Why am I here?"

Gaerwn answered, "Temijin is testing our border again. Thankfully we get plenty of warning since they have to cross the mountains. He has complete control of Moronland now. We need your help." Even though his Suwars were doing a good job of protecting the borders it was no longer enough. His Suwars were tired and many of them were young and inexperienced.

"What do you want from me?"

Gaerwn and Ioan glanced at each other before Ioan answered, "we need you to lead all of the Suwars and an army. He's coming with an army."

"Why have you not told me of this earlier?" Ozanus turned to Diego.

"I haven't been made aware of it." Diego glared at Ioan and Gaerwn who shifted uncomfortably under the gaze of the oldest man there.

"We thought we could handle it." Ioan admitted while playing with the edge of the map.

Diego rolled his eyes; he was probably the most experienced person in the room for dealing with full on warfare. This was a new era for Keytel after years of strong leadership and it wasn't looking good so far. It had been a long time since an army had attacked the country. He briefly clenched his fists, damn Kittal for his moment of weakness and leaving his sons ill prepared for leadership.

"We'll help." Diego said firmly.

Ozanus opened his mouth to protest but closed it when Diego gave him a warning look. He nodded, "fine."

"I'm taking control of this now." Diego announced.

The three young men looked grateful and relieved that someone else was taking charge.

"I need everything you have on them, men, weapons, more on this Temijin and where they are and when they are expected." Diego demanded, "how many have we got? How quickly can we get everyone back? How many trained soldiers have we got?"

Ioan and Gaerwn hesitated.

"Well?"

"I'll get the information." Gaerwn finally responded and pulled out scribbled notes from halfway down one pile of papers. He read from the list, "we have three hundred Suwars scattered around our borders and twenty more in Jukirla. The rest are split between here and their camp in the highlands plus there is your forty."

"And what are we up against?" Ozanus asked, starting to take some control of the situation himself.

"Ten thousand more or less from reports we've had." Ioan answered.

"Is that rumour, speculation or truth?" Diego asked sternly.

"Don't know."

"Well we need to find out, send someone over there and do a count."

"What are they armed with?" Ozanus asked.

"Rumour is scale piercing arrows."

Diego was frowning to himself and added to the questions being asked, "why is he wanting to attack us?"

"The dragons as far as I know or to show us his power?

We don't know as we don't have many contacts up there. There were a few people trading with them from out of Drukgang but that stopped suddenly." A new voice entered the conversation. Rafferty, Kittal's old secretary and now Ioan's was still going strong though looking old now. He looked tired but was relieved to see Diego, as a man of experience, present. They acknowledged each other with a nod.

"Do we have any trained soldiers?"

"None. We have never needed any. The Suwars and dragons have normally been enough."

Diego didn't know how to react but Rafferty was right. The Suwars, especially under Kittal, Ciara and Ifor, had always been enough but not now. "Right, we need to get as many men who can handle a weapon together then, as quickly as possible."

"I'll send Suwars out in the morning to every town." Gaerwn said.

"I'll get Kenene to bring the rest of my Suwars here." Ozanus also said.

"We'll need everyone to go here." Diego pointed at a bend in the River Nytel where it passed round the cliff top where Titan's old residence stood. He remembered Titan's army being encamped there though it hadn't been large, not as large as what they wanted to gather now.

"Are you sure?" Ozanus asked.

Diego took a deep breath, "I know its history but it's the best place to put a large number of people. Now, what can you tell us about this Temijin?" He turned to Rafferty who seemed to know the most for the moment.

"His grandfather started off as leader of one of Moronland's towns, Duntorn, named for the twin towers in it, I believe. He then started attacking neighbouring towns and taking control. Temijin has been consolidating that power for a few years now. Now he feels confident enough to take us on. He has been testing routes and our strength over the last year. The cataracts are no longer a natural defence." Rafferty answered confidently, "the first we knew that he was actually over was when Drukgang was attacked and held by him. He's going to use it as base to venture further into Keytel."

"Hang on." Ozanus stared at Rafferty, "Drukgang is lost? That is ours."

"Yes."

Ozanus turned on Ioan, "and we have done nothing to stop him?" He was well aware of the money that flowed through the town, filling the coffers of Keytel.

Ioan shrank back without realising, "they haven't asked for help."

"That is still our town." Ozanus turned back to the secretary, "how long before he gets on to the plains?"

"About seven days I think."

"Gaerwn, is it worth attacking the town? Distract him?"

Gaerwn was thoughtful for a moment, "I could try."

"Do it. We need the time to get ourselves prepared."

"Good. Can you support supplies, food, tents, weapons?"

"Sure."

"We can include it in the recruiting message." Ioan added.

It turned into a busy few days but Ozanus still made time for his two sisters, especially Lylya. He enjoyed the organising, something he could do, working with Diego, Gaerwn and Rafferty, until Lylya drew him away to their mother's pavilion.

Settling on the cushions she smiled, "I'm glad you are staying for a few days."

"Only because I have to. Temijin from Moronland has got an army heading our way." He answered stiffly.

"Oh. Is the valley safe?" She asked with concern, the

19

smile dropping.

He pulled her close, "you've got me and I'll make sure you aren't harmed. They are far from here so the Valley is safe and I won't let them reach here."

She smiled again, reassured.

That night was the last night before they headed out. They got together as a family for dinner though looking at them they didn't look like a family. There was a clear divide with Ozanus and Lylya on one side and Ioan flanked by Shuang and Bejou on the other. Conversation was stiff between them all and it was with relief that Ozanus retreated to the bedroom he was sharing with Diego.

It wasn't an easy night. He tossed and turned. This was the worst situation he had ever been in. He wasn't going to admit it to anyone but he was scared, really scared. He would be showing the country whether he was truly his father's son or not. He must have fallen asleep for he found himself dreaming or remembering a long buried memory.

He was four, five or six, studying the scars on his father's hand and wrist. Kittal was smiling down at him as he looked up into his face and asked, "does your hand hurt?"

"At first it does."

"How do you do it?"

"I cut it with my knife to offer my blood to the Gods."

"Why?"

"Because it is them that bestow success on us and bless our ventures."

"Can I do it now?"

His father had chuckled and then become serious, "the first time you'll do it is when you become a Suwar and that's when you earn a knife like mine."

Ozanus sat up and knew what he needed to do but how. He looked over to the other bed where Diego snored and knew the older man would be of no help. He got out of bed and pulled on his shirt and trousers and headed down to the study by the light of the moon. He lit a lamp and began scouring the shelves. He knew there was a book in here somewhere with all the ceremonies. He remembered Canaan showing it to him.

He began to get desperate and began pulling books off the shelves. Giving up he ran to Ioan's room and pushed open the door revealing their parents old chamber with the bed still in the centre of the room with netting hanging around it. The wind chimes that used to move in the breezes had been removed. He demanded angrily, "where is it?"

Ioan sat up, startled, and his mistress pulled the blankets up to hide herself. Ioan retorted, "you can't barge in like this."

"Yes I can! Where is it? I need it."

"Where is what?" Ioan asked with a frown, "Ozanus, it's the middle of the night!"

"The book with all the ceremonies in it." Ozanus demanded, "and the robe." He moved into the room and started opening chests and peering at a shelf of books.

"Why do you want them? You've never shown any interest before."

"Where are they?" Ozanus demanded angrily, hand going to his waist where thankfully his knife wasn't there. He could feel himself shaking with rage and fear. If he didn't do this right then he couldn't prove to them all he was his father's son. He needed to know the Gods were on his side.

"Just give them to him before he murders us." Ioan's mistress whimpered, seeing Ozanus' murderous look in the low lamp light.

"He won't kill us." Ioan retorted.

"Are you sure?"

Though Ioan glared at his brother, daring him, there was still the briefest of hesitations in his answer, "I'm sure. I am his brother and he needs me."

He remembered a conversation between Tania and Canaan he had eavesdropped on. They had been remarking over the fact it was Ozanus who had absorbed the rage and sexual tension reverberating round the Valley at the time and not Ioan who as a newborn had yet to develop a personality. He could see it all now in Ozanus' expression and stance.

"Just give him what he wants Ioan." She exclaimed.

Ioan rolled his eyes but asked, "why do you want them?"

"None of your business." Ozanus pointed out sternly.

"Fine. They are both back in the study in the chest under the desk."

"Why are they there?"

"You've never cared before." Ioan retorted.

Ozanus ignored his brother and left the room. Ioan and his mistress released their held breaths.

He found the chest while fighting back tears of desperation. He pulled it from under the desk and paused. He ran his hands over the worn carvings and closed his eyes. He muttered, "please let this work."

He took a deep breath and opened the chest. There lay the book lying on top of the Nejus' red robe. He lifted out the book and then the robe. So often he had rejected wearing his father's robe apart from the ceremony where he had been recognised as a man and took on the full responsibilities of Nejus. He pressed the robe to his face and breathed in his father's scent though it was tinged with a new younger scent which he suspected was Ioan's.

He pulled on the robe and felt the weight of its history and responsibilities bow his shoulders. He straightened them and picked up the book and hoped he could remember the way to the Dragon Lord's shrine.

He found the shrine in the side of the cliff, hidden by vegetation that had grown around it since he had last visited with his father at the birth of his brother. The stone statue of the Dragon Lord rising out of red painted flames snarled out of its alcove. Before it on a pedestal was a shallow dish of water reflecting the moonlight through the hole in the roof of the cave. He knelt before the statue, the robe pooling around him. He placed the lantern beside him and bowed to the God three times before opening the book.

He found the page and realised he couldn't read it. He had only the picture to go by and realised he hadn't brought his knife with him.

"So you have decided to finally honour me?"
He froze and glanced around but couldn't see anyone.

"Are you finally accepting your responsibilities?"

"I seek your blessing." Ozanus called out.

"Prove it." A golden claw appeared out of thin air holding a short bladed knife. The claw twisted and the knife dropped on to the rocky floor before him.

Ozanus looked down at the knife and then at the statue. He drew in and then exhaled a deep breath to calm himself. He picked up the knife and pressed it against the palm of his hand where only the barest of scars remained from when he had become a Suwar. Tears welled up as he sliced into the skin and blood beaded up. He cupped his hand and allowed the blood to pool. Slowly he stood and allowed the blood to drip into the dish of water as he said,

"O Great Dragon Lord, bless this misguided Nejus. Give him the strength to protect his country and his family."
There was no answer.

He sank to the ground, hand clutched to his chest. He couldn't believe how much it hurt. He could only hope that he had done enough.

Diego woke in the morning and found Ozanus' bed

empty but his flight clothes and his knife were where he had dumped them on a chair the night before. Diego got dressed himself before heading downstairs, not particularly worried yet as he could either be out swimming or training with some of the others. Arno appeared round a corner and he asked the servant, "have you seen the Nejus?"

"N...N... No." Arno answered nervously. He had stayed in the Valley as Ioan's servant, preferring the mild mannered younger brother to his Nejus.

"Not even in the study?" Diego frowned.

"No." Arno answered more confidently.

"Where's Ioan?"

"In the study."

He made for the study and found Ioan and Rafferty talking next to the big table and asked, "have you seen Ozanus?"

"Not since he barrelled into my room last night making demands." Ioan responded stiffly and then added accusingly, "I thought you kept him under control."

"I have never been his keeper. Where is he Ioan?"

"He finally decided to play at being Nejus."
Diego's eyes widened, "and you didn't think to send someone to find him when he didn't re-appear?!"
Ioan shrugged.
Exasperated, Diego exclaimed, "you need to grow up. Your father would be disappointed in how you are behaving."

"He only cares for himself." Ioan retorted, "he doesn't think about what I have to do."

"Which is why you need to be the bigger brother. You have no memory of anything, you were only months old but he saw and he felt. And now he is expected to lead the biggest army this country has ever seen and show he is of his father's blood and protect our country, while you, as heir and with no combat experience, and no dragon, stay safely here." Diego angrily said.

"I wanted to be a Suwar, but the Gods denied me." Ioan

sulked.

"Not everyone gets to be a companion to a dragon." Diego softened slightly, "now, I'm going to find your brother so we can head out. Make sure there's food and a hot drink for when we get back, Rafferty."

"Will do." Rafferty said without looking at either man, but he knew what Diego had said was right and he hoped that the Gods had responded favourably to Ozanus' offering.

Diego headed out into the Valley. He went to the ruined temple first but found only a few Suwars seeking last minute blessings from the Gods. He didn't disturb them and headed back down to the Valley floor. He hoped he would be able to find the shrine to the Dragon Lord for that was the only other place he felt Ozanus would be.

It took him an hour walking along the edge of the cliff to find the cave as he had to negotiate around trees, shrubs and rock falls. He spotted red and gold in the sunlight and headed for it. He found Ozanus curled up in the Nejus' robe on the floor with his cut hand in a small pool of blood. He leant in from the rocky step and shook him, "come on Ozanus."

Ozanus stirred and sat up looking nervous, something Diego had rarely seen in the young man. Ozanus asked, "do you think it will have worked?"

"Let's get you back to the house." Diego said, not answering the question for he didn't know the answer. Ozanus had ignored the Gods for so long he didn't know if they would honour any offering he gave now.

"I dreamt of my father last night and I thought that if I gave the Gods an offering like he would have…." He turned red eyes to his mentor and companion and the one person he considered his only true friend in the whole world.

"This is a time when we need the arrogant Ozanus who

25

thinks nothing can defeat him. Come, lets show the country that they should have faith in you." Diego held out a hand and Ozanus took it as he added, "and we'll get that hand seen to." He gave the young man a tense smile.
Ozanus just nodded.

Three

It was a sight to be seen. Ozanus and Diego led the two hundred and fifty Suwars across Keytel, leaving only a handful guarding the Valley. Animals, both wild and domestic scattered as their shadows flew over them. Those herding animals or in the fields looked up to see the multicoloured collection of dragons, some with four limbs, others with the claws on their wings; loaded with saddlebags and their riders armed with bows slung over shoulders, quivers of arrows at their knee and throwing knives at their waists. All wore their leather imitation dragon scale breastplates, and some wore pauldrons, protection on their shoulders and upper arms. Wrist guards were wrapped round the narrow sleeves of their coats, so clothes didn't get caught on bow strings. Knee high boots protected their calves, and the saddles protected their thighs.

No one was sure how the battle would go since there had never been any need to recruit an army from the general population. They had watched the men head out, the younger ones eager and nervous in equal measure. Some hoped they would be talent spotted and given an opportunity to become a Suwar. Those not going sent prayers up to the Dragon Gods that their sons, fathers and brothers would come back alive.

Titan's castle, claimed by the dragons as their roost, came into view with a large encampment on the opposite bank of the river in the shadow of the cliff. Gaerwn had taken up residence in a large tent at the centre of the camp with the circular tents of the Suwars around his set up and ready for them to arrive and then the assorted tents of the quickly gathered infantry. Fires were scattered throughout the camp with men around some of them. The majority were being trained to use their improvised weapons. They were armed with old swords, even more ancient, hooked spears, spears and halberds. Then there were the farming implements of pitchforks and scythes. Away from them butts had been set up for archers to practice.

The army scattered as the two hundred and fifty Suwars came into land. A lot of them dropped to their knee as they realised their Nejus was with the group. Ozanus barely acknowledged them as he heaved his saddlebag on to his shoulder and marched towards the centre of the camp, Diego limping behind him. He scowled at anyone who got in the way. He was still frustrated with himself for revealing a weakness even though only Diego had seen it.

Sweeping into the tent he demanded, "where's Temijin's army currently?"

"I'm waiting for the scouts to get back." Gaerwn answered from where he stood by a table with a map of the local area open on it.

"I'm not going to wait. I'm going to find out for myself." Ozanus decided.

"But Nejus..."

As Ozanus walked out the tent Gaerwn turned to Diego for help. Diego just shrugged and headed out after Ozanus. He called back, "just make sure there is some decent food and drink and a comfortable bed for when we get back."

Diego caught up with Ozanus, "are you sure about

28

this?"

"Yes. Find Kenene and Somon." Ozanus ordered as he checked the straps on Ozi.

"Where are we going now?"

"To see what we are up against. You up for it?"

"Of course." Ozi grinned.

"No attacking them." Diego added with warning.

"We'll do what we want." Ozi challenged.

"Not this time." Joli snapped towards the other dragon.

"You can't boss me around, I'm more important than you." Ozi snapped back and lunged at the mottled blue dragon, knocking Ozanus over in her eagerness to fight. Joli bowed his head and knocked Ozi sideways. She staggered, not prepared for him to hit her with the full weight of his head. He growled, *"but I am the elder."* She growled at him but didn't retaliate.

"You don't have to come." Ozanus said stubbornly as he got back to his feet and saw Deigo keeping out of the way of the dragons squabbling.

"Just for once I am." Diego answered sternly, "this is too important."

"Suit yourself." Ozanus climbed back into his saddle. Diego rolled his eyes and let Joli help him get into the saddle, his injured leg protesting.

"I thought I told you to get Kenene and Somon." Ozanus remarked as Joli rose into the air a few minutes later.

"They've been sent for." Diego answered calmly.

Once in the air they travelled in silence, Ozanus sulking. Kenene and Somon caught them up but sensed the tension and stayed quiet.

Ahead of them was a settling dust cloud. The year had been quite dry so far and he should have been concerned about the developing drought as Nejus, but he thought 'let Ioan deal with it.'

29

Coloured banners could be seen through the dust. Sunlight glinted off chainmail and shields. The shouts of men, muted by the dust cloud, still carried upwards.

As the dust settled lower it revealed large wooden war engines attached to two rows of 4 harnessed oxen that were currently being unhitched. Around them tents were being erected. Kenene called out, "what are those?"

"I've heard of them but never thought I would see them. They must have put them together once they were over the mountains." Ozanus remarked half to himself. He knew that back when his father had taken Jukirla some Jukirlans had left in protest at him freeing the dragons. Clearly they had found a new home in Moronland. He was glad he wasn't going to be relying on just the Suwars.

"What do we do now? When do we attack?"

"Let them come to us." Diego answered.

"Should we attack now? I've got enough fire in my belly." Ozi remarked with excitement.

"No you haven't." Ozanus retorted, *"you are still too young."*

"No I'm not." Ozi sulked.

No one knew how or when a dragon would suddenly be able to breath fire. There were plenty of observations noted but no obvious dragon identified. The ability did come with age but not all could do it.

"Not tonight." Ozanus ordered sternly, *"it's time to head back. I've seen what I needed to see."* The war engines worried him a little as they were designed to fire huge unfurling nets into the air to trap and pull dragons down. Ozi grumbled but couldn't resist letting out a roar.

Below, men looked upwards fearfully. Compared to their homeland they knew the dragons in Keytel weren't just wild but had riders who were just as fierce as their reptilian beasts. They were disciplined as well. The oxen

30

bellowed a reply.

Standing beside them was a large man, broad shouldered, broad chested and dressed in chain mail and plate armour shoulder pads. Hanging from his belt was a large sword. On his head he wore a conical leather helmet decorated with dragons' teeth cut in half. He gazed upwards through steely grey eyes and smirked.

He was Temijin, son of an engineer who had fled Jukirla when Kittal took it over. From his father he had inherited the desire to capture and use dragons and also the need for revenge. He had started out as a bit of a lone warrior and a bully but soon he had had followers and they needed to be fed, watered, entertained and supplied. And entertained he did, with dragons they had caught in Moronland, in a large arena he had built outside Duntorn.

They had started taking on the local tribes and towns and over ten years he had taken over all of Moronland and consolidating his power from Duntorn. Now had come the time to take on Keytel as it was currently a weak country with a young leader who wasn't interested in ruling.

Back above the armies Kenene asked, as they flew away, "what do we do now? When do we attack?"

"Let them come to us." Diego answered.

Four

But they did not come. Just as the Suwars stood their ground so did Temijin with his army.
Communications were sent after a week of stalemate and a place to meet and fight was agreed. The two armies drew closer together so that one could see the smoke of the fires of the other.

It hadn't stopped Diego sending the youngest Suwars out to target practice on the enemy, picking off men one by one at random while staying safely high above the enemy. Some of the older Suwars flew over to see what was coming. Those who rode dragons who could breathe fire tried to burn the war engines but all they could do was scorch the thick wood.

It was a restless sleep for Ozanus. He had never felt so nervous. Not even when he was on ones of his paid jobs did he feel this nervous. It was the fact he wasn't responsible for just his men and their dragons anymore. Now resting on his shoulders were the lives of the men of Keytel as well as their families scattered across the country as well as nearly every suwar and their dragon. Then there was the visitation of a scarred black dragon in his dreams which he recognised from his father's book on the Gods.

What was the Dragon of death appearance suggesting? Did it mean he would be successful or would there be plenty of deaths to feed the God?

And now with the morning they were on a slight rise facing Temijin's army, behind which were the two huge, scorched war engines swarming with men. No one knew what was going to be thrown from them. In comparison to his well trained and organised army Keytel's looked a ragtag lot of half trained town guards, farmers and those who thought it was all a big adventure. Lined up behind the disordered lot was a double row of Suwars. The newest Suwars and dragons, for whom this was their first chance to prove themselves, shifted nervously on their claws and in their saddles.

Gathered around Ozanus and Diego, who stood in front of Ozi, were the newly appointed officers of Keytel's army staring wide eyed at both each other and their Nejus. None had ever thought they would find themselves in such close proximity to him or finding themselves leading a group of men into battle. Standing a short distance away from them were a selection of young men known to be fast runners ready to take any urgent messages to the hastily organised bands of men made up of groups from towns and villages that were neighbours. Though supposedly united there had still been scuffles amongst them as old animosities had reared their heads. Suwars had had to wade in and knock a few heads together.

Ozanus cleared his throat and looked around at the men before him and silently prayed that the Gods were on their side. The best had been done in the short time there had been but even he knew it wasn't enough. He pointed at a group of four men, "you four take your men to the right of Temijin's army. And you three," he turned to point at another group, "take yours left. Who's leading the archers?"

Two men made themselves known by raising their arms.

"Good, provide cover for them. Who's leading those who have the war engine mission?"

A bearded man dressed in chain mail, with broken links, stepped out of the group, his chest puffed up in pride though he knew his job was a suicidal mission, "it's an honour Nejus."

"Go now, but wait until the fighting begins before attacking and good luck."

"Thank you Nejus." The soldier dropped on to one knee and saluted with a fist to his chest and bowed his head to receive a blessing. Ozanus placed his hand briefly on the man's shoulder before turning to the largest group of men waiting for orders, "this is going to be a hard fight."

The Suwars glanced at each other as what was being said didn't sound particularly inspiring.

"But this is our land we are defending and our families and our lives and together we will defeat the enemy threatening us. We will not let down those waiting at home for our return."

Diego turned and glared at the Suwars and dragons who realised they needed to cheer and roar.

The roar and cheer thundered across the no man's land buoying some of the Keytel men and sending shivers down the spines of some of Temijin's. The army joined in, though they hadn't heard what Ozanus had said, bashing spears, swords and farm tools against leather and wooden shields, rising the noise level even higher as they began to take courage and jeered and tormented the army opposite.

Within Temijin's circle of officers the men turned to him. He gave them a nod. Messages spiralled outwards and soon his army were responding with their own shouts, catcalls and shield bashing. The front line turned as one, bent over and revealed pink, white and brown buttocks to

34

all.

Slowly a tense silence returned. No orders were shouted but suddenly there was movement on both sides. The two ends of the Keytel army split away and bows were raised. Arrows sprung into the air and fell like a hailstorm on the enemy. Men began to fall. The majority of both armies clashed in the middle as the Suwars rose into the air, led by Ozanus and Diego.

On the other side of the battlefield the two catapults were cranked back and four large, muscled men heaved in a balled up net edged with heavy weights. A rope draped over the edge of the cup and was tied to the ground in the middle of a large coil which would then be released once the net had opened out. With a shout the men stepped back apart from one. With a large mallet in strong hands the releaser stepped forward and with a great swing knocked out the large metal pin that held the catapult in tension. With creaks of protest and a wallop against the rope covered cross beam that shook the frame and the ground, the cup swung upwards and threw the net high into the air. The net opened up and like a yawning mouth of death headed for its first victim as already the war engine was once again being primed.

The grey dragon and its rider had no chance to escape the net. It clamped round the dragon's wide jaw and the momentum of the weights pulled the net over its wings and pulled them back. The suwar found herself lying along the length of the dragon's back, pinned at an angle that made her cry out and tears run down her cheeks from the pain. Dragon and rider plummeted to the ground like a stone, crushing men that didn't get out of the way fast enough. The ground shook and then there was an echo as another dragon and its knight also landed, dust rising up around it.

From where he stood Temijin, with a single fingered gesture of a raised hand, sent a group of men, covered in leather armour and armed with hooks and spears, running past him. He felt it a great pity that he couldn't take the reptilian giants home with him alive to use in his arena but it would be too dangerous, so the next best thing was to kill them. He would try for some of the younger smaller ones.

High above it all Ozanus watched through the eye slit of his head scarf in horror as his trapped Suwars were run through with the long-shafted pikes while others swarmed over the dragons peeling back scales with their hooks to stab the soft flesh underneath with long sharp spearheads. The dragons withered in pain and fought the nets and men but couldn't move and didn't once their eyes had rolled into the backs of their head, blood pouring from now gaping wounds.

Out of the corner of his eye he spotted a metallic flash of copper and turned but couldn't see anything. He heard a chuckle in his mind and eyes widened. He wondered if he was going to turn mad like his great grandfather.

And they were only the first two. More nets were sent flying into the air, spreading wide like when a fisherman throws his into the sea and hoped to catch something. Some found their intended targets while others now began to fall, trapping men who changed from enemies to allies as they cut their way out of the nets. The Suwars and dragons began to anticipate and fly out of the way or burn them before they became no more than a flapping helpless fish themselves.

With no need to shout to each other a group of the more experienced Suwars gathered together to take on one of the immense war machines. The men operating it scattered as the dragons, in pairs, flew down. One reached with its back legs for the large cross beam wrapped in rope as the other circled, grabbing the pin mallet as it was swung upwards in defence. The catapult creaked in protest but didn't move as the dragon released its grip.

The second pair flew in. One tried the cross beam again, pulling on it, stressing the wood and shredding the rope. The other circled, breathing fire and disabling the catapult in a ring of flames before they also flew off.

The last pair were small enough to act together. They both grabbed the cross beam and flew vertically upwards, their muscles straining until with a crack it came away from its joints and together they dropped it on the machine. A roar of approval came from the dragons.

Though the catapult looked broken it still managed to spew out one more net before crumpling in on itself. It managed to extract its revenge and take down one more dragon and its knight before being torched by the fiery breath of several dragons; and there was still its twin urgently disgorging its nets.

And now the six dragons and their riders turned to the second war engine where Keytellian men were fighting to reach it. Below them the fighting between men raged on. But even with the aid of the Suwars the army of Keytel were losing against the strong and more skilled men of Moronland. It didn't help that the Suwars were struggling to identify their own people from the enemy and so weren't getting as involved as they wanted to while dodging flying nets and scale piercing arrow heads. They didn't dare swoop down and grab several men at a time and drop them from a great height that some of the more malicious dragons, including Ozi, wanted to do.

Gradually the Keytel army was pushed back and then men began to creep away and then the one or two men became a flood and sat on Ozi's back with an empty quiver at his knee, Ozanus' heart sank. He had failed and now no one was going to take him seriously as Nejus. He had let everyone down including the Gods and Ioan would mock him. His gloved fists became even tighter in his anger and frustration. He felt the wound on his hand and wondered if he would have to open it again to appease the Gods. He growled at Ozi, *"we are going home. Let the others know."*

"I could take them all now." She responded with one hungry eye on the now celebrating Moronlandians, *"or we could make our men turn back round and fight."*

"No." He answered sternly, *"we go before it gets any worse."*

With reluctance she let out a cough as if she was clearing her throat. Those that were part of Ozanus' band of Suwars recognised the signal and turned to look at Ozi. With a jerk of her head she signalled to them that it was time to go.

They turned reluctantly away from the battlefield to follow Ozi and Ozanus. Diego, on Joli, caught up with Ozanus, frowning. Angrily he demanded, "what are you doing?"

"Going home."

"Home?! Seriously?!"

Sensing the agitation between the two men Joli snapped at Ozi. Ozi returned it and there would soon have been a full-on fight if both riders hadn't shouted, *"enough!"*

Joli and Ozi returned to being sullen, grimacing at each other, baring their teeth.

"This is your army and you can't leave them to fend for themselves." Diego pointed out sternly.

"Stay then if you must but we are going." Ozanus retorted without looking at Diego.

Diego glanced back and saw the rest of the Suwars looking confused. He wanted to go back but felt Ozanus was going to need him more and so reluctantly remained. He knew Gaerwn would soon take charge, but it still didn't look good for the survivors to see their Nejus flying away like a coward.

Their pride was in tatters and they were angry and dangerous because of that. Never had they failed. They took their anger out on the male servants, shouting and cursing at them. They in turn took it out on the nervous townsman who was sent up to get news. He got a snarl and the small door in the large gate was slammed in his face.

As for the women in Linyee Fortress, at hearing the angry shouts they had all fled to Salli's chamber, including the lowliest of the maids. If they weren't to be seen then no one would be harmed. There were only a few of them but they huddled together on Salli's bed listening and waiting for the fortress to fall silent.

The Suwars emptied the cellar of beer and wine to drown their sorrows and dented pride. They got drunk enough for fights to start amongst themselves and then they began to fall asleep. Only two didn't drink so heavily, Ozanus and Diego. Ozanus drank a few and then departed the hall. Diego sat in his quiet corner, undisturbed, nursing his tankard. He wondered what, if anything, he had done to lead Ozanus to abandoning his army. Was there anything he could have done differently to make Ozanus a better Nejus for Keytel? He silently sent up an apology to Kittal though he knew he had done the best he could.

All Ozanus wanted to do was wallow in self pity. He wanted to talk about it but knew that everyone, including Ozi, would say the same thing. They should have stayed. With the catapults in ruins they could have turned it around.

In that first hour of flying away he could have turned them all back but it soon became too late. He hadn't wanted to stay with defeat staring him in the face and Temijin laughing. He felt sure there was more he could have done if he had been warned earlier. Temijin's army could have been easily picked off in the mountains, especially with the two war machines slowing them down.

He hadn't been able to cope with an open arena where two armies stood face to face. He didn't know how he could face the dragon knight's chieftain, who would certainly be angry. He stared at the two mannequins in his room, wearing his father's old clothes, agitatedly twisting the signet ring round his finger. He didn't even want to think about what his father would have said if he had been alive.

Five

     Diego limped quietly through the corridors on his way up to the towers where Ozi and Joli perched in the red glow of dawn. A few maids slipped past him, now able to go about their work undisturbed. He looked in on the Suwars in the hall. They all still slept either sprawled on the floor or slumped against each other or across the tables. Cups and jugs lay on their sides with their contents dripping on the floor.

     They may have all been sleeping but he was heading to the Valley of Dragons for news. He wanted to know how many of his kin had survived though it was unlikely that would be known yet. A messenger would have reported back to Ioan and he needed to know what was said so he could then talk to Ozanus. A new plan was needed. They had to carry on fighting, Temijin could not be allowed to win. It was only one defeat and if the infantry had held out they would have won. Ozanus had given up too easily. He felt sure they could gather their make-shift army back together and try again.

     Once in the air with Joli he was tempted to head anywhere but the Valley. It was peaceful soaring through the cloudless sky on the back of a dragon with only birds for company. The pair flew in silence, each in their own thoughts. They wanted to speak their conflicting thoughts out loud but neither dared to. It felt like they were back when neither could communicate with the other all those years ago when Kittal had first introduced them to each other. That felt like a long time ago now.

It was with reluctance that Diego finally said with a heavy sigh, *"let's head to the Valley."*

"We aren't in a good place are we?"

"No." Diego sighed again. There was nothing he could do about it.

"What are we going to do?"

"We can't do anything. It is up to our Nejus to remember who he is and decide what he wants to do." Diego carefully said. He would be there if Ozanus wanted his help but for now the young man had to decide for himself what fate he wanted for Keytel and the dragons.

"Can you....?" Joli cautiously started.

"I have tried. We will take back any news but it us for the Nejus to decide." Diego answered firmly.

They fell silent again as the Valley emerged from the ground ahead of them, its cliffs rearing upwards. For a moment their hearts and souls soared in anticipation of returning home.

The Valley soon opened up below them, the land dropping down and forming the crate of the long extinct volcano which was now hidden by vegetation. One corner revealed the crater's ancient history where the hot water and mud pools bubbled and steamed, and young dragons splashed. At the centre was the Nejus' family home in a large expanse of lawn. Radaring out from the lawn were several paths. One led to the arena, another off into the valley which split to head towards the cliffs, and the last to the Suwars' camp of large yurts and stone surround campfires.

42

A few young dragons came up to meet them. They flew around their elder asking, *"did we win? Did they have any dragons?"*

"Later." Joli responded sternly.

"Pittaan wouldn't tell us anything either." The first, a slim brown dragon with growing horns, protested as he flew under the slower moving Joli.

Joli reached out to swipe him with a growl, but the young dragon quickly manoeuvred out of the way and with a laugh he and his friend headed back to the valley walls.

Joli circled once more before coming to land on the lawn. Diego slipped off his back and stretched aching limbs as he looked to the house, expecting someone to come out. No one did. He sighed with relief that no one was going to demand answers from him. He remembered a time when he preferred to be at the house but now if there were in the Valley for any length of time, which was rare, he preferred the village and his family. Once the house had been full of laughter and happiness when there had been Kittal and Lulizen and then with the children under the care of Canaan and Tania, but now it had a tense atmosphere.

With a deep breath he turned and headed to the Suwars semi-permanent camp to pass on his condolences to those who had lost loved ones. He hadn't got far when there was a shout from the house, "where do you think you are going?!"

Diego turned and saw a young knight standing on the veranda and said, "I've come for news."

"You don't deserve any since our Nejus abandoned us."

"You have no right to criticise your Nejus you little twerp." Diego marched towards the knight with a stern expression on his face. He knew the Suwars were a close-knit community of their own and they felt every loss keenly for it could take years to find the right dragon and then train them. The younger knight flinched but stood his ground.

43

Once Diego was before the knight he added, "we all knew what we were getting into. Now, are you going to tell me what you have told Ioan."

The young knight with fluff for a beard scowled but said, "most of us are protecting our retreat. A few of us are harassing the enemy."

"Which way are they going?"

"They were following us still. We are trying to rally what's left of the army to try and fight back." His eyes had widened revealing to Diego that this was the young knight's first taste of true violence. The young man gulped. Diego put a hand on the man's shoulder and gave it a squeeze as he softly said, "you're safe now."

"But…?" The youth gasped while trying to hold in a sob.

"I'm sorry if you have lost a friend but this is what you have been trained for." Diego answered solemnly and gently as he remembered his own experience when the Valley was attacked by Titan, Kittal's brother, "go let your family know you are alive. They'll be glad to see you well and unhurt."

The young man gulped and brushed a tear away as he nodded his head.

"You've done your bit for the moment." He pushed the young man towards the steps.

With him on his way Diego turned to the house with a deep breath of trepidation. Now it was time to see Ioan's reaction. He entered the house with a call, "hello?" Lylya appeared with a frown which soon became a smile, "Diego!"

"Lylya." He returned the smile.

"You survived. How is Ozanus?"

"He's fine, a little stressed." Diego carefully said.

"Oh?"

"Where can I find Ioan?"

"In the study." She stepped back to let him through.

44

Her eyes lingered on him as he stiffly walked past. What had once been hero worshipping as a child when she had seen him working with Ozanus and the fact he had known their father had turned into a secret attraction but he never looked her way. She retreated before anyone caught her gazing after him.

Diego rapped on the door frame of the study before entering. Ioan, head bowed over the paperwork, glanced up. He signed the piece of paper in front of him as he calmly accused, "why didn't you stop him from leaving?"

For a moment Diego saw Kittal the strict ruler in the young man. Calmly he responded, "because I am not the Nejus."

"But you are his advisor." Ioan looked up and stared at Diego.

"I was his teacher, nothing more." Diego frowned, "it is up to him how he uses that knowledge. He is Nejus."

Ioan scowled. That wasn't what he wanted to hear. If he was Nejus he wouldn't have run from the field like a coward. Why couldn't Ozanus just admit he wasn't up to the title and abdicate? He, Ioan, would make a far better Nejus than Ozanus and his feasting and fighting in his fortress at Linyee. Could Diego not see that or was he too loyal to his student to speak out? Ioan clenched his hands into fists in frustration, not caring that Diego could see it. He demanded, "what are you doing here anyway?"

Ignoring the aggressive tone of Ioan's voice Diego replied, "for news."

"Well you probably know more than me since you were there." Ioan sneered.

"This attitude does not suit you." Diego pointed out with a harsh tone.

"How else should I be since my brother quit the battle like a coward? I would made the better Nejus. I practically run this country while he plays." Ioan slammed a fist on the desk as he leapt from his seat.

Diego's eyes narrowed, "I know it's hard to be the younger brother, but you should know it's not worth being bitter. There's already been one fight between brothers and this land doesn't need it to happen again so soon. You should be working together to get rid of the invaders."

"Tell him to get his arse here then and tell me how we are going to get rid of Temijin."

Diego slowly blinked before responding, "tell him yourself. I'm not here to act as a messenger. I think it's time I left if you have nothing informative to tell me." He turned and walked from the room, holding back a strong desire to punch Ioan.

"Come back here! That's an order!" Ioan commanded but Diego ignored it as he headed back to the lawn and Joli.

Ozanus stomped along the corridor, annoyed by how his brother had sent increasingly angry messages to go to the Valley hourly. He'd rather be out harassing the enemy especially while the sun was glowing blood red which hinted at the fact the gods were eager for more. Instead he had had to send Kenene with some of the riders to support the retreat of Keytel's ragtag army and frustrate Temijin's army as they marched deeper into Keytel while he went to see Ioan. He had no idea where Diego had gone.

His brother was acting far too much like the Nejus. His anger up, he stomped into the study and angrily demanded, "what do you want now?!"

He added with a growl when Ioan ignored him, "if you dragged me here to waste my time you'll live to regret it." His eyes flashed red though no one saw it and he wasn't aware of it but he did twitch when he thought he heard a chuckle from behind him.

Ioan bristled as he tried not to look up. He was irked by his brother, why couldn't he take his role seriously? Finally he looked up, carefully he said, "we cannot win."

46

"Yes we can. We need to regroup first."

"No we can't. We have no army, not one like theirs anyway. Even if we managed to organise them into any resemblance of a fighting force again it would collapse."

"Is this what you dragged me here to say?" Ozanus didn't want to believe his brother, however much he knew Ioan was right.

"No." Ioan's hands were tight fists under the desk where Ozanus couldn't see them, "that was just explaining the reasoning behind why I have offered Temijin a truce and he has agreed."

"A truce?!" Ozanus exploded and fought a desire to leap at his brother and shake him.

Ioan leapt from his chair, which tumbled with a crash to the floor and retreated to the back of the room, hand on the plain handle of the knife at his hip, "we had to. We are not a prosperous country considering our size. We need to trade with Moronland so we have agreed he can have Drukgang."

"No!" Ozanus protested, "the cataracts were our natural defences. If we let him have Drukgang then he can try again anytime he wants."

"It will still take two weeks to get to and from Drukgang over the mountains. Our borders are not strong anymore. Though you may pretend otherwise we are not a strong country. While you go out playing mercenary the rest of the Suwars are fighting to keep our borders safe. It was our father and his grandfather who kept the wolves at bay. No one wanted to test their strength but now we are an easy target."

"Is there anything more I should know about?" Ozanus asked warily.

Ioan gulped, nervous again. He couldn't look his brother in the face, "as part of the deal Lylya is to marry Temijin to cement our new alliance."

Ozanus slowly blinked, then without a word turned and left

the room. Ioan let out a long breath as he sank to the floor, relieved to still be alive and that he hadn't had to justify the marriage alliance as well.

Out in the corridor Ozanus bumped into Lylya. Impulsively he grabbed her by the arm making her squeal from his tight grip. As he began to drag her along with him he growled, "you are coming with me."

"You're hurting me." She protested, trying to dig her heels in and pulling at his fingers to loosen his grip, "where are you taking me?"

"I've got to keep you safe." He didn't look back as he carried on tugging her along.

"I'm safe here."

"Not any more you're not."

"Ozanus? Stop! What are you talking about?" She exclaimed, wide eyed.

"Our brother has betrayed us." He answered but didn't stop pulling her. They had now reached the veranda and he could see Ozi out on the lawn waiting for him.

"Don't be silly." She laughed though it sounded too high and tense to defuse the atmosphere, "you are Nejus, he should be obeying you."

"Ha! He craves it all for himself."

Lylya stumbled on the steps. Ozanus caught her and swept her into his arms to carry her across the grass to Ozi. He ordered, "get on."

"But..." She weakly protested, too confused now to fight her brother's sudden madness. She pulled herself into the dragon's saddle as Ozanus jumped up, using Ozi's clawed wing as a springboard. He wrapped an arm round her to hold her in place as he ordered, *"let's go."*

"What's going on? Why is Lylya with you?" Ozi asked with a frown as she pushed herself up into the air.

"My brother has betrayed us and is using her as a bargaining chip to satisfy the barbarian Temijin."

48

Ozi said nothing in reply. She had her opinion on the matter of the two brothers but felt sure her Nejus would not want to hear it. Although she enjoyed their mercenary life, fulfilling her bloodlust, she knew that Ozanus really needed to settle down and become the Nejus he could be if he put his mind to it; and then that would resolve the issues between the two brothers as no longer would Ioan think himself persona Nejus and crave the title for himself.

"Have you nothing to say?" Ozanus demanded and kicked at his dragon.

She reached up with a back claw and swiped at his foot as if it was an annoying insect. She scowled, *"not at the moment as you wouldn't like what I would say."*

He scowled as well but didn't add anything more.

The rest of the flight occurred in a moody silence with Lylya clinging tight to her brother for warmth as the clothes she wore wasn't suitable for flying in. She was relieved to see Linyee come into view. As Ozi came into land on her tower Lylya started to change her mind.

Below in the courtyard servants scurried around, shoulders hunched, as if in fear. This was the first time she had visited the fortress and she didn't like the atmosphere that lingered over the place. She wondered if her brother really behaved like a tyrant in his own home?

In the tight confines of Ozi's walled nest Ozanus slipped from his dragon's back before helping his sister down. As he did he remarked, "you'll be safe here."

"Safe?! You practically kidnapped me." She exclaimed and would have shrugged her brother's hold off if she could have, but there wasn't the space.

As he led her down the stairs she demanded, "what has happened?"

"Ioan has struck a deal with Temijin without me."

"Who can blame him? You don't act like the Nejus. You

play at soldiers and let Keytel go to ruin instead of ruling like you should. Now, take me home." She stopped on the steps and stamped a foot.

"No. I will protect you from those savages."

"What about the ones that live here? You can't say that they are particularly civilised." She exclaimed, "and I have only the clothes I'm wearing."

"You are staying here and that's that." Ozanus turned to look at his sister. He wanted to do what was right by her, "they won't touch you as they know you are my sister."

"Where's Diego?" She demanded. He would make Ozanus see sense and get her back home to the Valley.

"Away." He responded stiffly.

"Oh." She deflated. With heavier steps she followed her brother down an empty plastered corridor.

"We'll get rid of Temijin and then you can return to the Valley, safe and then we'll find you a more suitable husband." He reassured her as they stopped at a door. With a small bow he let her enter the room first.

It wasn't the most comfortable looking room, just a bed that had seen better days and a table and chair by the cold fire. Before she could object the door was shut and locked behind her. She turned and stared at the door, stunned that her brother had just become her jailer.

She sank on to the bed and could only hope Diego came back soon and sorted everything out. Maybe he would whisk her away from everything and they could live a quiet life somewhere far away from her squabbling brothers. She wondered where Diego was, normally he stayed close to Ozanus.

Six

With a heavy sigh Diego headed through the fortress. He wished there was some way he could get the brothers to stop arguing. They would be a force to be reckoned with if they would unite and then Keytel would be safe again.

He passed two Suwars talking and caught Lylya's name. He swung round ready to tell them off as he demanded, "what's that about Lylya?"

The two men shrank back but replied, "sir, Lylya is here sir. The Nejus brought her back with him from the Valley."

"What?!" He turned and headed back the way he came in search of Ozanus.

He found his Nejus in his antechamber at his desk. Ozanus spun round, "what is it? Oh, it's you. Where have you been?"

"I have just heard Lylya is here."

"Yes she is. She will be safe here, away from Ioan and his deals with Temijin." Ozanus spat, "he has promised him Lylya and Drukgang in exchange for peace."

"Oh? He didn't mention that when I saw him." Diego remarked in shock.

"Where have you been anyway?"

"Places." Diego answered vaguely. He had needed space

to calm himself and also think about whether he wanted to stay with Ozanus. Reluctantly, for the moment, he knew he would be staying, "where is she?"

"Safe."

Diego sighed, clearly he was going to have to find Lylya in the fortress himself, "you can't keep her locked up otherwise she'll start to resent you."

"I'm doing it for her own good. I can't have her marrying Temijin just because Ioan wants her to. He's a thug."

"But if it protects Keytel from his attacks." Diego tried to point out so that Ozanus would see the sense of peace.

"No! Not him."

"It would be one less border to worry about."

"I said no!" Ozanus snarled and stood to make it clear the conversation was now over. His hand was a fist and his eyes flashed red.

Diego took a step back, his eyes widening and without a word he turned and walked out of the room. It was no use trying to get Ozanus to see sense for the moment. He had seen the young man's eyes flash red and wondered what Gods were getting involved in the issues of man.

He found a maid and asked, "where is Lady Lylya?"

"This way sir." The maid hurried on ahead and stopped at a door, "here sir, he left the key in for us but the door is locked."

"Who's there?" A shout came through the door then there was the sound of a hand palm hitting the door, "let me out!"

"You can go. Get some food and drinks please." Diego ordered softly.

"Sir." She fled.

With her gone he turned the key. He carefully opened the door just in case Lylya tried to attack him.   As the door opened Lylya flung herself at the person standing in the doorway, hands as fists. Realising who it was she exclaimed, "oh thank the Gods! I am glad to see you. Where have you been?"

"Places. How long have you been here?" He glanced round the shabby room, "he could have put you in a better room."

"A couple of days."

"Are you alright? I hope he has been looking after you."

"Yes he has. Please sort this out Diego."

"His heart is in the right place even if his reasoning isn't."

"You've spoken with him already?"

"Yes."

"Talk to them both, please." She pleaded.

"We'll see." He replied without committing to anything, "let's find you a better room at least."

There was nothing he could do. Neither Ioan or Ozanus would talk about it and Lylya and Diego were trapped in the middle. Before anyone was truly prepared Temijin showed up at the Valley with his entourage. His men were made to camp outside the Valley with the dragons eyeing them warily. Only a few men were allowed to join their leader in the Valley.

The village came out to stare at the strangers in their midst, all bullish looking men dressed in dusty leather and chainmail over heavy sleeved surcoats, loose trousers and boots with a curved toe point. They were all sweating in the heat they weren't used to.

There were enough manners in them to wait to be invited into the house, but not enough to make themselves presentable. For once Ioan and Ozanus were in agreement, they would see their visitors in the morning once they were clean and tidy. The messenger reluctantly passed it on. Temijin growled in annoyance; he wanted his prize and to be gone. Ceremony was not his thing.

The following morning Temijin and his group came to the lawn in front of the house. They were surprised to find that overnight poles flying the banners of both Keytel and Moronland had been put up. A large triangle canopy had been set up to create shade over the chairs and table that had been placed on the lawn. One side had the Nejus' engraved chair with its dragons twisting around its back. On either side were chairs for Ioan and Gaerwn. Further away were chairs for Lylya and Shuang. On the other side were three chairs for Temijin and his two senior advisors. There were benches set up behind for the rest of his entourage.

They became wary as Suwars started to quietly filter out from the undergrowth. They all appeared casually dressed but they all noted the dragon headed knives at each man and woman's hip. The Suwars began to spread out to form a double rowed square round the edge of the canopied area. A gap was left at the house end. They causally spoke amongst themselves while also glancing at the strangers in their midst sweating in their clean clothes.

The visitors' faces were covered with beards or moustaches. Those with long hair had washed it and tied it back with strips of leather and some of the beards had leather thongs or beads tied into them. They were dressed in long brightly dyed tunics embroidered round the neck and cuffs. Their trousers were wrapped in straps or tucked into their calf length boots. All of them were feeling a bit warm in the heat of the Valley.

Fear came to them when they heard the flapping of large wings and felt the back draft from them rising dust. The vegetation protested as the dragons, with large medallions hanging round their necks, landed to observe the big occasion. There was a snort or two as they settled to wait and watch.

As the morning drew on Temijin became impatient,

54

stomping up and down under the canopy and muttering to his men. Finally there was a horn blown.

The Suwars turned to look at the house. On the veranda, at the top of the steps, stood their ruling family in full splendour. Ozanus stood at the front dressed in a long red coat embroidered with dragons in gold thread with a large medallion resting on his chest of a dragon cut out within the circle. His brother and sisters stood two steps back also dressed in a brightly coloured outfits and jewels to show off the wealth of the land.

The men from Moronland stared at the two women dressed in woven short shawl jackets with elbow length wide sleeves over loose linen blouses and long skirts all with embroidered borders. The folds of the fine linen protected their wearers modesty. At their waists, nipping them in were wide leather belts dyed red and green. Round their necks they had two chain necklaces each of different lengths, the longer one with a large jewel pendant on it.

They wondered which of the two young women would be coming back to Moronland with them. Diego, Gaerwn and two other Suwars stood behind them in ceremonial uniform buffed till they shone. They rarely wore their metal breast plates. They were too valuable to be worn during battle. Temijin muttered to his chief aide, "finally."

Temijin had mixed feelings about the young man advancing towards him. He recalled the boy's father, Kittal, a man who was known in Moronland in his youth as being vicious and strong but also considerate in equal measure. He knew that the magic powers bestowed on the Keytallian family by the dragon Gods had also gone with the death of the father. Ozanus was a bit of an enigma as Nejus. He was known to be a fighter and didn't have any control of his temper. He left most of the governing to his younger brother. He wondered how it would go today, especially as

Ozanus had a look on his face as if he didn't want to be present. Today was also the first time he had seen the young man close up.

They all sat down as two servants walked round pouring drinks. Temijin clicked his fingers and one of his men stood up and cleared his throat as he unrolled the parchment he held in his hands, "we come together today to sign this peace treaty between Keytel and Moronland. As has been agree between the two countries Drakgung will be given to Moronland and the hand of Lady Lylya in marriage to Temijin."

There were gasps from the Suwars. Ozanus scowled though thankful there wasn't any pomposity from the winners in the deal. They clearly wanted to just get the treaty done with and take their prize home. Lylya squeezed her sister's hand tighter and fought back the tears. Ozanus had reluctantly brought her back to the Valley for the signing of the peace treaty. Now she wanted to be back at Linyee. Under lowered damp eyelashes she studied her husband to be on the other side of the table and fought to keep her facial expression neutral and hide how she was feeling about all of it.

Temijin leered at the sisters across the table and twirled his freshly washed and oiled moustache. In honesty neither of them were the sort of woman to arouse him. He preferred a larger woman with some flesh to grab, but at least who Lylya was would give him a legal heir to start his dynasty with and give him the future opportunity to claim a right to Keytel if needed. Ozanus didn't look like he was planning marriage and creating the needed heir any time soon.

His thoughts were brought back to the moment as his man placed the treaty on the table and a servant of the Nejus' placed the ink pot and pen next to it.

He tried to keep his face neutral, though he was

56

quite gleeful over it all as he was definitely the winner in this treaty. Give it a year or two and then he would push on and try and take all of Keytel and the dragons. He would set up another arena that could cope with the size of the Valley ones and then force them to breed and fight for everyone's entertainment. He willingly signed the treaty.

On the other side of the table Ioan reached for the pen once Temijin had finished with it. He turned the treaty round and held the pen out for Ozanus to take. Everyone held their breath to see how their Nejus would react. It was a long drawn out few minutes where Ozanus scowled at Temijin and at himself for letting this come to pass. Ioan thought he would have to nudge his brother into action but finally Ozanus took the pen from him and dipped it in the ink. With a surprising flourish Ozanus signed the treaty. Then the next second, showing his disdain he was up on his feet and walking away before anyone was ready for the ceremony to be over.

Ioan grimaced at his brother's departure. Remembering his manners he turned to the Moronland delegation and Temijin and remarked with a forced smile, "now we have a marriage to organise."

"Definitely." Temijin remarked stiffly as he looked to the sisters again.

Ioan noticed the look but didn't remark on it, "you will have to follow our traditions since you are here."

"Whatever. As long as this happens quickly." Temijin shrugged his shoulders. The marriage was to cement the treaty, nothing more. It wasn't going to stop him doing anything permanently. He'd wait for Keytel to be lulled into false sense of security before attacking again. He stood and walked away, showing he was in charge of the meeting's end.

Ioan opened his mouth to protest and then changed

his mind. Now was not the time to start an argument when he would have to brave his brother's wrath later over the marriage.

Seven

Over the next two weeks it was not a happy house excitedly looking forward to a wedding. The sisters wept and the brothers argued or stomped around the house. The servants tried to stay out of the way. Diego was thoughtful and pensive. He didn't like the atmosphere the peace treaty had created. The usually tense atmosphere between the brothers was now positively murderous. The only thing stopping Ozanus from doing anything foolish was his sisters. They needed him as much as he needed them.

Before they knew it the wedding was a day away. With surprise Temijin had organised a feast on the eve of the wedding and everyone in the Valley was invited. Before they attended the feast Lylya and Ozanus was to be found sitting on the edge of a cliff overlooking the Valley. So often, when they were younger, they had sat up here, escaping their carers, just to sit and feel the sun on their skin and sit in quiet, away from the hubbub of the house. They would watch the dragons flying and the wind in the trees and bushes.

Behind them Ozi crouched, watchful but restless. The strong scent of the Moronland camp outside of the Valley kept drifting in and it was disturbing all the dragons. They didn't like the smell of filth and dried dragons' blood that it seemed to consist of.

They sat with their legs dangling off the edge. One of them finally spoke. Ozanus, studying his rough hands, said, "I can't stop this though I have tried."

"I know."

He reached out and took one of her hands in his, "if he treats you badly, if he hurts you or neglects you I will come for you and bring you home."

"I know you would and I would be forever in your debt but would that be wise?" She looked at him with concern, "he might start the fighting again and I couldn't do that to Keytel. However much I don't want this it is my duty to keep this country safe for our people." She leant into him and he put an arm round her.

Reluctantly he said, "as you wish but remember what I have said."

"I will, I promise. Now we'd probably should get back before we are missed as we are the guests of honour." Ozanus grunted, expressing his discontent at that idea. He remarked, "he just wants to show us that he can do something just as spectacular as us."

"Do we have to do the traditional ceremony? It doesn't feel right?" Lylya asked as she drew back from the cliff edge before standing up.

"Blame Ioan, not me." He retorted.

"It's not a ceremony suitable for such barbaric people. It's one that deserves the respect of those who understand."

"I know, I know." He held his hands up in surrender though he didn't really care anymore. He thought the ceremony barbaric itself, which would have surprised everyone if they found out.

Ozi circled the house and front lawn before landing behind the house. The whole of the lawn had been taken over by the Moronlandians for their feast of celebration. A huge bonfire had been built and set alight to cook the pigs and sheep that slowly rotated on spits being turned by boys from the Valley's village. Tables had been set up to encircle the fire with benches and chairs facing in.

The Nejus and his siblings waited till the last moment to leave the house. Temijin was gracious as they stepped out in their finery. He bowed to Lylya as she was finally introduced to him as his bride and held out a hand for her to take. He pulled her to his side as he announced, "my bride to be!"

A cheer went up amongst the gathered Moronlandians.

The Suwars and villagers glanced nervously at their Nejus to see his reaction. Ozanus was stony faced. With as much graciousness as he could muster Ozanus spoke, "on behalf of all who live in this Valley I thank you for organising this feast in celebration of the marriage between our two countries that happens tomorrow."

The clapping was a little forced on one side while the other banged the tables and stamped their feet.

"Come, sit and eat." Temijin bowed his head and directed an open hand to the tables.

At the table Temijin sat with Ozanus one side and Lylya on the other. A plate loaded with cuts of cooked meat was presented to them and with surprising graciousness Temijin served Lylya before filling his own plate. Servants went round putting plates of food out from spits and swapping the jugs of wine and beer as soon as they were emptied. The Moronlandians were clearly having better time than the Suwars and villagers who, though they ate well, did not drink so deeply from their cups. They stayed on the alert for any trouble that might break out amongst the Moronlandians who were quickly becoming drunk.

Lylya picked at her food while Temijin shovelled it down, laughing if he heard a joke nearby. Temijin turned to Ozanus, "I hear you are known to be a strong fighter here in Keytel."

The family stiffened, wondering where this was going.

61

"I am known to be further than just Keytel."

"True. You should come and visit. I have a brilliant fighting arena where you can truly test your mettle." Ozanus frowned, "and why would I want to do that? Why should I support you in your killing of dragons?" Temijin laughed, "they love it. They are vicious blood thirsty killers at heart. You know that, you've seen it."

"I think," Ozanus pushed back his chair and stood, "we should leave you now. There is another long day ahead of us tomorrow."

His siblings stood as well. As Lylya stepped away to leave Temijin grabbed her by the hand and sneered, "till tomorrow mi'lady."

Lylya angrily pulled her arm back and forced herself not to run to hide her distress. Temijin laughed and returned to his feasting.

She stood numbly and didn't help the maids as they dressed her in the morning. The maids worked silently as they manoeuvred limp limbs into the dress. They pretended not to see the red eyes from the crying they had heard during the night. None of them wanted to see Lylya gone. In another world she would have made a strong leader of the Suwars like her long dead aunt but instead she was being used as goods to be bartered with. They dabbed her eyes with a cool damp cloth to try and reduce the swelling.

Stepping back they couldn't help admiring their work. Her plump breasts were barely hidden by the low square necked bodice. The long mutli layered flounced skirt hung perfectly from her hips, hiding her bare feet and the ankle bracelets she had on. Her long hair was up, pinned in place with pins topped with dragons. The long veil was then placed over her, hiding her from view.

It was a quiet procession of friends and family who followed Ozanus and Lylya to the ruined temple on the

62

cliff. There was none of the music that normally followed the procession making the bells at her ankles sound even louder and wrong. Today was not a joyous event for anyone.

New cloth banners had been hung up between the stone pillars with dragons carved spiralling up them. One side hung Keytel's symbols of swirling dragons the other had Moronland's symbols of a sword pointing to a star with a dragon arched over it. Once dragons had flown free in Moronland but that was several centuries ago now. Once Moronland had also worshipped dragons, now they were seen as another animal to use for man's entertainment.

Temijin and his men were already at the temple near the altar with its weathered blood staining. Some were unsure what was going to happen having seen the old blood on the altar and cracked floor of the temple. They knew of the sacrifices that had happened here in the past including the immortal dragon who had needed a human sacrifice to return to the heavens. They glanced skywards with fear as they were weapon less. None of them wanted to be the next one as dragons started flying in. They huddled together hoping that if they looked like a group they would deter the dragons.

Ozanus, in all his regal glory, stiffly went through the ceremony. Finally he lifted the veil revealing Lylya to Temijin. He then stepped out of the way so that Temijin could take possession of her.

Lylya turned her head away from the stench of alcohol on his breath. Clearly he had needed some liquid courage to be able to proceed. She saw his men leering at the scene and her and closed her eyes against them. She tried not to cry as he pawed at her breasts, kissed her with rough lips and then thrust a hand under her skirts and shoved a finger up her. She felt his mouth form a grin and he sneered, "perfectly tight."

He pushed her up against the altar, turned her around and lifted her skirts out of the way. He fumbled for the belt of his trousers. He pressed his erection against her buttocks before guiding it into his bride.

Lylya looked up from where she was bent over the altar and saw Ozanus watching with an agonised expression on his face. She looked away. Looking down at the altar she realised soon her own virgin blood would be added to her ancestors' and even her mother's. She had so hoped to marry for love not because of diplomacy as at least the ceremony would have been that much easier to go through. She bit her lip as Temijin thrust himself in as deep as he could and grunted in the process. There was still a squeak from the pain as she squeezed her eyes shut as he broke through her hymen.

Once he came he stepped back, panting a little from the experience. He turned and grinned at his men who cheered and clapped. He pulled Lylya to his side while blood and semen ran down her leg and announced, "my bride, my woman!"
As a quiet aside he murmured to Lylya, "I'll show you what a man can truly do later."

Lylya gulped nervously. What was life going to be like with this beast of a man? Could she perhaps persuade everyone to let her stay in the relative safety of the Valley where there was some resemblance of civility? She sent up a silent prayer, hoping her virgin sacrifice would be enough to ensure the Gods protected her.

Eight

It was a restless night for Ozanus. He had barely ate or drank at the wedding feast. He didn't want to think about the fact a member of his small family, and what could be said, his best friend, would soon be leaving. He left before the feasting ended. He was not in the mood to be around people. He had gone to bed in his parents old bed, Ioan having moved out of it for the two weeks he was in the Valley, but kept thinking about what was to come.

As silent fell outside, the sober party having come to an end, much to the relief of the Valley residents, Ozanus got up and pulled on the Nejus robe over his naked body. He wandered out into the cooler air of the outdoors. From the veranda he looked over to the Moronlandians' temporary camp which was winding down as well. There was still some singing and drinking happening but only a few now. He hoped Lylya was alright in Temijin's tent.

He looked up where the full moon was shining bright over the Valley and wondered what the Gods were making of the events of man. He thought he saw the shadow of dragon flit across the surface of the moon. He certainly was not as dedicated to the Dragon Gods as his father had been but an urge came upon him to give them an offering to ask for their protection of Lylya once she was in Moronland.

An invisible force led him deeper into the Valley, hand running through the foliage, until he came to the high cliffs that protected the Valley from the outside world. He saw a cave in the cliff, a short climb up and remembered being there a month ago, just before going up against Temijin on the battlefield.

He climbed into the cave, pushing ivy and brushing clinging cobwebs off his skin. Ahead of him was the statue of the Dragon Lord half covered in ivy, one claw outstretched over a shallow bowl of water reflecting the moon coming down from the hole above it.

He hesitated then. Last time he had come he had been in such a state of fear and anguish that he had been unable to make sense of the place. He felt he didn't deserve to be in this sacred space. This was once his father's place and now it should have been his as Nejus but he had neglected it, forsaken it. He couldn't remember why he was even there now that he had arrived. He was about to leave when a voice spoke from the statue, *"you leave without paying tribute? You wish to be your father but cannot be."* Ozanus glared at the statue before retorting, *"you've done nothing for me so why should I."*

"What has kept you from injury, from death in all those fights?" The voice coldly replied.
Ozanus scowled.

"You wear your father's robe but you do not deserve it.... Yet."

"Yet?"

"Go to Moronland when you are invited. There is work to be done there."

"The arena?"
Ozanus turned to leave when he didn't receive an answer.

"Do you forget something? Clean the bowl and give me the offering. Now!" The voice snarled with warning. The statue glowed bright forcing Ozanus to cover his eyes and

drop to his knees.

Ozanus looked around to find something sharp to use to offer up some of his blood to the Gods. An obsidian knife appeared out of the gloom. He felt a presence gently guiding him, a human presence. He whispered, "father?" There was no answer.

He took up the black glass blade and felt hands on his, big warm reassuring hands. They held his left hand open, fingers uncurled and guided his right with the knife to slice into the palm of his left, through the heeling scar. No drops were lost as his hand was cupped and he was drawn to the bowl with its scum covered water. One by one drops of blood dripped into the water until it was red.

Suddenly he felt a peace within him that he hadn't felt in a long time. He released a long deep breath that he hadn't realised he had been holding. Had his father felt this when he offered his blood to the Gods?

He held his left hand as a fist to try and slow the blood. Carefully he stood and this time nothing stopped him from leaving.

Ozanus didn't think anything of the order given to him by the Dragon Lord for a couple of days as everyone was getting ready to see Temijin and Lylya off. It was only as they disappeared over the horizon, dust their only reminder that there had been anyone on the quiet savannah round the Valley, that he briefly thought about it.

He wasn't his father he reminded himself, he wasn't a hero. He put it to the back of his mind. There was plenty of time and other things to worry about like what his next mercenary job would be.

It was several months later when his father came to him in his sleep. He came to him, as he lay caught up in his bedding, like a wave of anger. He felt pinned to the bed by the weight of his father and the Gods. It was a whisper but it sounded like a roar of several voices in his ears, *"how dare you?! How dare you ignore the commands of your Gods?!"*

Ozanus opened his mouth but no words could come out.

"You are my son and our family live to serve and protect the dragons."

He found his voice, "but I am not you. I don't have the magic."

"You don't need it and you would never have had it as it was all bestowed on me before you were born." His father's voice was calmer now though there was still reproof in the tone.

"How can I do it?"

"Why have you lost faith in yourself?" His father challenged.

"Feed me more....." A whisper came from somewhere else.

Ozanus hesitated as he registered the new voice, *"Because..... because.... I could not protect Keytel, because I could not protect my sister. I promised to protect you and I couldn't stop it."* Tears ran down his face at the memory.

"Be a man!" Kittal snarled and disappeared. Ozanus could only stare at the canopy of his bed, taking deep breaths in as all the weight on his chest had vanished.

His breath calmed. He untangled himself from his sheets, pulling on his father's bedrobe against the chill of the night before hurrying through the fortress. He threw Diego's door open and declared, "I have to go to Moronland."

"Err…. What?" Diego struggled to wake up. He sat up and stared blurrily at Ozanus' outline in the doorway.

"I have to go to Moronland, now!"

"Can't this wait till morning?"

68

"And you are coming with me."

"And who will look after this place?" Diego responded, more awake now.

"Kenene."

"Ozanus, it's the middle of the night, I think. The stars and moon are hidden so we wouldn't be able to see to fly and there are things to organise. You'll have to wait till morning." Diego replied sternly as if Ozanus was a child.

"I am Nejus and you have to obey me." Ozanus stamped a bare foot.

"You are behaving like a spoilt child." Diego retorted. A snarl echoed round the room and Ozanus froze. Diego looked around, "what was that?"

Ozanus hesitated before saying, "nothing. It can all wait till morning, I'm sorry to have disturbed your sleep." He backed out the door and closed it behind him.

Back in Diego's room, as he settled back down to sleep he sensed a presence, "who's there?"

"Look after him. He's a boy in a man's body. You have done your best."

"Nejus? Sir? Kittal?"

"He needs you now more than ever. Don't let him fail."

"Will he ever find peace?"

There was no answer and the sense of a presence dissipated.

It was an impatient couple of days for Ozanus while between him and Diego they organised their departure. There were protests but the Suwars were finally convinced that they couldn't all go. They were still mercenaries and needed to make money. Ozanus' mistress was sorted out with money and a small set of rooms in Linyee. Ozanus had no idea how long he would be away and anyway he had grown bored of her.

Then it was time for one last feast before Ozanus

and Diego left. While the rest of them ate and drank as normal Diego and Ozanus sat apart finishing off the planning. They planned to fly to the foot of the mountains and camp for the night before flying over the mountains and entering Moronland with the new day.

With the planning put to one side they nursed a last tankard of ale each. After a while Ozanus murmured, "I don't think I can do this. I don't have the powers like my father did."

"I think your father was the end of an era, the end of a long generation of Nejus who were High Priests as well. Even if he could have trained you I don't think you would have had any of them. You are a new era who has to use the skills of man." Diego tried to reassure him.

"Hmm." Ozanus was sceptical, it wasn't like his father's 'powers' had saved either him or his mother from the Gods. He still wasn't sure whether he believed in the Gods but they seem to have decided to use him like they had used his father.

"We may not worship them anymore but we still have to protect dragons from us." Diego added, "and that's why we are going to Moronland isn't it?"

"Suppose." Ozanus shrugged his shoulders, as he wasn't really sure why they were going. Only the day before he had finally received a letter from Lylya and it hadn't been a joyful letter. There was a hidden undercurrent in it which angered him. He had wanted to drop everything then and bring her home. He had resisted the urge but one thing was certain he would bring her back to Keytel. To hell with the treaty! She was more important than whatever mystery thing the gods wanted him to do.

Nine

Coming over the mountains the dragons snorted and grimaced. Diego asked, *"what's wrong?"*

"Can you not smell it?" Ozi asked as the dragons used the updraft to soar.

"Smell what?" Ozanus' thighs tightened on Ozi and a hand went for his sword. He glanced around warily.

"The fear, the despair." Joli snorted again as if to try and get rid of the smell in his nostrils. He could smell the dragons hiding deep in the mountains, not willing to show themselves to anyone.

"They're trapped and if they reveal themselves they will end up in the arena, worse than being enslaved." Ozi remarked bitterly.

"I think we should stop soon." Diego suggested after a few minutes of quiet where each were in their own thoughts, hunkered down in their head scarves against the cold.

"Why?" Ozanus glanced round, thinking there was some ominous weather front coming. In fact the skies were clear from being high in the mountains. Every so often they would in fact circle through a white cloud. Far below them their shadows skimmed over bare rock, grass and the occasional scrawny tree, "we can get to Duntorn by this evening if we keep going."

"We need to remind them of who you are and that you are not someone to be taken lightly. Lets rest up, clean up and scare them." Diego advised.

"Never leave me Diego." Ozanus remarked, "I seriously don't know what I would do if you weren't with me. You are right, impressions are going to be everything tomorrow."

"Keep an eye out for a lake or waterfall with a deep pool. We are going to give both of you a wash." Diego said to the dragons.

"They certainly won't miss us flying over their country then." Ozi laughed.

"And that is the point."

A new day and the scales of the dragons shimmered in the sun.

"Who knew under all that dirt?" Diego remarked with eyes squinted as he put the saddles on. Behind him Ozanus finished shaking their clothes of dust before starting to get dressed in the now polished dragon knight armour. Ozanus pulled on a clean linen shirt from his saddle bags which he had been keeping for once they had arrived in Duntorn.

"What did you say?" Joli asked.

"I've never seen you so clean." Diego replied, *"did Kittal ever see you this clean?"*

"Enough talking, we need to get moving." Ozanus ordered sharply.

Diego and Joli raised an eyebrow at each other, clearly Ozanus was nervous. Joli shrugged his shoulders to settle the saddle on his back while Diego pulled on a white linen shirt and then his padded jacket dyed blue to match Joli's colouring. He roughly wrapped his headscarf round his head. He would pull it tight once in the air.

Ozanus held his father's chest plate, engraved with dragon scales in place, and let Diego buckle him into it over his padded coat. As Ozanus shrugged on his sleeveless robe over the top Diego commented, "I don't think they are going to miss us."

"I should hope not after all the cleaning we did last night." Ozanus remarked stiffly as he began to wrap his red headscarf around his head until only his eyes could be seen. He tucked his leather gloves into his belt before, with the aid of Ozi, pulling himself up into his saddle.

They finished the descent from the mountains and swept over the arid land sheltered by the mountains and then on to the green and wooded farmlands dotted with farms and villages. The further into Moronland they went the more the dragons reacted to the rancid smell of fear and death that only they could smell, snorting and grimacing, lifting their lips to reveal sharp teeth in their disgust.

Spotting a wide road busy with people and horses moving in both directions they began to follow it, their shadows making the road travellers look up and making the horses nervous.

Both dragons and man's eyes were intent on the horizon and they ignored the effect they were having on the ground. By lunchtime, which they ate on the go, the landscape had started to change again. Still following the road the villages along it were starting to merge with each other and were busier with industry. Tall chimneys were sending smoke into the air and there was the stench of tanneries and rotting meat.

Ahead of them the city of Duntorn could now be seen, more built-up roads leading into it like tentacles. The walled city had broken out of its walls and sprawled outwards creating new districts that filled the gaps between the roads. None of them had ever seen anything like it. Within the walls was a large tower built up against the wall rather than in the centre. The other was opposite with the gated entrance into the walled part of the city. A wooden roofed rampart linked the two. Banners hung from the gatehouse tower, the twin towers with a sword between them, the city's insignia. It looked to be large enough and strong enough to support the weight of a dragon.

Off to one side, with a road lined with banners hanging from T-shaped poles, was a huge arena that dominated the outskirts of the city.

"If you go there, we aren't coming." Ozi declared, *"can you truly not smell it? I can even taste it now."* She tried to spit the taste out.

"I'm not agreeing to anything." Ozanus replied sternly.

"Let's destroy it now." Joli remarked, *"then we can go home."*

"No." Ozanus said, *"we are coming peacefully for the moment."*

"But you promised to protect all dragons." Ozi protested. *"That is not why we are here."*

"Then why are we?" Ozi demanded.

Curious to see what his reply would be Diego looked over as he didn't know why yet either. Ozanus scowled, apart from checking on Lylya, he didn't know why they were in Moronland and didn't want to reveal the fact he didn't. He hoped the Dragon Lord would tell him soon. Sensing the reluctance Ozi didn't challenge her rider.

Temijin stood on top of the tower watched the dragons and their riders steadily approaching Duntorn, his double breasted coat hung open. He had had news of them several hours previous and had already sent orders for them not to be attacked. He gripped the stone battlements, trying to control and suppress his excitement, anger and trepidation. He wondered why they had come considering his invitation back in the Valley had been rejected. He wondered if one of Lylya's letters had managed to get through. As far as he was aware they had all been handed to him, read and then burnt. He glanced behind at the men who stood waiting for him to say something before making a decision, "let's give them a Moronland welcome. Make ready the Great Hall."

"And the dragons sir?"

"They'll have to look after themselves unless they want to end up in the arena."

"And afterwards?"

"For the moment they are guests. Let's see what they want first. They'll soon be here."

The men left to prepare for their visitors while Temijin turned back to watching the dragons. The two very healthy, strong dragons would be ideal for his arena, and the two men as well. He wondered what reason he could create to arrest the riders and capture the dragons.

The two dragons circled the city a couple of times, seeking out the best place to land which wasn't near the arena. Diego pointed to land by what looked like a water storage area or fishponds. It was a series of large ponds linked by stone-built canals, "down there will have to do." Ozanus nodded, *"Ozi, by the ponds."*

"If you are going to be in the city, where do we go?"

"We won't stay in the city, I don't trust Temijin. We'll camp out with you down there."

"The tower looks strong enough to hold me." Ozi offered.

"Let's be peaceful for the moment. You would be suggesting that we were a threat if you were on the tower. Anyway, I think Temijin was up there watching."

Ozi grumbled but didn't reply.

By the time the saddles had been removed they had visitors. Gathered at a safe distance was a group of the local populace whispering and pointing. They split as a group of riders came through. At the front leading the group was clearly an official in a fine red woollen coat, the crossover collar folded back to reveal the lining. Round his neck was a gold chain and his round face was half covered by a neatly trimmed beard. This was a man who had never left his city. The four others were armed and in chain mail. With his nose in the air the official demanded, "who are you?"

Diego approached, "you are rather rudely addressing the Nejus of Keytel and his chief advisor."

There was an audible gasp from the audience. They had all heard of the Nejus since his sister was now their leader's wife. The official blinked and lowered his chin a little, "his Lordship, Temijin, asks that you come to the Khorin, the large tower you can see in the city walls."

Ozanus stepped forward, folding his headscarf over his arm, "I accept his invite, but do you expect me to walk?" He raised an eyebrow.

Just about still unperturbed by the surrealism of the situation the official clicked his fingers and two of his guards slipped off their horses, "horses for you sir."

"Thank you." Ozanus hauled himself on to the horse with slightly less dignity than he would have if it had been a dragon.

They were led into the city's narrow streets where second floors leant into the road and the muddy streets were crowded with people who pressed themselves against the buildings to let the five horses pass. Unlike the murmurs of the crowds, those in the courtyard of the Khorin fell silent as the visitors were led in through the double arch into the courtyard.

Slipping off his horse the official pointed to the large studded double doors at the top of 3 wide steps, "this way."

The official led the way through two small ante chambers

before another pair of doors were thrown open by two spear holding guards.

Inside the Hall was Temijin's hastily gathered group of men and women that he called his court. He sat in a heavy wood chair on a dais with his personal banner and Moronland's behind him. Beside him was Lylya standing looking pale but with a red flush to her cheeks. He kept a firm grip of her hand so she couldn't run to her brother. Ozanus was now in his territory and he wanted to give him a demonstration of his own power to the Nejus.

Ozanus and Diego stopped a couple of metres before Temijin. With barely a nod Ozanus said stiffly, "Temijin."

His whole body was tense and one hand was on his knife handle while the other was rubbing his thigh as he observed how Lylya looked. Her clothes didn't quite fit and her hair had lost its lustre. Her eyes had a slightly hollow look to them as if her soul had been battered and bruised and it had only been a month.

Temijin stood and with open arms said, "welcome, welcome Nejus. What an honour to have you visit us and a surprise. What brings you here?"

An unspoken force inside Ozanus threatened to speak for him but he forced it back down; now was not the time to make demands. With controlled calmness Ozanus replied, "I thought I would take you up on your invite."

"You should have let me know and I would have organised a better welcome." Temijin stepped down from the dais and approached the younger man, "I could have met you at Drukgang." He couldn't help smirking. He watched for a reaction from the younger man who gave nothing away much to his disappointment.

"I had some free time."

"There will be a feast tonight and we'll have to organise something in the arena. And in fact you might be able to help me."

"With what?" Ozanus asked with curiosity.

"We'll talk later. I will get someone to show you to your room, I hope you don't mind sharing?"

"That is fine but we will actually stay with our dragons."

"Oh? I can put guards down there to protect them?"

"No thank you." Ozanus responded sternly.

Temijin raised his eyebrows and held his hands up in mock surrender. With forced jollity that was starting to slip since the beginning of the conversation he said, "very well."

"Now, may I see my sister?" Ozanus demanded.

"Of course." There was hesitation in Temijin's reply. He turned and beckoned Lylya down. He possessively put his large hands on her shoulders, "we've been getting to know each other haven't we?"

Lylya glanced up at Temijin and then at her brother before nodding silently. Her pained expression said it all to Ozanus and he had to fight the urge to grab her out of Temijin's filthy hands and take her home there and then. He would have to be patient and find the right time even if it meant restarting the animosities between the two countries. At least this time he would be better prepared for Temijin's army.

"Lylya, why don't you take your brother out to the garden? Diego, would you care for a drink and something to eat?"

Diego glanced at Ozanus. He was fighting the urge as much as his Nejus to take Lylya away from her obvious hell. Ozanus gave him a look and a nod that Diego understood and knew meant, 'find out information'. Turning to Temijin he said, "thank you."

"Sigwear!" Temijin shouted.

A man dressed in a woollen jacket with a clean linen shirt underneath stepped out from the crowd. His red beard was trimmed to follow the line of his chin and his hair had also been cut. He looked civilised compared to the rest of the men, intriguing Diego. He felt sure there was a story to be told in the man. The man bowed his head, "sir?"

"Get this man some food and drink and keep him company."

"Yes sir." He turned to Diego and quietly said, "come with me where we can have some peace."
Diego was surprised by the comment and reacted, "thank you, I could do with a rest and some good conversation."

"That I can sort out." The man smiled friendly as he led the other from the hall, "do you need anything for you limp?"
Diego wondered whether he could make Sigwear an ally, "just a good seat."

Ten

From beside a pillar set into the wall to hold up one side of the arched ceiling beam a woman dressed discreetly as a servant in a long-sleeved brown dress and apron, watched the scene. Her brown hair was hidden under a headscarf knotted at the nap of her neck. There was an aura about her that caused others near her to keep their distance so she had ended up with a clear view of the meeting of Temijin and Ozanus. She felt and saw the anguish coming from the three Keytellians and realised there was an advantage to be taken when the time came, but she would need help.

She slipped along the wall and followed brother and sister out into the small garden which was through a door in the city wall that abutted the tower. A high palisaded fence kept it hidden from public view. It consisted of an overgrown square flower bed edged with scraggy box. It was clear it was rarely used. A stone bench against one fence was half hidden with ivy. The woman hid in the shadow of the door and watched and listened.

Ozanus hadn't realised but Lylya's long dress had hidden her bare feet and he only noticed as she gingerly walked along the path and avoided the muddy puddles. The sleeveless dress with a square neckline, she wore, had seen better days and didn't properly fit her. It had clearly once been a sumptuous dress but in places the velvet had become worn, embroidery had been picked at and the skirt's hem was stained and had holes. The white long sleeved dress underneath was in better condition but still looked stained where the lace had turned yellow from age. While everyone else was wearing a coat she wasn't. She had her arms crossed to stay warm against the high steppes cooler weather. He took off his own robe, warm from his body and wrapped it round her as he asked with a frown, "where are your shoes? You aren't dressed as you should be as my sister."

She shifted uncomfortably under his criticising gaze, "he says he has ordered me a wardrobe of clothes and shoes and that this will have to do for the moment."

"Why hasn't he made it clear that its urgent. You were sent off with clothes, where are they?"

She gulped and picked at the embroidery edging the cuff of the white dress.

She felt such shame that her brother had to see her like this but clothes like what she wore was all she had as Temijin's mistress had claimed all of the ones she had come with. She may be Temijin's wife but here in Duntorn she was nothing more than a trophy. His mistress ruled the place with an iron fist as hard as Temijin's. If she became pregnant, which she prayed every time he visited her that she wouldn't, she knew he would use it as an excuse to invade Keytel again, claiming the right as having produced Ozanus' heir.

She fought back tears. All she wanted was to go home to Keytel, far away from Temijin. She hoped Diego would have her.

"Does he treat you well?"

"Most of the time." She lied, "I'll be brave and good and stay for the sake of Keytel."

"Are you sure?" He studied her face where he knew her eyes would not lie.

She turned her face slightly to break his studying, "what are you doing here anyway? You should have let me know you were coming."

"I got your letter and there wasn't time to warn you and I didn't want Temijin to know. Why didn't you write sooner?"

"What do you mean? I sent you several." She exclaimed as they sat on the bench.

He frowned, "I have only received one."

"You can't have come just for me." She said, staring down at her hands, not thinking she was important enough. He turned her head and lifted it so her face looked into his, "I promised to protect you didn't I?" He didn't like how his sister had lost all of her personality so quickly and hoped this was why the Dragon Lord had told him to go to Moronland.

"Did the Gods tell you to come for me?" She asked hopefully.

He grimaced, "He didn't tell me to come here."

"Maybe you are here to save the dragons from the arena?" She suggested thoughtfully.

"Who knows. He hasn't told me. He has never spoken to me before until the night of your marriage."

"Hopefully the answer will come to you soon then." She gave him a tight smile.

"Hopefully. He did say I hadn't earnt the right to wear father's robe." He remarked with a frown.

"Oh?!" She was surprised by that but thinking about it Ozanus had fled the battlefield. Unable to say that she added with positivity, "but you have earnt it, you are Nejus."

He shook his head.

Looking at him with confusion she added, "he has

never spoken to you before so you must have earnt it."

"I know. But all He has said is come to Moronland, and I ignored it. Then father came to me in my sleep to tell me off." He reluctantly revealed.

"You fool." She hissed, "if you had acted sooner I could have been back home."

"I know, but I didn't think I could do what He asked. I'm not our father."

"You were six when he died, how can you know you are not like him?"

"You heard the stories. He was a saviour and hero to the dragons. He rescued a God and got it back into the Heavens."

"And that killed him and mama in the process." Lylya exclaimed.

"I don't have the powers he had."

"And you never will so don't dwell on it." She softened and took one of his hands, stopping it from playing with the signet ring, "look, tell me what they want you to do."

"I really don't know. He didn't give me anything specific. Do you think this is some sort of test?" He looked at her. She was thoughtful for a moment before saying, "you are here now so that's a start. Maybe, whatever they want you to do will reveal itself in the next few days. There is the arena where dragons are being used as entertainment. You can rescue me." She half laughed, trying to make a jest of her pitiful situation.

"I don't think it will be as easy as that." He looked at her. Her shoulders slumped, "I suppose not. This is the Gods we are talking about."

Changing the subject Ozanus asked with concern, "what do you think Temijin wants me to help him with?"

She was quiet a moment as she had a think. She then said, "I have heard him ranting about someone who calls themselves the Daughters of Scyth."

"Who? I have never heard of them."

"Neither have I. Do you think father would have known of them?"

"If we were back in the Valley we could have had a look. He did all that travelling didn't he. Who are they then?"

"They seem to be attacking in some way but I don't know how or why?" She shrugged in defeat at the lack of information.

Changing the subject again to bring it back to his sister he asked, "does he treat you well?"

"I must go." Lylya abruptly stood up. She wasn't ready to reveal her woeful life to her brother who was clearly dealing with a more important issue involving the Gods. She knew she would have to wait, "I need to go and get ready for the feast later."

Ozanus stood, "oh…" His sister had changed. He felt abandoned as she hurried back into the tower, not even noticing the woman in the shadows of the door.

The feast was noisy as those gathered enjoyed themselves on long tables while on a wooden balcony at one end, accessed by a ladder, was a collection of musicians. Their pipes and hand drums drowned some of the laughter and talking. On the dais sat Temijin with Lylya on one side and Ozanus and Diego on the other. Beside Diego was the red-haired man he had been with most of the afternoon, Sigwear.

Down at the top of end of the left hand table was Temijin's mistress pouting over the fact she wasn't in her usual spot on the dais but it didn't stop her from preening in one of Lylya's outfits, filling the voluminous blouse and skirt with her large body so it didn't drape attractively. Vanity made her ignore the fact they weren't suitable for the climate. At the beginning of the feast Diego murmured, "is that Lylya's clothes?"

Ozanus' eyes narrowed and he growled as he looked to the mistress and then at his sister with her cast down eyes and tired clothes. Seeing his reaction Diego added, "patience." Ozanus nodded.

As the feast went on Temijin grew impatient with Ozanus' sullen quietness, "so you like a good fight?"

"Maybe." Ozanus answered warily, "why?"

"I mentioned I needed your help earlier. I am being attacked within my lands. I have their leader but that has not stopped them. In fact she is going to be part of my next event in the arena."

"Doesn't sound like you really need me."

Diego leant towards Sigwear, "who is he talking about?"

"The Daughters of Scyth." Sigwear answered quietly.

"Who are they?"

"Have you not heard of them?" Sigwear was surprised and then went on, "they are a tribe of women who live on a flat-topped mountain where there is no easy way to reach them but they somehow get around."

"How are they bothering you then?"

"Some of them ride dragons like you. They've been a problem for a Temijin for a few years now."

"Let me guess, since the arena was built?" Diego couldn't hide the scathing tone in his voice.

Sigwear glanced to his leader who thankfully wasn't paying attention and then nodded and whispered, "before then to be honest. As soon as he started organising dragon fights the dragons started disappearing and then these Daughters appeared, trying to break up the fights which is when he had the arena built. They have been quiet of late. We don't have much information on them. Occasionally we hear of a man returned from their mountain home but he can never tell us anything of what is up there."

"Interesting."

"Oh definitely." Sigwear remarked with an eager nod of

his head, "they have been there a long time, mainly peacefully. It is odd that you are unaware of them. I'm sure your previous Nejus must have known of them since they are riders like yourselves. We don't know how many there are but there aren't a huge number of yourselves either?"

"More than enough to deter most people." Diego answered gruffly.

It was late when they returned to Ozi and Joli. They sat tucked against the warm bodies of the dragons staring into the fire, wrapped in blankets. Ozanus finally spoke up, "what did you make of all of that? Did my father ever mention these Daughters?"

"What do you talk of?" Ozi asked.

"A group known as the Daughters of Scyth. Kittal never mentioned them. I don't think he even knew of them. Have you heard of them Joli?" Diego answered so that everyone could understand.

"No. Who are they?" Joli asked.

"A group of dragon riders. I'm surprised my father didn't know about them." Ozanus replied.

"Perhaps we should go check this mountain out?" Ozi remarked.

"We do not need to get involved in someone else's battles." Diego commented.

"But isn't that what we do all the time?" Ozanus challenged back.

"Yes we do but this is Temijin. Do we want to get mixed up with his issues when his intent is still suspect?" Diego replied with consideration.

"I'm curious. Is it not my job to defend and protect dragons?"

"Doesn't sound like they want to be found or protected. I'm sure they'll soon hear we are here and make contact if they want to." Diego advised.

Ozanus nodded thoughtfully, *"for now then we will stay here. We have been invited to this arena of his."*

"You can't really be planning to go?" Ozi exclaimed.

"Do you want me to help the dragons that are there?" Ozanus asked sternly.

"Of course."

"Then I need to go and check the place out."

Ozi grumbled but knew her Nejus was right.

Eleven

Everyone they passed on the way to the arena was in a good mood. A fight between dragons always had a good draw and today there was the captured leader of the Daughters of Scyth whose fighting skills would be put to the test against the captured dragons. The crowds heading towards the arena made room for Temijin and his guests. They stared at Ozanus and Diego and murmured amongst themselves. They wondered if they were going to end up in the arena along with the woman. They had heard of Ozanus' fighting skills and wanted to see them in action.

Travelling on horseback, pass two huge boulders wrapped in chains, with Temijin the Keytellians weren't sure whether to be amazed or to fear the arena that was rapidly taking over the skyline ahead of them. Half of its height was made of courses of large stones carved into blocks. These supported a wooden frame that contained all the seating though currently there was also a large charred hole in it surrounded by scaffolding. Around the base of the huge arena were throngs of people heading for the stairs that led to the seating squeezing into narrow corridors lined with permanent and temporary stalls.

Drinks were being poured from huge barrels into tankards while others were shouting out betting odds for the coming fights. Others were buying food for now and later. Temijin asked with a raised eyebrow, "tempted?"

"By what?" Ozanus replied as he watched a child handing out the day's programme.

Temijin laughed, "food, drink, a bet or even perhaps a fight of your own down in the arena."

Diego's frown went unnoticed while Ozanus asked, "who normally wins?"

Temijin shrugged, "depends. If its man versus beast then the animal. He didn't mention the dragons they had captured from Keytel. He had brought the smallest two of the ones brought down on the battlefield but even they had proven too big and powerful to be kept contained and to fight with. Temijin had originally thought all dragons would have been the same size as the ones captured from the Daughters of Scyth's mountain home until he had crossed over the mountain. The ones in Keytel had been huge in comparison. He had therefore had to return to his original source, the Daughters of Scyth's smaller dragons but there were less and less of them. The country had been scoured a few years back and no other wild dragons had been found.

The two injured ones he had brought back over the mountains, well secured to large carts with a lot of rope had been too big for his arena. He had anchored one to each side of the arena with the boulders they had passed but they had refused to fight. Instead, one had sent a fireball into the wall of the arena before managing to break its chains and flying off and seemed not to have returned to Keytel. The other had been killed trying to escape.

He remarked to Ozanus, "it would be an honour to see a man of your skill and talent in the arena. I'm sure I could find another soldier equal to you." The few Suwars that had been captured had put up a good fight for their survival and false promises of freedom but eventually they had all sacrificed themselves to his dragons rather than harm them, "well?"

"I will pass."

"I'll leave the offer out there." Temijin remarked with a smirk. He knew that a hot-blooded young man like Ozanus would probably want to get in the arena after watching a few fights, "would you like to meet today's main show?" Curiousity piqued Ozanus and he nodded.

"Very well, come."

Hidden under the arena was another floor with barely any light apart from smoky oil lamps hanging from the ceiling. The corridors were wide and lined with large iron barred cells. Temijin led the way past the cells where dragons, wings folded against their bodies and one even had a torn fanned neck frill, grumbled about their confined quarters.

In one corner were smaller cells where human prisoners were being kept. Most were criminals who knew their fate and sat on benches with heads in their hands, already defeated. A few appeared to be professional fighters, come to test their skills, as they sat at a table together, dressed in armour, eating and quietly talking. Their cell wasn't locked but there was a guard to ensure they didn't wander far. In a cell on her own was the Daughter of Scyth. She stood as the men approached. Her clothes were torn. She wore a waist length bolero padded jacket with a raised collar. Off centre toggles kept it closed, a wide sash covered the linen shirt and top of her trousers. Her loose trousers were tucked into high ankle boots. Her black hair was in a long plait lying over her shoulder. Her face was bruised and smeared with dirt but she held herself proudly. She spat, "come to gloat again?"

Temijin stepped to one side to reveal Ozanus and Diego. Her eyes widened. She had heard tales of the Nejuses of Keytel but never thought to meet one. She physically spat at him before hissing, *"traitor. Are you in league with this*

90

man?"

"No."

"I don't believe you." She crossed her arms and turned her back to Ozanus.

"Feisty isn't she?" Temijin chuckled, "what did she say?"

"Nothing." Diego replied.

"Come, let us head up top." He turned and beckoned over his shoulder to head back the way they had come.

Compared to the hushed contained atmosphere of the under croft the arena was loud and bright. People ate, laughed and argued. A few fights had even broken out. The group headed up to an empty box where chairs were set up in a row and a table at the back was laid with food and drink. Seeing it was empty Ozanus asked, "where's my sister?"

"She didn't want to come." Temijin lied. She hadn't been invited as he felt she would bring the mood of the entertainment down with her sullen moping. "Come, sit, have a drink, eat. Have you had breakfast yet?" He added with forced brightness.

While Temijin went to the table to pour himself some beer Ozanus and Diego went to the edge of the box and peered over. Below the seating at various points were barred gates. Down on the dirt floor were two pairs of clowns bumbling around though very few of the audience were paying attention. Occasionally there was a laugh from the crowded seating. Ozanus, leaning on the cloth covered edged box quietly asked, *"what do you think?"*

"Mmm. Impressive. That hole is definitely from one of ours so Joli and Ozi could destroy the place between them but we would have to ensure there is nothing underneath. I wonder how he got ours over the mountains and where they are now?"

"Dead probably though I hope they escaped but they haven't returned to Keytel. Did you see any guards?"

91

"Once this starts I'll see if I can slip off."

"What do you talk of?" Temijin interrupted loudly. He looked down and laughed with his mouth full.

"Nothing." Diego carefully answered with a glance at Ozanus who nodded in response to the question previously asked.

"Sooo, once those fools have entertained the crowds we'll start with a few animal and man fights before we start on the dragons and then the bitch that has been a thorn in my side for the last year. Sit, sit." He gestured at the chairs.

Back in the city it was quiet apart from the occasional roar of the crowd in the distance. Lylya was in her room, sitting at the window reading a book. If she kept quiet and unnoticed Temijin's mistress wouldn't come to bother her or mock her depending upon her mood. Thankfully she made a lot of noise if she was going to enter her chamber. Though her ears were on alert for the mistress she didn't hear the door whisper open or the footsteps until she felt a presence.

Lylya looked up from her book with surprise. She asked, "who are you? Have I seen you about?"
The brown haired woman dressed in servant clothes whispered, "are you definitely Lylya, sister of the Nejus and daughter of Kittal?"
Lylya sat up straighter, "I am, who are you?"

"I am a Daughter of Scyth. When we heard you were coming here I was sent to watch over you."

"I don't need your protection." Lylya protested and then asked with curiousity, "how come we have never heard of you in Keytel?"
The woman crossed her arms and pursed her lips, "I think otherwise."

"I have no power here. What do you want from me?" Lylya demanded.

"We have kept ourselves to ourselves because of the recent rulers of Moronland. Once, we were a respected part of this country. Now we have become isolated. We try to protect the dragons who live with us but the youngsters like to spread their wings and some get caught by Temijin and never return."

"So what do you want from me?"

"Your brother is here."

"Talk to him then."

"We can't be seen to be speaking with him. It is too public where he is camped."

"I could organise a meeting?"

"No." The woman answered sternly, "you are going to come with us."

"Like a kidnapping?"

"If that is how you want to see it."

"Why should I trust you…?"

"Taleba." She bowed her head briefly.

"Well Taleba, how are you going to get me out? And are you ready for both my brother's reaction and Temijin's?"

"That's what we want."

"I don't think you will be able to change Temijin. I am just a trophy to him."

"Will you come? You will have a better life with us. We chose the men we wish to bed." She didn't admit that it was Lylya's brother they wanted to attract the attention of. It was her who had sent the letter when she had realised all of Lylya's letters were being burnt. They reluctantly needed his help against Temijin.

"I need to think." Lylya hesitantly said. Would she speak about this with her brother or not? She knew nothing of these Daughters of Scyth and if she went she may find herself in a worst situation than she was currently in.

"I can't give you long. I'll come back later. We must be gone before they return from the arena." Taleba said sternly and then left before she could reveal her frustrations. How could Lylya not know of them considering who her father was? How could she not want to live a life with the Daughters of Scyth away from the cruel world ruled by angry destructive men? Lylya's brother was just as much evidence of that but as he was Nejus, defender of all dragons, they desperately needed his help, not that all would agree with that.

The clowns were quickly harried off by the arena stewards to make way for a group of armed men who began to fight each other. Even then not all of the audience were watching and that included Ozanus and Diego. Such fights did not hold any interest for them unless it was practice. It seemed that Temijin was rapidly bored as well as with a gesture of his hand a wild animal was released to charge at the fighting men. They scattered in panic before regrouping and working together to corner the bull that pawed the ground and snorted at the men with their spears and swords. With a chuckle Temijin gestured again and another fiery tempered bull was released and lowered its head and aimed its long horns at the group of men.

There was a pause as the corpses were pulled out of the dirt arena and fresh sand was spread across the worst patches of blood. Temijin asked, "would you care for the horns of the bulls as a souvenir?"

"No thank you." Ozanus answered after a brief moment of stunned silence.

"Oh well," Temijin shrugged, he didn't really care, "now we move on to the animals. I believe it's a couple of lions and a bear. Shall we add the star of the show as well? No, let's see how she does against an angry dragon." He stood at the edge of his box and waved a hand. There was a rumbling from beneath the arena.

Temijin beckoned Ozanus and Diego forward to

peer over the edge again. They hadn't noticed before but there was a large rising gate below them. A scarred dragon ran out with a roar, swishing its tail. It span round in a circle much to the delight of the audience who cheered. Temijin remarked, "this one is a tough one, we've yet to kill him. He's now a crowd favourite."

The dark green dragon with ridged horny plates along its back took up a lot of the space but not enough to fill it. It had clearly been dragged out from the darkest depths of some forest. Its wings had been sawn off leaving scarred stumps not that it would have been able to fly with them.

Another gate opened and two male lions with shaggy manes ran out to get whacked by the dragon's tail. They lay stunned for a few seconds before getting back to their feet. Sticking to the edge of the arena they began to circle, eyes warily on the dragon.

From the other side of the arena another gate was raised and a pack of large hunting hounds swarmed out baying for blood. Some of their bodies carried the scars of previous fights. Some had lost ears, a few had shortened tails and others had bald patches from healed wounds though deep scars remained. They charged at the dragon and there were too many for it to attack. Soon it had to shake to loosen their hold.

Some landed near the two lions and then a smaller fight broke out much to the delight of the audience. The dragon roared as a dog found a spot where a scale had dropped off from a previous fight and the tender flesh underneath could be bitten.

Temijin turned to the men at the back of their box and demanded, "more!"

The two men glanced at each other and then hurried away. Their leader was quickly getting bored today or was it because his guests weren't looking particularly impressed with it all? Hurrying down the corridor and stairs they discussed their options, "another animal?"

"No. He's bored already."

"Another dragon?"

"Mmm, don't think that would be good considering the guests. Have you seen the ones they flew in on? They are even bigger than the two he brought back with him."

"I hear they are fed virgins to make them that big." One whispered with a quick glance around.

The other rolled his eyes and then said, "we only have one choice then. We are going to have to go for the big one."

"What?! Already? It will make it a short day."

"What he wants is what he gets." He shrugged, "we don't have any other options."

"Fine. Let's get the she-devil up there then."

"Without her leading them I hope we don't get any more bother from the bitches."

A hush descended on the arena as those who felt the vibrations from the under-croft realised this was different from normal. It quickly spread through the crowds. People moved to the edge of their seats. Those in the front row peered over trying to work out what was happening, which gate was going to open. The animals sense something as well and paused in their attacks. A few sniffed the air.

Temijin leant against the edge of the box and hissed, "yes! Let's see that bitch die!"

Diego and Ozanus glanced at each other and then curiosity got the better of them and they joined Temijin in peering over to see which way the Daughter of Scyth would come out.

The gate below them opened and the Daughter of Scyth was marched out between two guards. They left the chains round her wrists and thrust her forward causing her to fall to her knees. They threw a sword and spear on to the dirt for her to use. The dogs and dragons turned to look at her. Ozanus couldn't take his eyes off her. Though she had been locked away she still stood with a straight back as if her ego hadn't even been bruised. He wondered what she would do. Would she actually fight the dragon? Would she sacrifice herself to it? Or would she be merciful and end the dragon's life? His hands gripped the edge of the box.

The audience was quiet as they waited to see what she would do as well. They held their breaths as they watched her roll her shoulders, stretch her back and adjust the hold of the sword that she had picked up. Would she use it?

The dogs growled at her as they started to approach, she was now in their territory. From the other side of the dragon the last lion standing limped round to see if it could win against the new smell in the arena. The dragon shifted and its tail swept the lion against the stone wall of the arena, stunning it. It growled at the woman, *"who are you?"*

"I am a Daughter of Scyth."

"You speak as if I should know what you are. Clearly you are not someone to be heard of if you have foolishly been captured."

"I could say the same of you." She retorted, *"how could you let yourself be caught?"*

"Because they went far to find me and I was a foolish youngster once. You age quickly here." The dragon replied.

"I am sorry." She bowed her head.

"Don't be."

Up in the box they all strained to hear what she and the dragon were saying. Temijin looked to the Keytellians, "can you hear?"

"Not clearly, but it is simple small talk from what I can catch." Diego politely replied without taking his eyes off the scene below.

Temijin grunted, disappointed and relieved at the same

97

time.

Back down on the arena floor the dragon asked, *"is it true that the Nejus is here? I heard it from another dragon."*

"Yes he is though I'm not sure why." She reluctantly answered.

"The answer is obvious. He is here to save us dragons."

"You have been listening to the ancients, it is just a story." She laughed.

The dragon growled and it was only then she felt fear and took a step backwards. The dragon snorted approval.

"We are both here and only one of us will be allow to survive. Who will it be?" She asked, changing the direction of the conversation.

"I think today both of us will be dying, whatever we chose to do. I am ready to go, I've fought to stay alive in this arena for too long. I'm tired. With the Nejus here, this arena will be coming to its end. Kill me but be prepared to have to fight for your life."

"They have given me this sword." She lifted it.

"I have plenty of partly healed wounds, stick it deep into one of them."

"Are you sure?"

"Yes." He replied firmly.

She nodded.

The audience couldn't take their eyes off the woman and dragon. Even the surviving dogs knew something was about to happen and circled the edge of the arena occasionally whimpering. The audience leant forward in their seats, holding their breaths as they watched the leader of the Daughters of Scyth bow to the dragon before stabbing it in a place that had lost a scale, going deep into the flesh, up to her shoulder. It roared in pain as the blood started to run out. In the box Ozanus flinched as if he could feel the dragon's pain.

There was a roar of shock and disappointment from the crowds. Temijin stamped his foot in rage, "no!" He turned to the attendants at the back of the box, "kill her! Destroy her! Send everyone in. I will not let her shortchange me."

Diego whispered, *"what do we do?"*

"Her fate is decided."

Diego frowned, *"how do you know? We must rescue her."* If he was younger he would have jumped over the edge of the box and joined her in the arena.

Ozanus turned and looked at his blinking his eyes, "what?"

Diego stared at him, "did you not hear me?"

"What? Why? What did I say?"

Diego realised then that the voice that had replied to his first question hadn't been Ozanus'. It had been older and deeper.

Twelve

Decision made Lylya went in search of the servant who had offered her freedom. A new life with the Daughters of Scyth would be better than where she was now and the closest she would get to the Valley. She found the woman in the laundry and pulled her out into the corridor, "take me away from here."

Taleba smiled softly, "it is the right decision. Come, we will leave now. We can give you everything you need."

"How?"

"There is no time." It was Taleba's turn to pull as she led Lylya down the corridor and out of the tower through the stables and to a narrow half-forgotten door in the wall. By it was a bundle of clothes, "put these on, quickly." She threw it at Lylya who opened it to find a pair of worn boats and a coat.

"Where do we go? We can't really be going on foot?" Lylya asked as Taleba headed out down the street towards the back of the fishponds and to fields beyond, "will we not be seen?"

"Everyone is at that foul arena." Taleba spat out her disgust, "we will not be seen."

As they began crossing the fields Lylya hesitated and glanced back at the tower and the city. She saw Ozi and Joli crouched on the far side of the fishponds and wondered whether she should instead make a run to them and get them to protect her till Ozanus returned. She decided she would be safer, with no opportunity for Temijin to drag her back if she carried on. She turned back to Taleba and ran to catch up.

"Everything alright? No misgivings?" Taleba asked as Lylya caught up to walk at her side.

"No misgivings." Lylya carefully smiled. The only regret was she was leaving her brother and Diego behind and they wouldn't know where she had gone. Would Temijin take it out on them? She knew Ozanus and Deigo could look after themselves.

They walked for at least two hours though Lylya had no way of tracking the time as the sun was hidden behind clouds. They walked through the worked fields that turned into scrubland and quickly into woods. They stepped in and out of small clearings and across streams that split the woodland floor. Finally they came to, by all appearances, an abandoned farm. The house roof was caved in but the barn seemed too big in comparison and apart from a large quantity of ivy climbing around one corner was in good repair.

Out of the dilapidated house came a woman. Her golden hair hung in one long plait down her back. She wore trousers tucked into high ankle boots and wore a waist length brocade coat with an upright furred collar. It currently hung open showing a fitted shirt. She demanded, *"who is this Taleba? Were you followed?"*

"They were all at the arena." Taleba replied, "and this is Lylya."

The other's facial features softened and she smiled, "welcome Lylya. I am Elaheh."

"Where are we?"

"This is a waypoint for us so my dragon can't be caught

by Temijin and so we can then get home." Elaheh said carefully so as not to give away the fact that there was actually a group of them using this as base, attacking at random on foot any of Temijin's men.

"Is there one here?"

"Yes." Elaheh turned to the barn and shouted, *"Calluna, show yourself!"*

The side of the barn trembled and then from under the ivy a dragon's pale grey snout appeared and snorted, *"glad to hear it. It's rather dusty in there. When was it last cleaned?"*

"Oh don't fuss. You know full well we can't."
More of the dragon emerged and it shook itself like a dog once in the clearing. It stretched its wings and snorted again and swung her spiked tail round, *"why do I have to hide in there?"*

"Just stop Calluna. You know why. We don't want you getting caught by Temijin."

"I wouldn't let him." She growled. She turned and saw the visitor, *"who is this?"*

"This is Lylya."

"Who? Is she wanting to be saved from the world of men? It's no easy life where we are." She stared straight at Lylya expecting to unnerve her. Lylya stared straight back, unperturbed by the arrogant dragon. The dragon's eyes narrowed suspiciously, *"you are not scared of me?"*

"I am sister of the Nejus." Lylya calmly replied with a brief bow of the head to acknowledge the dragon.

"Now, why don't I get that respect from you Elaheh?" Calluna turned to her rider.

"Because we have been with each other since you were born." Elaheh sighed. She had never worked out where Calluna had got her high opinion of herself.

"We were Gods once. I bet she still worships us." Calluna retorted.

Elaheh rolled her eyes, *"because, we, several generations ago, agreed with your ancestors to co- exist without ceremony or holding one or other of us higher than the other. Who has been filling your head with nonsense?"* Changing the subject Calluna asked, *"why is the sister of the famous Nejus here?"*

"Taleba?" Elaheh turned to Lylya's companion.

"Because we need the Nejus to help us destroy the arena and Temijin. If we have Lylya, she will help us convince him to be on our side."

"When have we needed a man's help?"

"Since Esfir got captured and they have bigger dragons."

"He won't need persuading." Lylya interrupted, "the Gods have set him a task and maybe this is it."

"But will he?" Elaheh challenged, "I hear he spends his time fighting and feasting and that it is your younger brother who rules on his behalf."

Lylya bowed her head to hide her brightening cheeks of shame. She was right, would her brother do the right thing?

"Stop Elaheh! She is our guest. We need her on our side and so far we are showing that neither us, nor our dragons," Taleba glared at Calluna, "are united when we know we are. I made the decision to invite her to come with me. We need her brother's help even if no one else thinks we do. I live in that tower and see and hear a lot."

"But we are currently leaderless. We should be trying to rescue Esfir, not hiding here." Elaheh protested.

"She cannot be rescued with the six of you and one dragon. That's not a rescue force. Now we need to decide on a new leader and be even stronger."

Lylya interrupted, "sorry, but how do we get to your home? Will Ozanus know to find us, me, there?"

"We fly, which is why Calluna is here. Now, you and I get to leave, now." Elaheh beckoned Lylya forward.

"No saddle?" Lylya queried.

103

"Dragons aren't packhorses."

"I know but saddles are definitely more comfortable than bareback."

"Sorry, no saddles, just the quilted blanket." Elaheh replied with a shrug as she helped Lylya up on to Calluna's back, "hold on with your knees."

They were flying for at least two hours before the flat topped vertical sided mountain came into view. Halfway up the mountain was a layer of thick cloud that rose and fell depending upon the weather creating a microclimate of its own. Circling the bottom was trees. A river fed by a waterfall broke through the woods. Near the river was a camp. Elaheh remarked with a chuckle, "Temijin's men keeping an eye on us."

"Do they even see you?"

"Occasionally, it cannot be helped."

"Why don't you attack and then they'll be gone?"

"It's not worth it. We did once but they came back better prepared. We'll circle round to the other side and then up through the clouds and they won't see us."

With a roar Calluna flicked her tail to propel them up through the clouds. Lylya closed her eyes against the water droplets as they rose through the clouds and back into the sun.

Opening her eyes at the feel of the sun she stared in wonder at the sight below her. The source of the waterfall was a large pool of water with the barest hint of the spring rippling its surface with a stone wall enclosing it. Spread across the rest of the ground was fields of crops, round houses and workshops. A few young dragons rose up to greet the arrivals while others briefly glanced up from the cliff face. Lylya asked, "how many dragons are there?"

"Enough.... Not many."

"How many ride?"

"Not as many as use to." Elaheh frowned, "we have found it to be safer for all that only a select, honoured few will now be allowed to fly. It has not been safe for many years. Youngsters, both girls and dragons, encouraged each other to be reckless and that is how they get caught. The camp is mainly there waiting to catch any that are foolish to go near."

Calluna lazily circled a few times before landing. She sniffed with a hint of disdain. Elaheh rolled her eyes and remarked, *"you don't have to stay here if you don't want."*

"I didn't even get to see the Valley dragons." Calluna muttered.

"I'm sure you will if my brother can find this place." Calluna turned to Lylya who now stood by her side, *"are they really bigger than the dragons here?"*

"I've only met you so far so can't say but yes they are bigger than you."

"Come with me Lylya, I'll take you to the council." Elaheh beckoned Lylya away from the dragon who she guessed was already plotting a mating. She had to hope the council was in the council roundhouse.

Lylya was taken to a roundhouse with a large porch. Hanging between the wooden pillars were banners embroidered with dragons curling upwards, clucking eggs in their tails. Large stones held down the rope netting that in turn held down the thatched roof. Smoke seeped through the thatch. Elaheh ducked in and announced Lylya who hesitated on the step.

Inside a fire burnt both wood and incense. Around the edge was laid out benches and chairs. Directly opposite the doorway was a high-backed chair painted and carved with a dragon clasping an egg. The chair was currently empty but either side ranged 6 women of various ages plus two empty chairs. They looked surprised to see the windblown Lylya step around Elaheh.

The eldest, white hair plaited with ribbon running through it, leant across the table, one eye cloudy and the other a piercing green, "are you truly daughter of Kittal?" Lylya glanced round at all the women. They were all wearing similar outfits to Elaheh, fur collared double breasted coats, some done up with a toggle on their shoulders, others with it loose from the heat of the fire apart from the elder. The elder was dressed in a undyed blouse with a pinafore dress over the top cinched in with a belt that held a bag and various tools Lyla couldn't identify. She answered carefully, feeling a little intimidated by them all looking at her, "I am." She shifted in her boots.

"I am sorry that the world of man has not been easy for you."

"How… How do you know?" Lylya asked warily.

"I see much, even more so now that everyday life does not interfere so much anymore. Though you may not know of us, which I think is true." She paused as Lylya nodded and opened her mouth as if to ask a question before changing her mind. The elder went on, "we know of your father, as we have always known of the Nejuses of Keytel."

"Were you all originally from Keytel?"

"That is a question for another day."

"Did my father know about you?" Lylya asked out of curiosity.

"He never came this far north however we heard of what he was doing through the men we have taken as lovers. I would have loved to have met him, even have him as my lover."

Lylya blushed as one of the women beside the elder hissed, "Mada, behave yourself."

Mada chuckled and sat back, "a woman can dream. Image a child of his and Esfir's."

"I'm sure Lylya is a good example. She must have some

106

of his spirit if she is standing before us."

The woman, with beads and ribbon braided into three auburn plaits which in turn were plaited together, who sat to the left of the big empty chair, stood and remarked without emotion before tersely saying, "welcome." Her face had a sprinkling of freckles on a high boned face with a slightly pointed chin. Currently she was revealing nothing of her thoughts which made Lylya think of Ozanus and his hidden moods.

The elder interrupted, still on her train of thought, "perhaps Lylya should become our leader. Imagine her bloodline joining with ours…."

"Mada!" Miryama exclaimed, "that is not up for discussion yet, she may still live. Elaheh," she turned to Elaheh who stood to one side of the doorway, "any news on Esfir?"

"Everyone was at the arena today so might have news next time."

"Hmm."

"He won't let her go or escape." Lylya injected.

Miryama raised an eyebrow in surprise at Lylya's boldness.

"Told you." Mada crowed and then chuckled again.

Miryama rolled her eyes, "enough Mada."

Mada stood, "I'm going to go see how the next generation are doing. Lylya, walk with me while these ladies talk boring stuff."

"Umm." Lylya glanced at the council and then at Mada, "sure."

Mada smiled as she slipped round and to the round house entrance. With a free hand she tucked her arm round one of Lylya's, "come, let me show you round."

Thirteen

Temijin was angry. His longest surviving dragon was dead by the crazy Daughter and now she was dead as well. There hadn't been the fight he wanted, expected. He looked to his guests to see if they were disappointed but their faces weren't revealing anything. He shook himself to compose himself, "come, we are done here, let us return to the city."
He walked out of his box and waved away the two men that approached and growled, "not now."

Diego and Ozanus peered over the wall at the scene of death on the arena floor. The living lion was now dead after taking a few soldiers with it who lay moaning from the claw and tooth induced injuries The dogs had taken the safer route and fled. Esfir had left a circle of death round her. She went down fighting and for every injury she received she gave back two, till she became too weak to hold her sword up and the last two men standing took their vengeance by stabbing her again and again even once she was clearly dead.

The two dragons riders glanced at each other, both had been impressed by the Daughter's persistence and stamina, but Temijin hadn't been. Would they now find themselves in the same cages? They each gave the other a small nod. They weren't going to let that happen. They would have to stay alert.

Their morning breakfast was disrupted by ten riders on horseback driving their horses hard the short distance and then pulling hard on their mouths to get them to stop. At the front was a red faced Temijin. He stood in his stirrups and pointed at Deigo and Ozanus, "take them!"

The dragons swept their riders off their feet with a wing each and the two of them retreated to the safety of their dragons' backs.

"Don't let those dragons take off!" Temijin roared. The riders moved closer, the horses shying at the size of the beasts.

"What do you want from us?" Ozanus enquired, trying to stay calm, a hand on Ozi's neck telling her to stay put. If he dug a hand under a scale she would know to take off.

"Where are you hiding her?" Temijin demanded.

"Hiding who?" Ozanus frowned.

"You should know. Your sister." Temijin spat, "give her back right now. She is rightfully mine."
Diego and Ozanus looked to each other. Had Lylya decided to act herself? Or had she found someone to help her?

It dawned on Temijin then and he hissed, "them! Those damn Daughters of Scyth. This is revenge."

"Well, he did kill their leader." Diego remarked and Ozanus tried not to chuckle.

"They must have kidnapped her. I need your help to rescue her."

"Do you think she will want rescuing?" Diego asked.

"Perhaps we could find her and then take her home with us?" Ozanus considered.

"But we don't know where she is."
They both looked at Temijin who impatiently waited.

"We'll have to use him then." Ozanus said with a nod in the horseman's direction.

"What if he tricks us?"

"I don't think he can get away with that. We've got these two and these Daughters might be willing since their leader has just been killed by him."

"True."

"Are you going to ask our opinion before you put our lives at stake?" Ozi snorted.

"Lylya has been taken..." Ozanus told the two dragons.

"Or gone willingly." Diego added.

"True. Either way we need to go find her."

"And the arena?" Joli asked, *"that can't be allow to stay standing."*

"We will see about that. I can't promise anything."

"Get the Daughters of Scyth involved perhaps?" Diego suggested, *"I don't think they would say no to destroying that place. It can't be allowed to stay."* He finished with a frown.

"Now, that is a good idea." Ozanus grinned.

"What do you speak of?" Temijin demanded. The two dragon riders looked down. Ozanus nodded, "we will help."

"We need to destroy that band of troublesome women once and for all, teach them all a lesson they'll never forget." Temijin growled.

Some of his men grinned. Diego became nervous. Ozanus glanced at his friend, *"we'll take as much as we can and give as little as possible in return."*

"One of us should stay with the dragons."

The two Keytellians glanced at the dragons and then at the group from Duntorn. Ozanus nodded, *"I'll go, you stay."*

"Got your knife?"

Ozanus half pulled his dragon headed knife from is sheath.

"Be careful."

Ozanus turned to Temijin, "I will come and we will make a plan."

110

"Excellent." Temijin grinned, "we'll go now then."

With an order for refreshments to be brought Temijin led Ozanus to a room off his bedchamber. A large table was in the centre of it, taking up much of the space. Several maps lay half unfurled on it including one of Keytel. While Temijin was distracted by the arrival of food and drink Ozanus had a quick glance and was relieved to see the Valley didn't have much detail to it. The Valley, for the moment, was still safe. It could defend itself.

With a roll in his mouth Temijin shuffled through the maps till he had his own country's map on top. He stabbed a chunky finger at an area marked with several hills, "here, this is where they breed. I have a camp at the bottom, watching, picking off dragons when they can but I haven't managed to get anyone up there to get the lay of the land. Your dragons can." Temijin looked to Ozanus who appeared to be half listening.

Ozanus turned to Temijin from where he had been pouring himself a drink, and peering at drawings on another table of what looked like Temijin's war engines, "why have you not managed to get to their base?"
Temijin turned to a pile of papers and pulled one out. It showed a sketch of a vertical sided hill with no hand holds to use to climb up. Even if there was any climber would be exposed to the weather, wind, and any circling dragons.

Ozanus didn't say anything but was impressed. It was certainly one way to ensure your dragons were safe. He asked, "what do you want me to do then?"
"Fly over, have a look at what they've got up there."
"What does that achieve? It's not like you can then attack them? You won't be able to draw them down to the ground." Ozanus pointed out, his strategic mind starting to try and work out Temijin's plan and how he could use it for himself.

111

"I know that." Temijin growled with warning.

Temijin knew he was grasping at straws but he hoped with the Keytellians on his side that maybe he could demoralise or weaken the Daughters of Scyth. Their leader was dead, whether they knew that or not so that would help him. She had been fearless and stubborn, almost worth admiring. She would have made a good wife if she had been inclined and then he would have been stronger and undefeatable. A little smiled danced on his lips at the thought of her in bed with him and his imagination went wild. Remembering who he was with he demanded, "are you going to help me?"

Ozanus shrugged. He would go out of curiosity and decide then. He never made a decision till the last minute, even if it was minutes before the fight. Diego tended to know what the decision would be and smoothed the way beforehand. Sometimes the presence of his Suwars and dragons was enough but he would still expect a payment.

His shrug frustrated Temijin who exclaimed, "is that it?! Is that your answer? That doesn't tell me anything."

Ozanus turned and looked directly at Temijin who fought the urge to step back, "you ask me to help. You ask me to agree to do something blind. I do not agree to anything until I know what I am up against."

Temijin didn't look impressed by the answer but knew he currently had no other options. Reluctantly he grumbled, "fine."

"Now, tell me where I need to go and then I will take my leave and prepare."

Being offered control again Temijin beckoned Ozanus to the table, "this is us." He pointed at the city of Duntorn on the map, "and you need to head here," he pointed to where a camp was marked at the bottom of a mountain at the far side of the map, "it's a three day march there but I'm sure it will be faster on your dragons. What else do you need to know?"

Ozanus studied the map, mentally noting the direction he and Diego would need to go in, "no, that's it. I will go prepare now."

"I want to know everything, numbers, how they live, their defences, any way up that has not been spotted before." Temijin demanded as Ozanus headed to the door.

Fourteen

Mada slowly led Lylya around the top of the mountain with the new day, leaning on her stick. She liked the young woman who was now dressed in the warmer and more practical clothes of the Daughters, patched in a few places but still in good condition. She knew that if given the opportunity she would make a strong leader.

Lylya was surprised by how big the area was. In the centre was a large pool with a spring bubbling in the centre. This fed a man-made stream with a water wheel turning on it and it then drained into the pools above the waterfall. At one end there were strip fields with a selection of grains and vegetables being grown and being cared for by women and a few boys. There was also an orchard of fruit and fields holding sheep and goats.

At the opposite end was the practice grounds. Mada and Lylya paused to watch two groups of young girls training dressed in long sleeved blouses and trousers, wide belts or sashes round their waists. One group were practising with short bows at butts while the other was in a circle standing or crouching watching two fight with wooden knives. A woman stood supervising them with her arms crossed, a scowl on her face. She shouted, "stop!" The two that were fighting paused in their positions breathing heavily. The woman approached, "watch your hold on your knife. You need it loose enough to be able to adjust your hold but tight enough that you can put your strength behind it."

She pulled her own knife out from her hip and showed how flexible her grip and wrist was. Lylya asked, "why do they need knife skills? Where are the dragons? Where are the men? I have only seen a few boys?"

Mada replied, "the dragons have nests in the cliffs. You may get shown a way to them when you are trusted. Men think us incapable of defending ourselves once close so we train them on close quarter attack and defence. As for men, they are invited up but aren't allow a permanent residence here. Any male heirs are allowed to stay till about eight or nine where they then go to their fathers."

"Why?"

"Who says a woman needs a man to protect her? We are as strong as them are we not? I believe your aunt led the Suwars. What more proof do you need?" Mada pointed out calmly, "come now, let us return to the village, there is still more to see."

As they turned another Daughter of Scyth, tears running down a dirty face, ran up crying out, "she is dead! We must all convene."

"Now calm down. Who is dead?" Mada demanded while behind them all the girls and young women stopped and stared.

"Esfir." The woman exclaimed, brushing tears off her cheeks and smearing soot, "Temijin has killed her."

"Did my brother not save her?" Lylya asked.
She turned and stared and asked in bewilderment, "your brother? Who are you and who is your brother?"

"Ozanus, Nejus of Keytel."
The woman spat at Lylya's feet, "he just watched as she was slaughtered."
Lylya's hand when to her mouth to hide her shock, she couldn't believe that was right. If only she could see him

115

and find out the reason; there had to be a reason.

The three teachers came over and one asked, "what's going on?"

"Our leader has been murdered. We must all convene. The council has requested we all convene here on the practice grounds. We are soon to be at war."

"We already were." One of the archery teachers pointed out, "we can't decide on a new leader till we have mourned."

"We need the stability of one now though." Mada said. The four women looked to her and the archery teacher asked, "what do you mean?"

"This is Lylya, a daughter of a Nejus, sister to a Nejus and reluctant wife of Temijin. It is likely he has now noticed she is missing, plus we must exact revenge on him for the death of Esfir."

They all stared at Mada, surprised by the anger in the old woman's voice. The four Daughters looked at Lylya with more curiosity now. Mada added, "and Lylya will join us. She will have knowledge that might be useful."

"She can't have a vote. She is not one of us."

"We'll see. Gather the girls."

Wooden benches were fetched from houses and brought to the practice grounds as it began to fill as word spread through the village and fields. Conversations happened while children ran around and babes were being breastfed. Gathered in the centre of the practice grounds was the council. They looked round as Mada and Lylya approached. Mada asked, "is it true?"

Miryama nodded, "we can't mourn as we should. Life is too fragile at the moment."

"We need the Nejus."

"No we don't." Another of the council objected, "we don't need a man's help. Now, let's get on with this."

Lylya moved a little closer to Mada, "what is about to

happen?"

"We must choose a new leader. Those that want it step forward and then it's a mixture of speeches, votes and then a dual between the last two. This will take a day or two, normally it would be better planned."

"Sssh, Miryama is about to speak." Someone hissed. Mada and Lylya turned to look.

Miryama stood a few steps forward of the rest of the council. She pulled her jacket down where it had ridden up. Her hand gripped a knife handle tucked into her sash. She gave a nod to someone holding a large bell and they rang it. Everyone stopped talking and the children running around stopped and sat where they were or ran to their mothers.

"As you know our bold strong leader was captured by Temijin. News has reached us that she is now dead. She went down fighting to the last. Normally we would mourn her loss and give ourselves time to look into our hearts and decide if we are worthy enough to put ourselves forward. This time we cannot. We have a guest in our midst and Temijin will want her back and currently we don't know what side the Nejus is going to be on."

"Yours." Lylya remarked quietly to Mada.

"Ssh." Mada murmured, "you do not know that."

"Yes I do." Lylya frowned.

"Ssh."

"Who will step up and take on the mantle of our leader and guide us forward?" Miryama went on.

"Miryama would have been perfect but now she has taken the lead on this decision making she cannot. She was Esfir's second." Mada remarked to Lylya.

"Oh."

There was quiet as the gathered women looked to each other and their sisters and their friends. Who was going to be bold enough to step forward?

After a few minutes there was movement and seven

women stepped forward.

"Thank you ladies. Please speak up now on who you are and then you'll have time to prepare for speeches this evening and the first vote." Miryama said loud enough for everyone to hear.

Names were declared and those who would second each one announced themselves as well before the gathering broke up. The council stood together talking once everyone had left. Lylya interrupted them, in support of her brother, "my brother **will** support you."

"Quiet! You are only a guest here. You should be seen and not heard." Miryama snapped, starting to feel stressed from her responsibilities and the fact she had had to step away from her desire of becoming leader of the Daughters.

"Why bring me here then? You say that you don't know which way my brother will fall but I can tell you."

"Why was he with Temijin at that hell hole that they call entertainment?" Miryama challenged.

"Curiosity, check the arena out, not to offend Temijin." Lylya listed off the possible reasons.

Miryama scowled at her before walking away. She had enough to worry about and didn't need this woman thinking she could tell them what to do.

That evening Lylya stayed away though she was curious about the proceedings. She had been invited to stay in Mada's roundhouse which was tidy but filled with a lot of belongings from generations and generations of Daughters. Two thirds of it was lived in with a couple of beds, chests, benches, stools and a circular fire hearth. This was where the meat, plants and vegetables hung from the rafters. The other third, divided away from the rest with a short wattle wall was crowded with old weaponry and several narrow unmade beds crammed in. Mada had remarked, as Lylya looked round, "just me and my assistant

118

live here now. Sometimes we tend to patients here. I'm one of a few medicine women up here. I've taught all of them."

Concerned that Mada wasn't going to the practice grounds after dinner Lylya said, "don't let me keep you from the speeches."

"Don't worry about it. There's plenty of the next generations to decide who will lead them forward. The girls can vote as well if someone captivates them enough. I prefer the warmth of the fire these days as it gets very chilly up here. Now wrap yourself in a blanket and join me. Tell me of the Valley." Mada gestured at a stool.

"Thank you." Lylya answered as she perched on a stool feeling a little like being round one of the campfires when the Suwars were visiting. Recently they hadn't been visiting as often due to Ozanus not living there and their new leader distancing himself from Ozanus and his own activities, "can I ask something?"

"Go on?"

"Why am I here? I'm grateful to have escaped Temijin but don't really understand why I am here. If feels like I'm not really wanted."

"We could not let you suffer. And though you haven't heard of us we are aware of you, your sister and your brothers. You are your father's daughter from what we have heard. If he had remained alive I think he would have encouraged you to lead the Suwars. I think, if you were to stay, you will become one of our leaders and tales of you will be told to generations to come."

Lylya's eyes widened, "how...? What....?"

Mada chuckled and then poked at the fire with her poker.

Fifteen

The camp had fallen into lazy habits. There were still watchers but as the women on their mountaintop didn't bother them they just kept an eye out for dragons. The dragons were a different matter. They came out of curiosity or they dared each other to get as close to the camp as possible. The huge arrows weren't used, too much of a waste but the men did use the dragons as target practice if they came too close. Occasionally they would manage to net one to send back to Duntorn for Temijin but that was getting rarer and rarer and half of them weren't arena material either from inbreeding.

Therefore the sentry on duty in the wooden tower facing the vertical sided mountain was starting to doze off. He only woke as he heard the sound of air being moved by wings. He recognised the sound enough to realise that this was a bigger beast than the Daughters' dragons. He peered out just as a shadow flew over. Shouts came up from the camp. He strained to see what it was but they seemed to have already disappeared. He leant over and shouted down, "what was that?"

"You're the lookout, you should be telling us!" Someone shouted up from below, "keep a better eye out for them while we set up the big one." The shouter walked away muttering, "we are going to need it."

Standing in the open centre of the camp the camp

leader stood with hands on hips supervising the setting up of the large arrow war machine. He wanted the two dragons brought down before they spotted the camp and destroyed it. Hopefully they would come round again and they would be ready next time. All the men were eager as something was actually happening for once.

High above, Ozanus and Diego, on their dragons, began their first circle of the mountain to get the lay of the land. They skimmed the top of the clouds, the dragons snapping at any small bits as if they were young ones again having fun. Their riders observed the flat mountain top taking in the fields, the roundhouses and the practice ground. There were plenty of people about and some were looking up, hands shielding eyes against the sun. Diego called out, "what do you think? I can't see any dragons."

"Where do you think the dragons are?" Ozanus asked the dragons.

Ozi snorted, *"I can smell them but can't see any."*

As they continued round they came to a wide vertical crack in the cliff. The floor of the crevice was littered with skeletons tumbling out of it. At the back were carved steps looking like they came from the top rather than the bottom. They led to ledges in the cliff face. On the ledges were nests and the dragons. The youngsters took flight to check them out. Joli growled a warning but they just chirped and chattered. They swooped around the two giants, dipping under their wings, flying through the clouds and popping out to startle the visitors. Ozi snapped angrily as one sprung up a metre in front of her. Ozanus and Diego glanced at each other. They were both surprised at the size of the dragons that had come to greet them. Seeing Ozi getting angry Ozanus said, *"let's leave these distractions behind. I want to check out the camp."*

With some relief Joli and Ozi turned their bodies

towards the high sun and with a few large beats of their wings left the youngsters below them. They then dived down through the clouds. Ozi asked, *"anyone following us?"*

"No." Ozanus turned to look behind.

"Good. We didn't need a childish escort." Joli snorted.

The lookout shouted and pointed in the direction, "here they come!"

The large arrow on the ballista was quickly turned to face the flying dragons. The angle was raised so it would be sent high into the sky. The camp leader glared at the dragons through narrow eyes against the sun, and raised a hand. Everyone that was gathered held their breathes so they could hear their leader's command. The air was so still they could hear the flap of the dragons' wings. The camp commander called out, "fire!"

The tensed coiled rope was released and the arrow smoothly slid up its groove towards the dragons. For the two dragons it was spotted too late and though Joli called out Ozi could only pull up at an angle. The arrow pierced through her scales and got caught in her ribs, puncturing a lung. Ozanus clung to her, *"hold up!"*

"Joli, break the shaft, it's pulling her down." Diego called out as he watched the unbalanced Ozi tipping forward even though she was trying to fly upwards. Joli flew in and snapped the shaft of the large arrow in his mouth.

A whimper escaped Ozi as she fought to hide her pain. With most of the weight of the arrow shaft gone she turned and flew upwards into the clouds. Ozanus shouted, *"where are we going?"*

Ozi didn't answer, she was concentrating on flying, getting away and finding somewhere safe. If she could get to the top of the mountain....

The women and girls on the training ground was stunned to see a red scaled dragon fly up and scramble with its claws on the edge, bits of the rock face breaking off and falling. It slumped forward on the dirt packed ground, pushing the remains of the arrow further into its chest. They watched as a man threw himself off the dragon's back and almost got swept off the edge as the dragon's clawed wings scrapped the ground to try and stay on top of the mountain. He went tumbling over the wide wing and landed on his back.

Another dragon emerged with a rider on its back. It grabbed the injured one by its tail. The audience couldn't work out if there was a fight happening or whether one was trying to save the other. The blue scaled dragon pulled upwards on the tail of the other but it was clearly weakening. The desperate movements were slowing and the blue dragon couldn't get the right grip to help her.

She began to slip and with one last look up to Joli and Diego she gave up. Joli roared out in rage and sorrow as he watched his mate fall through the clouds and hit the ground with an audible thud. Forgetting he had Diego on his back Joli dived below the clouds.

Diego held on tight but he could feel his leg muscles on his damaged leg tiring. He gripped the front of his saddle as he began to feel himself rising out of it.

The dust hadn't settled from Ozi hitting the ground as Joli crash landed and threw it into the air again. Diego found himself being thrown off into a tree as Joli landed and crashed to the ground himself.

Joli crept closer to Ozi who lay on her side, *"Ozi?"* She lifted her head, blood dripping from a huge gash, to look at him, *"we never had the chance."*
Joli nuzzled her and moaned.

"I will be with the Dragon Lord."

"But you should be with me."

"He clearly has a plan for the Nejus which I am not part of. Look after him like Diego does."

Joli nodded.

"At least they can't take me to that horrible arena." She tried to laugh. Becoming serious she added, *"destroy that place for me."*

"I will."

"And burn me as well, don't let them take my body to crow over their success."

"I will."

She lay her head back on the large rock fall boulder it had landed on, blood staining it and dripping from it to the ground and creating a stream of steaming blood running down under her body. She closed her eyes.

Joli nudged her with his head but now she lay still. He roared and high above, like a flock of disturbed birds, the mountain's dragons rose into the air calling out in fear and commiseration. He knew he needed to find Diego first so his rider didn't burn to death. He shuffled the best he could around Ozi's body, the boulders and the broken trees. He found Diego lying in a crumpled heap under a tree. He muttered, *"please be alive."*

Gently he lifted Diego and was relieved to feel the man's chest rising and falling in his claw though he was limp.

He pushed off the ground and flew up to the top of the mountain where he knew Diego would be safe and cared for while below his beloved would burn. He placed Diego carefully on the ground and looked for Ozanus. Already women were gathered around his Nejus. They turned as he landed and lay his rider down. Gruffly he said, *"take care of him, I will be back."*

He turned and pushed off.

Never had he used the flames that burnt within him.

He felt them heating up inside his belly. With a roar the flames poured out of his mouth as he swooped down to Ozi's still warm body. The white hot flames engulfed her body. He circled round and came in low again, spreading the flames further over her body and now spreading across the ground, consuming the trees, the sap spitting as it boiled in the heat.

He turned away from Ozi's burning body and turned his attention to Temijin's camp. He circled round the back of the mountain so they wouldn't know he was coming. He was sure they would have heard his roar but would have no idea where he would come from.

The flames burnt inside him and he wondered if he would be able to contain them once his anger and sorrow had subsided. He turned the last corner of the mountain and roared, announcing himself. They had nowhere to run as the flames licked up the buildings and reached out for the running men. In the heat of the flames metal melted and wood rapidly became charcoal. Joli then turned away from the mountain, away from the circle of flames that surround it now. He turned away from his Nejus and his rider to find somewhere to hide and mourn.

Sixteen

Lylya was on the far side of the fields with Mada helping gather herbs and plants for medicinal purposes. Both saw the two dragons fly past. Lylya turned with excitement to Mada, "they are here! Where will they land?"

"Mmm. They look like they are getting the lay of the land first. Come, lets start back to the village and be there to greet them." Mada picked up her basket and gestured at Lylya to pick up hers. Mada smiled to herself as she began walking. Though no one had listened in the past, she knew a new era was soon to begin and the two dragons heralded the start of its arrival.

They both froze as they heard the sound of the ballista and then thud of its arrow entering something solid. They moved even faster, not sure what they would find once they reached the village. Mada called out as they saw women and girls heading for the training grounds, "what's happening?"

"I was coming to find you. They are here, they've landed by the training ground but one of the dragons is injured." Miryama shouted as she headed towards them, "leave the baskets, we will need your skills Mada."

Lylya paused at the edge of the training ground while the other two hurried on. She saw women and girls gathered round two prone bodies and no dragons in sight and black smoke rising through the clouds behind them. Miryama came back to her and with more kindness than previously shown said, "they are both alive. Come, can you identify them for me?"

"I...?"

Miryama took Lylya by the wrist and gently led her forward, "Mada will look after them, she is good. She is the best"

They all stopped as they heard Joli roar. Lylya remarked, her hands tight fists, "Ozi is dead. Temijin will pay for this."

"He will, yes, but first lets look after your brother and his companion."

"Diego, he's call Diego." Lylya whispered.

"Come on." Miryama led her forward again. They went to Ozanus first. His headscarf had been unwrapped, his padded coat undone, and his thick leather gloves had pulled off. His eyebrows were pinched in silent pain above closed eyes. Mada knelt beside him, "no broken bones as far as I can tell, just a big bump on his head."

"He got off." One of the girls remarked, "but got knocked out by the dragon. He landed hard on his back."

"It was huge." Another added, still amazed by its size.

"He's young, he'll be fine." Another of the medicine women remarked.

Mada nodded in agreement, "we'll move him carefully."

"And Diego?" Lylya asked with fear.

Mada was helped to her feet and together the two medicine women with Lylya went to where another knelt by Diego's prone body.

Lying so still his age seemed more apparent. He was no longer the young man Lylya remembered from her childhood. He had greying hair and his hands were curled from the beginning signs of arthritis. Lylya realised that Joli would outlive his rider. Tears gathered in her eyes and she brushed them away as she fought to hide her feelings from everyone. No one needed to know she still had her little girl infatuation for him.

The three women quietly consulted over Diego's body before gesturing some others forward. Very slowly they lifted him on to a makeshift stretcher and was taken off towards the village. Mada approached Lylya and Miryama, "he is worst then your brother I'm afraid. It looks like he has taken a serious fall, probably off his dragon's back and looks like through some vegetation though I can't tell you from how high. He has quite a few scratches on him. There is a couple of bones which I'll set once back at my house. Come, they are bringing your brother as well."

The roundhouse was beginning to feel full. The three spare narrow beds were now full and Lylya had the fourth. Two of them now held the injured men while the third, squashed under the eaves, had an injured girl who had been caught by Ozi as she had scrambled to stay on the mountain top. A friend sat with her.

Space was at a premium as Mada murmured administrations and instructions and another medicine woman and her assistant looked after Diego. Lylya sat at the foot of her brother's bed, fiddling with the end of the sash she wore where there was a loose thread. Knowing what had happened to her brother and Diego she knew she couldn't let Temijin get away with it. She sat up straight and with determination said, "I want to put myself forward to lead."

"Not now Lylya." Mada replied without looking up, "revenge is not a good enough reason, and you need to learn our ways."

"Let me ride a dragon." She demanded, "I know I can."

"Maybe. That will be up to Aryana and the dragons." Mada turned to Lylya as her assistant wrapped the last bandage, "now, look after your brother and his friend while

128

I go and check on the birthing hut with these two, I believe we have two preparing to birth in there and you girl," referring to the injured girl's friend, "stop gawking. Your friend will be fine tomorrow and will have a scar to talk of in the future."

The girl, with a glance at her friend, ran from the house, embarrassed she had been caught eavesdropping. Mada rested a mottled hand on Lylya's shoulder, "have patience. We need your brother awake first to find out what is happening. We must also finish voting in our new leader. Now, give your brother this if he wakes and feels sick. It will let him sleep for a little longer and let his head settle." Mada gestured at the cup on the table behind Lylya.

"And Diego?"

"If he wakes, find me, it will be too soon for him."

Lylya nodded.

The roundhouse was quiet with no one else in it but Lylya still hesitated to touch her brother and let him know she was there. She froze as he stirred and watched as his hand reached for his head and moan, "ugh, my head."

"Ozanus?"

He slowly turned his head as he heard his sister's voice, "Lylya?"

He opened his eyes which quickly widened. He sat up too quickly and felt dizzy. He clutched his head in both hands, "ooo, Lylya is that really you? I feel sick and ache all over. Where am I?" Remembering what happened he demanded, "where's Ozi?!" He tried to get out of bed but his body protested.

"Umm, Ozanus, not now, you need to drink this and we'll talk properly later."

"No, tell me now!" He spotted Diego opposite him and calmed, "is that..?"

"Yes, we aren't sure what happened to him. Please, drink this, you need to let your body rest." Lylya reached for the wooden cup behind her. She held it as he drank from it. As he lay back down, feeling the infusion working he remarked, "I'm glad you are safe."

"So am I." She smiled at him, "now rest." She pulled the blanket up him.

Seventeen

He was woken by the noise of cooking but wasn't sure by the smell of it if it was any good. Sitting up more carefully than the previous day the nausea had gone but the aches and bruising remained. He asked, "is something burning?"

"Most of it has stopped. It burnt fierce most of the night. Everywhere is going to smell of the smoke for a while." Mada sat on the stool by the fire and looked at Ozanus. She studied him for any hints of anything wrong, "how do you feel this morning?"

"A lot better, thank you…?"

"Mada." She bowed her head in acknowledgement of his status, "I suggest you stay in bed today and then maybe tomorrow you can get up."

"Where is Lylya?"

"Asleep. I made her." Mada answered firmly, "now, hungry?"

"Yes, thank you."

He looked round the roundhouse from his bed as Mada organised some of the pottage and fried bacon into a bowl. There was a chest at the end of the bed and at his head was a stack of spears. In a dark recess he could make out a sleeping form who he guessed was Lylya. Opposite him was Diego with a bandage round his head and another covering half the bare arm that lay bent on top of the blanket. He frowned as he realised that the injuries made Diego look his age. He asked as Mada handed him the bowl, "how is he?"

"We aren't sure. We can only wait and see. He is fit for his age." Mada smiled.

"He is." Ozanus observed back, "he has been with me a long time and with my father before that. Thank you. Our dragons, do you know what happened to them?"

"One of them died we think."
His breath caught as he knew which one and hoped Joli hadn't suffered the same fate.

"The smoke is from the fire created by the other. Temijin's camp has been destroyed but it has not returned."

"Joli will return. He and Ozi were close though you wouldn't always know it." Ozanus remarked with a chuckle as he raised the spoon to his mouth.

A new voice interrupted the conversation, "oh, you are awake? Feeling better?"
Mada and Ozanus looked to Lylya and he smiled, "I am and it's good to see you. How long have you been here?"

"A couple of days." Lylya replied as she pulled on trousers and a Scythian jacket. She accepted the bowl from Mada and sat on Ozanus' bed. Mada crossed the space to check on Diego. They both watched and Lylya quietly said, "he's bad Ozanus."

"I've heard. Maybe it's time he should stay home."

"I don't think he would agree, you need him too much."

"He is like a father to me and perhaps I need to grow up." Lylya rolled her eyes and exclaimed, "finally!"

"What?!"

"Ozanus, you are an idiot sometimes. Maybe the Dragon Lord has set you this mission so you do grow up and step into father's shoes as much as you can?"

"I don't think I can ever be as good as our father."

132

"No one can be like their father." Mada remarked, turning back to look at the siblings. She sensed their closeness. "You can only try to be your own best."

"And I don't think I have been." Ozanus remarked thoughtfully. He studied the contents of his bowl feeling guilty of what he had put Diego through and not just in the last few days, over the years as well. He handed the unfinished bowl to Mada, his appetite gone. Lylya looked at him with confusion. He gave her a tight smile, "I'm fine."

"Let's leave you to rest. Come on Lylya, let's go see what's happening with the candidates." Mada took the bowl from Lylya and gently pushed her out the door. She glanced back at Ozanus and saw a small boy who was confused sitting in bed, the arrogant young man currently absence. She had to blink as she felt sure she saw two shadows of Dragon Gods on the wall of the roundhouse, behind the young man glaring at each other. The next second they were gone as she thought it must have been her imagination.

It was early when he woke the next morning. He could hear Mada snoring in her bed close to the tamped down fire. Lylya was at the back and opposite him Diego still hadn't moved. Slowly he got to his feet, aware he might feel unsteady but thankfully didn't feel dizzy or nauseous. He pulled on his tunic top, coat and boots and crossed the few steps to Diego. He placed a hand on Diego's still hand and silently prayed to the Gods to keep him safe and let him heal. He felt a twitch of a finger and saw movement in Diego's face but then he was still again, "take care friend, I'll be back and hopefully so will Joli as we are going to need him."

He stepped out of the roundhouse into the cool early morning air. A heavy dew rested on everything. He took note of the roundhouses before choosing a direction and heading away from them, trying to remember what he had observed from the skies two days earlier. He found his way to the edge but couldn't see anything from the layer of cloud that he had flown through on Ozi. He wondered whether there was a temple or altar to make an offering to the Gods and would they even accept it from him?

He turned away from the edge and began walking along it and came across the pool that fed the waterfall. Close up it was divided up into several pools flowing into a bigger one. He spotted the small mill a bit further into the mountaintop. One had steps leading into it, another had washing drying on stones and the third was fenced off with a bucket on a rope attached to it. The pool looked very tempting after the last few days.

He abandoned his clothes at the top of the steps and waded in before diving under. He let the water hold him under the surface till his body demanded oxygen before rising back up.

Suddenly he felt himself being pulled down. He tried to keep on the surface but whatever was pulling him was stronger. He didn't know how deep the pool was but it seemed to have become bottomless. He glanced down and saw a yellow glow, *"grow up now! You have lost your dragon because of your indecision and your best man lies unconscious."*

"I...."

"You are the Nejus."

Ozanus kicked at the claw holding his ankle, fear growing in him as even the Dragon Lord had seen through his bravo to his inner turmoil. He didn't want to be told what he already knew but wouldn't admit. Finally he broke free as below him the God snarled, *"get on with it. Remind these women that if it wasn't for me they wouldn't even exist any longer. They would have been raped and re-enslaved long ago."*

Ozanus broke the surface gasping for air. He could still feel the rage from the Dragon Lord around him, tightening his chest. He had so far let everyone down. Ozi was dead, Diego unconscious, Lylya had rescued herself somehow, Keytel had been entered and nearly lost and he couldn't even cope at being the Nejus and chose to run away from it leaving Ioan doing most of the work.

Slowly the feeling of rage subsided and he began to relax enough to start planning war, something he could do. He knew he needed to prove to not just the Dragon Lord but himself that he was truly his father's son. He needed to destroy Temijin and the arena and take Moronland as his like his father had taken Jukirla. He needed to be feared by his enemies again.

He was interrupted from his thoughts, "so you are awake?"

He turned to find one of the Daughters of Scyth standing at the top of the steps, hands on hips.

"You know we don't normally let men wander round on their own but I think we will have to make an exception for you Nejus." She gave him a mocking bow.

Ozanus took his time studying her. Her woollen dyed green tunic coat embroidered with pine trees and closed with a dark green sash accentuated her slim figure. Her auburn hair was braided with ribbons and beads framing a lightly tanned face with a sprinkling of freckles over her nose. Her hazel eyes glared at him from the fine boned face. She stood with feet wide and hands on her hips, alluding to a power that she wanted to keep hold of.

"Are you the new leader?"

"No." She snapped and then realised she had revealed her feelings on that matter.

He smirked, getting into his comfort zone, "but you want to be?"

135

"Get dressed, you must meet with the council." She retorted, ignoring his question.

"Your name?"

She thought about whether to reveal it or not but realised he would find out anyway, "Miryama."

"And you are?"

"Acting leader of the Daughters of Scyth until we have elected a new leader. And you are Nejus of Keytel, son of Kittal and Defender of dragons though you seem to be failing at that at the moment."

Ozanus bit back what he wanted to retort and instead smiled with a sneer, "glad you know how to boost a man's ego."

A smiled tugged at her lips.

"You'd best turn round unless you want to see all of me."

"Nothing I've not seen before."

"Don't blame me if you throw yourself at me."

She rolled her eyes, "just because we don't have men here permanently doesn't mean we are all sex starved. Come on, we've not got all day." She folded her arms, trying to hide the fact she was enjoying the banter.

He shrugged his shoulders, "you can't say I didn't warn you." He swarm across to the steps and headed up them, water dripping from his body.

Miryama kept her eyes lowered but still studied Ozanus' naked form, taking in the muscular arms and legs, the scar on his shoulder from some old mercenary job and the sprinkling of golden hair on his chest as well as the hair on his head. His body was suggesting a tough exterior but there was a look in his light brown eyes he hadn't quite managed to hide of inadequacy. He blinked and it was gone and a steely look appeared. He glared at her as if he knew she had seen something she shouldn't have. To break the tension she remarked, "you're safe, you aren't my type," and turned away from him.

He chuckled as he pulled his clothes on to his damp body. "Come on. I'll take you to the council."

She led him to the roundhouse used for council meetings. Inside he found Lylya standing to one side along with four other women. In front of him were five women all sat down, one of them Mada. Miryama took the seat next to the empty high back chair carved with its dragon and egg. Ozanus was curious about but he knew now was not the right time to ask questions. Maybe later Mada would be willing to answer his questions.

One of the councillors was the first to speak once Ozanus had been offered a stool to sit on, "how long before Temijin knows what has happened to his camp?"

"A week at least. They get a weekly messenger." Elaheh replied from the end of the row.

"So we have about three weeks, maybe four to prepare ourselves."

"We should just leave here, find somewhere new. There are those who are fed up of being always wary, we want to be free of Temijin." Someone spoke up.

"That is not the way of the Daughters." Miryama retorted.

"While Temijin lives we will never be safe."

"Why have you not tried to kill him?" Ozanus asked out of curiosity.

"Don't think we haven't tried but he always works out who we are and sends them to the arena. We have lost several good women to that damn arena." An obviously pregnant councillor remarked bitterly, "and how dare you ask such a question?! You have arrived unannounced, unwelcomed and we do not know what side you are on."

"Why take Lylya then?" He challenged.

"We rescued her from Temijin, something you clearly were incapable of doing." She sneered back.

"Calm down Dari you will make the babe restless." The defeatist councillor tried to soothe, putting a hand on Dari's

137

arm.

"Oh, sssh! We need warriors don't we, let it feel the anger." Dari retorted and turned back to Ozanus. She stood and demanded, "we should put him on trial."

"You do know who this is don't you?!" Lylya exclaimed, stepping forward to stand beside her brother who appeared remarkably calm.

He raised a hand to silence her, "let them rage and then we can get down to the real business."

"Who says you can dictate what we do?!" Dari spat and then demanded, "put him on trial, for letting our leader die in Temijin's arena. He is no protector of dragons if he allowed her to die there."

"Quiet Dari." Miryama ordered.

"No, you will not quiet me Miryama, you are not my leader."

"Quiet Dari, you'll excite the babe you carry. I was left in charge as acting leader by Esfir and until a new one is elected I will stay so." Miryama said sternly.

But Dari wasn't finished and continued, "why was he even allowed to roam free? You know men should stay in the men's enclosure. He could be a spy for all we know!"

"Would a spy from Moronland really come on the back of a dragon? He and his companion were injured and needed my care." Mada pointed out.

"His sister could be a spy as well." Dari exclaimed.

Elaheh stood, "I can vouch for her. She certainly isn't if you heard how he treated her."

Miryama stood and shouted, "enough!" More quietly she went on, "The Nejus is our guest and currently we are not giving him a very good impression. If you do not want to be part of this meeting then leave."

"Hmpfh." Dari sat down with arms crossed, "get on with it then before I need to go and piss."

Miryama restrained the urge to roll her eyes. Hopefully no

one saw her heavy sigh as she sat back down. She looked to Ozanus. Did she see mirth in his eyes? To give herself a chance to compose herself she requested drinks for everyone.

With the drinks passed out and Dari returned from the toilet Miryama said, "I have invited the Nejus here to answer questions if he is willing. We don't know why he is here. Nejus, are you willing?"

Ozanus nodded.

"Thank you sir."

"Sir…." Dari muttered scathingly but went silent at a glare from Mada.

Miryama ignored the comment. Dari had had the chance to be elected if she wanted but had chosen not to. She asked Ozanus, "why did you come to Moronland?"

He thought about whether to mention that the Dragon Lord had told him to but decided it was too early to be revealing the real reason, "I received a letter from my sister and I was invited a few months ago."

"If you are a defender of dragons why did you go to the arena?"

"Curiosity and would have been rude not to."

"Never stopped you before."

Ozanus declined to reply making Miryama raise an eyebrow in surprise. She felt sure the man was hiding something and wondered whether the Gods were involved like the tales of his father. She moved on, "why did you come here?"

"Curiosity." He shrugged.

Dari frowned, "why would Temijin let you come? Are you working for him?!"

"I work for no one..."

"Unless it involves money." An observer remarked with a sneer.

"Ssh." Her neighbour hissed.

139

Ozanus glanced round and then returned to look at the council, "she is right, but even then I don't necessarily do it. He may think I am here on his behalf but I chose to come. I will decide where I stand when I am ready. Now," he stood, "is that all? I would like to catch up with my sister."

The council looked at each other, their own self-importance writhing under his glare. Miryama answered for them, "thank you."

Ozanus, his straight back aching, walked out of the roundhouse, calling over his shoulder, "coming Lylya?"

Lylya smiled as she caught up with her brother, there was the arrogance she recognised, "I'm relieved you aren't badly hurt."

"How has it been here?" He asked without looking at her. He marched on, making her almost trot to keep up with him. He was trying to find somewhere where they wouldn't be overheard.

"It's been good, Mada has been welcoming but I think most of the others are wary of me. Ozanus, slow down, you were unconscious yesterday." She protested, "let yourself rest."

"In a minute," but he did slow down.

"Do you think Joli will come back?" She asked, trying to distract him.

He stopped and looked at her, unconsciously twisting his signet ring, "I don't know. He and Ozi were mates..., most of the time. I'm hoping his loyalty to Diego is strong enough to bring him back."

"And Diego?" She asked with fear.

"That is in the Gods' claws."

"Perhaps you should give them an offering?" She suggested quietly.

"I don't know." To hide the pain he was feeling he turned away from his sister and marched on, "where's a place we

140

can talk? There's got to be somewhere."

Ignoring his question she went on, "there is a temple here somewhere since there are dragons, I just haven't found it yet."

"You have no reason to know where it is. It doesn't seem they are that bothered with the Gods."

"I'm not sure. I haven't been here very long, only a couple of days before you arrived. How long was it before he realised I had gone?"

"The morning after he came for us, accusing me of stealing you. I thought I was going to end up in the arena myself. Instead he let us come and rescue you." He chuckled at the end.

"You aren't going to take me back are you?"

"Of course not."

"Are you going to help them with Temijin?"

"If they ask." He shrugged and added, "they seem to be some hot heads amongst them."

"They don't have many dragon riders but they are all trained to fight. You and Ozi landed on their training area. They have become wary of training new riders for fear of both girl and dragon being captured. I don't think Temijin is the first to have captured and used them as bait in an arena. Why haven't we heard about this before?"

Ozanus was thoughtful for a moment, "probably because we were protected by the cataract and we had other borders to worry about more. Ioan has never brought Moronland up until recently. You know, they won't defeat Temijin on foot, however well trained they are. I bet most of them have never seen real combat either. Their captured leader definitely had. I would have loved to have spoken with her." He remembered how bravely she had fought until she had been too weak from blood loss to continue.

"They are smaller than our Valley's dragons." She remarked.

"That could be an advantage, I'd have to ride one and see what they can do."

"Without Ozi, how are you going to get home?"

"I don't know. The Dragon Lord…." He paused and turned to look at his sister again, "he came to me this morning."

"When? How?"

"I went for a dip in one of their pools and he pulled me down. I thought I was going to drown." His throat tightened, "he told me that I need to grow up, that I was dragging this out, that these women need taking in hand."

"Oh, they won't like that. You heard what that pregnant one said." Lylya was shocked.

"They definitely haven't got the Dragon Lord's favour. I will have to do something but don't know anything about them to know how to go about it. Don't you dare tell them what I have just told you." He grabbed her wrist and held it so tight that it hurt.

"Ozanus, you are hurting me." She exclaimed.

"Promise me." He hissed.

"I… I promise." She answered in fear, seeing a flash of something in his eyes. Was that a dragon's face overlaying his briefly?

His grip relaxed and she shook his hand off her. She walked ahead to regain her composure and let Ozanus calm down. He watched her walk away and slowly released his hands from the fists they had become. He needed Diego to talk to but he lay unconscious in Mada's roundhouse.

Eighteen

He should have been in bed, Mada had even told him so, but he didn't want to though he had a headache and his bruised back ached. Lylya had already retired to bed. He sat opposite Mada and stared into the small fire, "Mada?"
Mada looked up from where she was sorting through dried plants, "yes?"
"Tell me about the Daughters of Scyth please?"
"Do you not know of us?"
"I have never read of you. My father probably would have found you in the end, he was always searching out dragons. He was a true protector of them and had the ancient magic of the High Priests. I am merely a man." He ended bitterly.
"Everything has a reason as you know." Mada tried to console him, "he was the last of an era and you were unlikely to ever receive the abilities he had been gifted." She tutted at a plant and threw it into the flame. Without looking up she carried on, "he did visit here once."
Ozanuse was shocked, "why did he not write it down?"
Mada shrugged and smiled a secret smile. Her mother had told her as a child of Kittal's visit and that she had been conceived at that time. Some of his God blessed power must have passed to her through his seed as that was the

only explanation she and her mother could come up with for her ability to occasionally see the future. Kittal never knew of her existence but that was the way it was as she had been born a girl. The young man opposite would never know that he spoke with a half-sister but she knew of all of his siblings and his other half-sister.

"So, how come you ended up here on this mountain top?" He broke into her thoughts.

"That I can't answer as no one really knows. It is in the distant past. No one knows who Scyth is any more either. They could have been the mother of those who fled or possibly the man who fathered all of the women. All I know is that it was a group of women who fled some fate that has been forgotten and they brought dragon eggs and one grown dragon with them. They got up here somehow and this mountain top has been a sanctuary for all women ever since. It is just the village up here now but in the early days there was a hut at the foot of the mountain where women and girls escaping their fates could come and seek refuge. There has been attacks in the past by Dragon Warriors as they were known then, and we have had a few generations conceived through those traumatic events.

"Dragon numbers grew at the same time as our numbers did. It is said that one time when we were raided for dragons a couple of warriors stayed and a few of us were trained on how to ride and fight on our dragons."

"How come there are no men now? Still?"

"It has always been that way. They are invited to stay for a bit but are not allowed to leave their enclosure, we don't want them telling others of what is up here. It is a rite of passage for our girls as they turn sixteen to go out into the world, find a suitable lover and bring them back if they wish. Once they have tired of the man or have become pregnant then the man goes back home. If a boy is born, once he is about eight or nine he goes to his father. Girls

144

stay with us."

"Are they just baby makers then?" Ozanus frowned. Mada chuckled considering women were often seen as being the baby makers, "oh no. If they have skills we invite them to teach us. We have a few men who have been here several years now. Neither them nor their lovers have wanted to end their relationship. Only one man lives here permanently and he looks after the temple with his apprentice but they aren't allow to leave the temple or rookery."

"Rookery?"

"Where the dragons all live."

"How do I get there?"

"I'll get someone to show you in the morning, now I think it's time you went to bed." They both froze as there was a moan from Diego's bed and then Mada smiled, "hopefully that is a good sign or he is just agreeing with me. He will be hearing everything we say though he is in a deep sleep."

"Thank you Mada and good night."

"Sleep well." She smiled and then returned to her basket of plants.

It was a restless sleep, dreams ebbed and flowed. He dreamt of flying on a skeletal Ozi burnt black from Joli's flames. Behind him flew an army of dragons and men and women, the biggest gathering of dragon warriors ever seen, bows in hands, arrows at their thighs and plumes flying out from atop helmets. Beside him was the serpentine burnished copper scaled War Dragon speckled with fresh and dried on blood, his red mane and tail feathers flowing behind him. It turned red eyes to Ozanus as it cackled at him, *"oh I need this, who will be my first meal?"*
An image of Diego flashed in his dream's mind.

As they all began to dive into a thick layer of cloud and on to the unknown he woke with a start shaking and sweating. He sat up gasping for breath and pushed off the tangled bedcovers.

In the dim light of dawn seeping through the door he crossed to Diego and touched him. His friend stirred at his touch but didn't wake. He sat down beside Diego's bed with his back to it and whispered, "Diego, I need you. I can't do this without you. The Dragon Lord is not happy with me. I must give him an offering. I just saw the War Dragon and he is blood thirsty. What do I do? Have I been too long under his wing but never realised? The Suwars are already depleted by Temijin so I need these women and their dragons but haven't got the time I really need to ensure they are truly trained. I've got to get back to Keytel and don't know how and I have no idea where Joli is. And," he laughed, "we both need some clean clothes." He looked down at the tunic shirt he had worn in bed, not even changing out of it from wearing it all day.

He looked up as he heard, "sir, I can help you."

"What did you hear?" He demanded as Mada's short assistant, clearly growth stunted, stepped into view from the other side of the roundhouse.

"You want some clean clothes. I can find some." She hesitantly said.

"No, that can wait, show me where your temple is."

"Are you sure? Not many of us are allow that way." Ozanus stood, "yes I am sure. You may be lax in honouring the Gods but I will not be."

She bobbed her head, "this way then." She opened the door and stepped out of the way to let him through. He pulled on his trousers and boots and tucked his knife into his belt before following her out.

She hurried him across the village, past the men's enclosure which he had yet to see. No one was up but a few cats out on an early morning hunt. They came to the point of the large crack he and Diego had seen two days previous. It was wide enough for a man to slip down. She pointed down, "there are steps."

She ran off before he could thank her.

He knelt down and peered down the crack. He wondered whether there was another route or whether this was some sort of test. He spotted a wide step a metre down and between it and the top a couple of hand and foot holds. They were certainly deterring any casual visitors to the temple and the dragons.

Carefully heading down, step by step, he followed them as they curved round the edge of the widening crevice till they came to a wide ledge that went back to the point. Running down each side of the cliff were more ledges holding the dragon nests, most of whom had sleeping occupants. Swallows flitted around catching the insects that hovered before returning to their own nests hidden in the overhanging rocks.

Close to the edge of the ledge was a boy teasing two baby dragons who were hopping up and down in front of him trying to grab a piece of meat he was waving at them and then pulling out of reach. Seeing what was happening Ozanus shouted, "stop that!"

The boy turned and glared at him, "you can't tell me what to do."

"Do you know what a dragon, even a baby one could do if it is angry? Continue teasing them and they will get angry."

The boy ignored him and went back to teasing.

In several strides Ozanus was by the boy and grabbed his arm. He yanked the strip of meat from the hand and tossed it. The two dragons turned and ran to it, snapping and hissing at each other to be first to the prize. Ozanus pointed, "see. Do you want to be scarred for life or live with a limp?"

The boy glanced at the two fighting dragons and back at Ozanus, "no."

"Leave that boy alone! Unhand him! What are you doing here?! You should be in the men's enclosure."

With a tight grip still on the boy Ozanus turned to see who was shouting at him and waking the dragons who were beginning to chitter behind him. In turn he demanded, "who are you?"

"I am the keeper of the temple and guardian to these dragons. Are you going to tell me who you are now?" He stood with fat hands on his hips. His robes were tatty and dirty which suggested he didn't care for his appearance, but his rotund belly showed he was fed well. His face was poorly shaved and his hair trimmed but looked like that needed a wash as well. Ozanus wondered why the Daughters of Scyth even bothered to keep the priest if he looked like this. He was sure there had been priestesses in the past and he had heard Lylya and Shuang being told of some of the ceremonies their mother had led when their father had been absent.

Ozanus threw the boy towards him, "you should train him better then."

The boy landed on his knees whimpering. The priest hissed at him, "get inside."

"Are you aware of what has been happening?" Ozanus asked unable to believe that this man didn't know who he was.

"They all got excited over two large dragons that flew past and to be honest we do need some new blood." Ozanus turned and looked at the dragons a little closer, the majority were on the small size due to inbreeding. Behind him the jaded priest continued, "then there was that stinking black smoke which seemed to sober them all up. Don't know where those two big ones have gone. Now, enough chit chat, who are you?" He stamped his foot in frustration.

Ozanus continued to ignore the demand. He was repelled by the filthy man before him. He clearly had no respect for the responsibilities of his job and had no idea what condition he would find the temple in, wherever it was. Maybe this was why both Mada and her assistant were reluctant to show him. Would they have had it cleaned up before letting him visit? With growing anger he demanded, "have you no respect for yourself or the Gods? Look at you! You don't deserve to be considered a priest."

"They don't care so why should I?" He sneered back, "no one comes here."

"Well, I have and I am Ozanus, Nejus of Keytel, Defender of Dragons and the High Priest of their Valley home in Keytel." He stood as tall and as imposing as he could with all the authority he could put into his voice. The priest's mouth dropped open in shock. He had heard of Keytel. He dropped to his knees and bowed his head, "sir, I apologise for my sorry appearance. Though I am a disgrace you will find the temple in a good condition. They are all heathens in this country and have no desire to worship the Gods as they should, even those bitches up top. They give lip service to the Gods by keeping me fed." All his pent-up frustrations were coming out now that he spoke to a fellow worshipper.

"Quit your whining. Take me to the temple." Ozanus ordered.

"Quick boy, go and add more oil to the lamp, you are standing before the famous Nejus of Keytel, son of the man who managed to return a God to the heavens at great cost." The priest turned to the boy who disappeared into the dark at the back of the ledge.

"Quiet! Enough!" Ozanus snapped, "I want to hear nothing more from you."

149

"Yes sir, of course sir." The priest bobbed his head and clasped his hands together.

The back of the ledge brightened as the boy returned with a lamp, revealing two openings carved into the rock. The priest led the way to the one directly in front of them, "this way sir."

They walked down a corridor carved into the rock and lined with smoky oil lamps that flickered in the wind that blew up the length of the crevice. The lower half of it was smooth, worn so by water, while the top was carved out by man.

The corridor came to an end, opening into a large cavern. Stalactites hung from the ceiling and glistened in the flickering light of the four large lit wide shallow dished lamps carved out of stone and with a carved dragon holding the end of the wick in their mouths. In the dark corners drips could be heard and the floor felt damp underfoot. Shadows danced and created strange shapes that would cause anyone of a weak heart to turn and flee.

In the centre of the large lamps raised on a dais carved out of the floor was the altar and like his father's little cave there was a stone bowl on it and above this, grey from smoke now but still dripping, was the longest stalactite in the whole cavern. Posed with one claw round the stalactite was a dragon made of quartz.

Mystical energies pulsed in the cavern as if it was alive. No one had harnessed any of it for a long time. He didn't mean to speak aloud when he said, "my father would have loved this place. How did it come to be here?"

"The waterfall that is on the opposite side used to flow this way and one of the early Daughters found the corridor as a tunnel while working out a place for the dragons to roost." The priest answered with pride, "the quartz was here as if waiting to be found and looked like a dragon in the light of the torch she held. Over the years it has been carved to create the form it is now." He paused, trying to remember more of the history he had been taught as an apprentice and should be passing on. He opened his mouth to say more but Ozanus said, "leave."

"Sir? Do you not need my help?"

Ozanus turned and glared at the priest, "I need to be alone." The shadow behind the young Nejus flickered into the form of a dragon before returning to a human shape. The priest's eyes widened and he turned and fled.

The atmosphere of the temple seemed to relax without the priest there and so did Ozanus. With the man gone he turned his focus to the altar. He took a deep breath and playing with the handle of his knife before pulling it out of its sheath. He approached the altar and saw the stain of old blood on the dais, *"sir, I wish to offer up my blood in thanks for allowing me to live so that I may complete whatever the task it is that you have set me."*

He cut the palm of his hand where the scar from the previous time was a pink line. He winced and then squeezed his hand to draw out the blood and let it drip into the bowl of water. It hissed as if his blood was acid before being absorbed and disappearing.

The quartz dragon flashed and Ozanus found himself covering his eyes feeling blinded by the light. The weight of the cavern forced him to his knees. He felt rage and anger swirl around him, followed by compassion leaving Ozanus confused. What did the Dragon Lord mean? What did he want to see from him? His mind was in turmoil, he couldn't think straight. He felt the weight grow heavier, pushing him flat to the floor. Ozanus cried out, *"what have I done to anger you?!"*

"Get on with it." The voice snarled.

"I can't." Ozanus protested, tears appearing and rolling down his face to the damp floor, *"what do you want me to do?"*

"Your own dragon is dead, is that not clear enough." The voice hissed.

"I need Diego." Ozanus protested.

"Grow up!"

The oppressive weight disappeared. Ozanus lay there, fearing it would return if he tried to stand. What did the Dragon Lord want him to do?

He knew he needed to get rid of Temijin, destroy the man who dared enter and try to take Keytel and show the country that he was a strong Nejus. He also needed to extract revenge for what Temijin had done to his sister and he had to stop him from killing any more dragons. But which one, if any, was what the Dragon Lord wanted him to do? One thing he knew was that he needed the Daughters of Scyth on his side as his Suwars wouldn't be enough if he took on Temijin in his own country. He needed fighters who knew the lay of the land.

There was a chuckle in the air and he remembered the dream with the War Dragon. He wondered then if his father had ever been visited by the same God before he led the Suwars to Jurkila.

He looked up to the quartz statue and there was no movement, no sense of a presence. Slowly he stood and bowed his head. He let some more blood drip into the bowl and this time it just rippled out as if it was another drop of water from the stalactite. He tore the edge of his tunic off and wrapped it round his hand.

He waved the priest away as he passed by the man's cave home, he didn't need the man wittering while he tried to sort his thoughts out. He went to the edge of the ledge and looked round taking in all the dragons. He turned as he heard someone behind him, "none of them will be big enough."

Behind him dressed in what he could best describe

152

as the standard clothes of the Daughters of Scyth was a stocky woman with auburn hair cut short. Her trousers and shirt were sombre and practical. Tucked into a leather belt were a pair of thick gloves like he wore when he flew. She carried on, "what do you think of them?"

"The priest says they are too inbred."

She shifted uncomfortably, "and he is right. We are rather insular here and wild ones don't come past anymore. Compared to yours they have always been smaller, but now we have defects. Now some can barely fly."

"Do you look after them?" He asked out of curiosity, "the priest said he did."

"Ignore him, he doesn't care for them. I look after them the best I can." She answered.

"How many are good enough?"

"I don't know actually. We have so few riders these days, only a few are selected each year to learn."

"And do they get much practice?"

"Not as much as they should. We have to be careful because of Temijin's camp and we don't always find a match for them." She admitted.

"Could you get me a list of dragons who can be ridden and a list of riders…. And a list of dragons who can fight?"

"Why?" She questioned suspiciously. She knew who he was, word had quickly gone round but she had also heard that they didn't know whose side he was on.

"At most you have three weeks to be ready for Temijin and he won't just build a new camp at the bottom of your mountain home. He will be out for the complete destruction of you and your dragons. How many of you would survive in his men's hands and then in that arena of his? I have seen what he is capable of but I don't have my own riders here to protect you." He informed her soberly. He wondered what huge war machine Temijin would have built to reach this female haven.

He eyes widened and nodded, "of course sir. I'll get those lists for you."

"Thank you." He looked back at the dragons who were now awake and many were in the sky stretching their wings and he could see some were struggling to stay aloft. He heard a lot of chittering as they called to each other but nothing he could understand, "do many speak?"

"You are on the wrong level for that. They live higher and further out."

"Can I meet them?"

"I can arrange it."

"Thank you."

They both turned as a dragon fell on the far side of the ledge. They ran across as it got back to its feet. Its wings folded in and rested on the ground with two claws at the fold points so it could cling to the rock. Cautiously Ozanus approached, *"hello?"*

At close range he studied the dragon. Its brown scales were perfect for camouflaging against the cliff face. One of its arms was deformed while the other ended in a claw with one larger than the others which tapped on the rocky ledge as it sat up. If his father had been alive he would have tried to decipher its genealogy. It was clearly carrying ancient genes from some species of cliff dragon like his father's dragon Kit. It snorted at Ozanus through overlarge nostrils and then shrieked a warning.

"This is probably one of the better ones." The dragon keeper remarked behind him.

"And the worst?"

"Don't survive to breed. You probably saw the bones at the bottom of this place. You'd best head back up before you start to be missed. I'll let you know once I've spoken with the dragons and identified what you need for your list."

Nineteen

Reaching the top of the steps he blinked in the sunlight and wondered how long he had been down there. He realised that there was a stench that lingered down in the crevice even with a wind blowing through and was glad to breathe in several deep lungful's of clean air.

He headed out across the mountaintop in roughly the direction of the training ground based on his bird's eye view two days previous. He skirted round the village so he wouldn't get stopped and spotting Lylya he ducked behind a short tree as he didn't need her distracting him either. Though they didn't know it he felt sure that their very existence would now depend upon him keeping them safe. To do this he needed to know their fighting strength. He clearly wasn't going to be able to depend upon their dragons. Now he needed to know their fighting skills. All of this was normally done by Diego but he was going to have to step up, grow up.

And then there was the biggest problem of all. How to get back to Keytel or even communicate with the Valley? He was going to need to muster all of the Suwars as Temijin would definitely not be going down without a fight now. He would soon realise that Lylya would not be coming back, nor his esteemed guests.

Reaching the dirt training ground there were already several groups out and more gathered around watching and waiting their turn. He wondered whether word had already spread about what might be coming. Use to having no men around a lot of them had stripped to their trousers with their breasts bandaged up to keep them secure in place. Sweat already glistened on brows and chests as they were put through their paces, some to the rhythm of wooden spears thumping the ground.

He felt a presence beside him and glanced to his right and nodded an acknowledgement. Miryama remarked, "you found the temple then?"
He glanced down at the blood stained rag wrapped round his hand, "yes."

"What do you make of the Daughters of Scyth then? Up to your standards?"

"Only time will tell." He gruffly remarked.

"They are all trained from a young age."

"But how many of them have experienced fighting, smelt the blood, the fear, the aggression? How many know what it feels like to cut into a man's body and hear the scream of pain and rage?" He challenged with no emotion in his voice. If she had been able to see his eyes she would have seen a glint of excitement and thrill Ozanus found in a good fight. It didn't mean what he had seen in the arena had turned him on. That had been staged and it hadn't caused adrenalin to course through his veins like a true fight would. Maybe that was why he enjoyed acting the mercenary.

She was thoughtful. She knew what he meant for she had experienced some of it herself just before Esfir was captured. She wouldn't admit it even to herself, but she had liked the power she had felt as she maimed and killed the men.

They watched in silence as the groups swapped and changed. An idea came to her, "if you feel well enough, would you like to test the skills of some of our best?"

He looked at her and wondered if she was reading his mind, "let's."

"Shall we wrap that hand up properly first? Why do you men do it?"

"Do what?" He asked as he removed the torn piece of tunic from his hand.

"Mutilate yourself."

"It comes with the territory for me, though I possibly haven't been as devoted as my father was."

"Our priest doesn't bother."

"Why even have one if you never use the temple?"

She shrugged, "there is a story that one of our leaders got rid of him and we then suffered sickness that spread quickly killing half of the tribe and we lost half of our crops that year as well. As soon as he was invited to return it was like we were blessed again. We ensure he is fed and clothed and let him do what he wants as long as he stays down there. No one has dared try to remove him again."

"Have you ever been down there?"

"No. There. A lot better though Mada will probably want to put some ointment on it later." She tied the bandage on tight, "what would you like to try first?" She turned to look at the training ground trying to guess what he would pick.

"Would you go down there if I took you?"

She turned wide eyed at the suggestion. She hesitantly said, "maybe." She had always been curious about the temple but had always chickened out of at the top of the steps. The narrowness and steepness deterred her. She didn't think anyone had ever been there, even her half sister Anyana had never gone in though she was often on the ledges with the dragons.

"There is something down there you are all missing out on. Close combat, have you got a sword?"

She gave a sharp whistle for attention and then shouted, "Anja!"

A tall woman holding a bow turned, "what?!"

"Anyone fancy a demonstration match?" Miryama replied and jerked a thumb at Ozanus.

Whispers sprung up as some of them recognised Ozanus from when he and his dragon had crash landed. Anja shouted, "silence! Have respect for the Nejus of Keytel."

They all knew of him and fell silent.

"Now, who would like to test their skills with the Nejus?" Two young woman and a teenager stepped out. Miryama looked to Ozanus, "what do you say?"

"I'll take them all on." A smile playing on his lips. A wooden short bladed sword was found and he tested the weight of it. It was a little too light for him but would do.

Everyone formed a large circle sitting or standing. Some of the older women weren't impressed with what was about to happen even if he was Nejus. Did he think he was the better fighter? He stripped off his tunic and pulled off his boots. He had always found it easier to practice bare foot. Miryama's eyes widened at the sight of the dragon tattoo on his back as he rolled his shoulders to prepare himself. Never had she seen anything like it.

Opposite him his three opponents were having a whispered huddle. He walked round the circle, feeling for any bumps or holes that might trip him up with his bare feet.

The oldest stepped forward first, "I am ready when you are sir."

"Let's begin."

The audience went quiet as the two combatants bowed to each other and then lifted their swords ready to defend themselves from whoever attacked first.

He beckoned her forward, sure she would be keen to show off then he caught movement out of the corner of his eye as one of the others charged forward with a spear aimed at him. He smiled and remarked aloud, "playing dirty?"

He spun out of the way and slammed the wooden blade on to the shaft of the spear sending vibrations up it and into its holder's arms. She gasped as she stumbled past him, surprised that he had spotted her. Ozanus, one eye still on what was meant to be his main opponent glanced round seeking the last member of the tag team. He bent his knees ready to spring in any direction.

The oldest, sword up and in both hands, leapt at him, ready to take him out. He ducked and raised his own sword up in defence. Neither would yield as they pushed against each other but slowly her arms bent and dropped but just then the third member of the team came in. Ozanus turned and their wooden swords met. They both withdrew as the first came in to attack again.

Ozanus grinned, he was loving the exertion of the fight. The second came in with a sword this time and soon he was parrying attacks off all of them, dancing on his feet. He finally spotted an opening and caught his second opponent in her ribs with the edge of his wooden blade. With an "ompfh," she withdrew, all air expelled from her lungs in surprise. There would be a large bruise there come morning.

Taking advantage of his brief distraction the other two charged him but now he was in the zone. He stuck out a bare foot and one went tumbling while with his hand he grabbed the raised hands of the eldest and bit his lip back against the pain. He came in with his sword hand and gave her a hard thump on the side with its pommel. If it had been a real blade he would have twisted the blade up diagonally through her stomach. He threw her backwards and she landed hard on the dirt surface gasping in pain.

Behind him the last one of the team had staggered to her feet but before she could even try to attack she received the butt of Ozanus' sword in her chest. She sat back down on the ground wincing and blinking away tears of pain.

He threw his sword away and pulled them both to their feet, "you did well."
It had been good to use some pent-up energy he didn't know he had had. He panted a little and wiped sweat from his eyes.

"Thank you sir." They panted in reply. The eldest added, "it was an honour."

"You have clearly trained hard, but do you think you'll remember it all in the moment of panic as an equally well trained soldier, who has tasted blood already, charges at you?" He started to turn on the spot and repeated it louder so everyone could hear, "do you think you'll remember your training in the heat of battle?! It will be coming. Do you think you are ready?!"
There was stunned silence. Very few of them knew and many didn't understand. Others were offended that he had suggested they were all training for nothing.

Miryama stared in horror and then in anger. She couldn't believe what he was doing. How dare he even speak so when he was merely a guest?! And an unplanned guest at that! She exclaimed, "what in Gods' breath do you think you are doing?!"
He calmly picked up his tunic and boots, walked towards her and then past her. She tried to grab his arm to stop him as she went on, "you have no right to say any of that. You are to go back to Mada's and stay there till I tell you differently."

He could have jeopardised everything. She knew they were currently living on a knife edge even before Lylya had been brought to them. There was a power vacuum and no one strong enough to lead them through the next few years now that Esfir had died.

160

With Esfir they would have eventually beaten Temijin but not now. If she had been able to take part in the leadership contest then maybe they would have been able to directly take on Temijin rather than dancing round the edges, almost to his tune. She would demand an explanation from Ozanus but not yet; she needed to calm down first.

Ozanus strolled into Mada's roundhouse as if he hadn't caused an uproar at the training ground. Mada looked up from her fire, "oh, you're back. You must be hungry? You look like you've been building up an appetite. There's some water over there if you want a wash first. I have found you some clean clothes and looks like you need them." She then spotted the bandage round his hand and tutted. She added, "your sister is out somewhere."
"Has Diego moved at all?" He asked stiffly.
Mada looked confused. His whole demeanour had changed. She wondered what he had been doing all morning.
He ate, pulled on the clean clothes and then left again. He was not going to stay in Mada's roundhouse. He needed to continue planning and he wouldn't be able to do that with Mada and Lylya hovering and Diego's unconscious body reminding him he was on his own for the moment.

Twenty

"Where is he?!" She demanded. She had been calming down until her sister had brought her Ozanus' requested lists. Now she was fuming again and this time she wasn't going to wait till she was calm. She entered Mada's roundhouse and couldn't see Ozanus.

"Where is who dear?" Mada asked as she and her assistant were dribbling water into Diego's mouth.

"That infuriating man who thinks he can come here and take over." Miryama spat out in her frustration, "how can you not have heard about what he did this morning?"

"I did and yes it probably was the wrong time, but they all do need to know."

"He's gone and got Anyana to make a list of the dragons."

Mada looked at Miryama, "and in all honesty we did need a detailed list of them. We don't really look after them that well."

"Mada!" Miryama protested.

"I've seen a lot and I'm an old woman so can get away with it." Mada chuckled.

Miryama sighed, "you aren't being very helpful. Where did Ozanus go? Please."

"I don't know and however much you probably all want to pretend otherwise we do need him. I know you see it as well. None of those who have stood to become leader are strong enough to lead us into the fight for our lives."

Miryama sat on Ozanus' bed, "oh Mada, what are we going to do? We shouldn't need a man to order us around. We've survived this long without one. If only Esfir was still alive. She would have put him in his place. I should have shut him in the men's enclosure as soon as he came round."

"I know you miss her. I miss her too. She was a good leader. Maybe the Gods are suggesting it's time to adapt."

"You don't believe in the Gods any more than I do." Miryama pointed out.

"But He does. Remember what his father had to do. He comes from a family that is intertwined with them. I wouldn't be surprised if there is immortal blood in there somewhere. I think there is more to him than meets the eye. He's got more than Temijin on his mind and needs a little kindness."

"Hmm." Miryama was thoughtful, "he did offer to take me to our temple. I'm not sure why. He said there was something down there."

Mada raised her eyebrows in surprise, "oh. I hope it's in a good state."

"I have no idea, the priest hasn't come to complain."

"Calmer now?"

"Yes, I'll see if I can find him."

"Go careful, you don't want to get on his wrong side."

Miryama left the roundhouse contemplating how she was going to approach Ozanus but first she had to find him. He had clearly visited the dragons and been down at the training grounds so what else would he be checking out? The weapons they had?

She wandered out of the main village to where the blacksmiths were in their own enclosure. It was also where they stored all of their arms and some of the leather armour they wore. Most kept theirs in their homes and a select few

163

even had old metal breastplates stored away, passed down from mother to daughter.

The fire was low when she entered the site. Sat, having a break were the three blacksmiths and their two apprentices. All of them wore large leather aprons over sleeveless shirts revealing strong arm muscles scattered with burn scars. One looked up, "Miryama, what are you doing here?"

"Has he been here?"

"Oh yes. Why isn't he with the others?"

Miryama ignored the question as she asked, "what did he want?"

The blacksmith frowned, "what's going on Miryama?"

"I'm not really sure. Have you heard what happened at the training ground this morning?"

"No." She looked confused, "he came here asking to see our weapons."

"And?"

"I refused, said he needed to speak with the council first."

"Thank you. How did he react?"

"He had a look at my bow that Dotti is working on." Another said, "he seemed to admire it."

"The Suwars of Keytel are known for their archery skills." One of the apprentices remarked, brushing a hair out of her eyes, "he will have lost his bow the other day."

"He's not having mine." The bow's owner retorted as she broke off a piece of bread from the loaf on the table.

"I wasn't suggesting that." The apprentice remarked, blushing.

Miryama interrupted, "which way did he go when he left?" They all shrugged.

"Never mind, thanks." Miryama tried her best to hide her frustration and left.

She wondered whether it was worth wandering all over the mountain top in search of Ozanus or wait until he

164

returned to Mada's. She remembered then that she had interrupted his swim the previous day and wondered whether he would be at the pool.

She spotted a bare back with the large, tattooed dragon with its wings outspread outlined on his back, sat on the steps to the bathing pool and a head of golden brown hair that curled neatly at the nape of his neck. She hung back as a hand swept through it with a motion that suggested stress. She took a deep breath. She couldn't let the gesture stop her. She wasn't going to let him get away with what he had been doing and marched over and demanded, "who gave you the right?!"

He turned with a frown, "What? Oh, it's you."

"Yes it's me. Get up, we need to talk."

"Yes we do." He replied with seriousness.

She hesitated, confused. Everything she had planned to say escaped her. Cautiously she asked, "what's wrong?" She feared he was about to tell her that they would never be able to defeat Temijin.

He stood and reached for his clothes and boots, "shall we walk?"

She nodded and hoped there would be an apology coming.

"What's that paper in your hand?"

She'd half-forgotten it and glanced down to where her hand had scrunched it up, "oh this, a list you asked for."

"Excellent. May I?" He held out a hand.

Reluctantly she handed it over and tried not to look at him as he had only got half dressed. It had been a long time since she had been with a man and was finding his body more attractive than she should have. She had been with Esfir for the last two years and they have been very contented together; and she really didn't need a man complicating it all.

He frowned as he read the list, it didn't look good. Out of an estimate of one hundred dragons he possibly had

165

twenty that could be flown with someone on their back and another twenty who could support. And he still didn't know how many could speak to be able to co-ordinate an attack. He was going to need Keytel's Suwars but he didn't know how he was going to get them to Moronland without alerting Temijin. He turned the signet ring on his finger as he felt his stress levels rising.

Miryama broke into his thoughts, "It's not looking good is it?"

He looked directly at her and shook his head, "no, it isn't." He handed the piece of paper back, "I'm sorry."

"Is there anything?"

"I don't know. There are two things to worry about."

"Two?"

"Maybe three." He replied thoughtfully as he pulled on the clean tunic Mada had found him.

"Three?!"

"Shall we walk?" He offered.

"Tell me what you are thinking." She demanded.

They started walking away from the pools and into the fields.

"Joli has unwittingly given them an advantage. Temijin can now see every cliff face of this mountain. He'll do one of two things, well I would, based on what I know of him. He'll either seek out any weak spots, your dragons' nesting area for one and break it down so that they can get up." He glanced sideways at her to see how she was reacting, but her face was emotionless. "The other thing he will do, which is more likely, is that he will probably use one of his big catapults to just bombard the top of this mountain until he thinks you are all dead. His catapults are big enough to throw nets big enough to pin my dragons down so they can probably throw large boulders up and there are plenty of those at the base of this mountain. That is why you have three weeks at most as he will have to get his war machines

166

here and set them up."

Miryama had paled at the thought of huge boulders landing haphazardly all over their mountain home destroying and killing. Cautiously she asked, "is that one or two?"

"One." He answered without emotion.

"Do I want to hear the next one?"

"All I am doing is telling you the truth."

"You didn't have to tell everyone this morning." She protested, "you had no right to."

He shrugged. He didn't care. They would have found out sooner or later, "is that what you came to talk to me about?"

"Well, yes, but I think you have some important things to say. Compared to us you do have more experience. Tell me the worst."

"That list," he gestured at the piece of paper she had folded up several times, "tells me that you are not capable of defeating Temijin. You probably would have a fighting chance if you could get all of your women down to his level quickly without him knowing but you would eventually still be defeated as he would overwhelm you with his manpower. If you attacked from the air you have nowhere near enough dragons that can be ridden or controlled to survive. Without them you cannot send enough of you down safely to attack from both the air and the ground."

"So what do you suggest?"

"That's the second half of this issue. If you, we, are to defeat him we are going to need my Suwars. I need to get them here without alerting Temijin and walking, as I no longer have Ozi, will take too long."

"What about the other one?"

"Joli? I have no idea where he is or if he'll come back. He's lost his mate, or the dragon he considered his mate."

"You said there were three things to consider. What's the

167

third?"

He paused in his walking. She didn't notice straight away. Realising he wasn't beside her anymore she turned, "Ozanus?"

"I don't seem to have enough faith or belief in the Gods but in Keytel they are an important part of life."

"We heard what your father did." She softly remarked. He frowned as that was not something he wanted to talk about.

"Sorry."

"The Gods have decided to grace me with my own mission to prove myself worthy." He said carefully.

"Oh? What do you have to do? I hope it's not to convert us?" She tried to lighten the mood.

He glared at her. She blushed, "sorry."

"I don't really know but it involves all of you."

"Do the Gods really care that much?" She scoffed and received another glare from Ozanus which she ignored.

He realised she wasn't going to take his mission seriously so didn't push it. At some point he would need to convince her of the importance of his mission. He didn't want the Dragon Lord to remain angry with him as He could easily take it out on the rest of Keytel in revenge. If only she could see the power the Gods controlled, then she would realise that they needed the Gods too.

They began walking back to the village in silence. There was a shout off to their right, "I've found you." The looked to see the dragon keeper jogging towards them. She stopped in front of them panting. While recovering her breath she studied the two and realised they made a handsome couple. She knew she would have to tease her sister later. Miryama asked, "what is it Aryana?"

"Well..." Aryana shifted uncomfortably, remembering Miryama's reaction to the list she had presented earlier, "… I've gathered all the dragons who can talk."

168

Ozanus brightened, "excellent, lead the way."

"Hang on." Miryama exclaimed, "Aryana you didn't mention this earlier?"

"That's because I had been working on it. Come on, I don't know how long they will hang around, they are all a bit egotistical though they also want to meet you sir."

"Come on then, I'm intrigued to meet them." Ozanus remarked.

Seventeen dragons crouched on land beside the crevice. Approaching them Ozanus wasn't sure what to expect as he hadn't seen any of them when he had made his way down to the temple's ledge. He wondered where they nested as he hadn't seen them when he and Diego had flown past. They were definitely smaller than the dragons he was used to, by about a third, otherwise they were similar in appearance. A couple had blue scales as if a coastal dragon had passed through at some point. A green shaded one had a large frill at the rear of its skull streaked with brown veins. Two had nose horns and another had two horns on their foreheads. One other was distinctive by the spiked tail meaning it would be deadly in a fight. Most were of a pale brown colouring to blend in with their cliff home.

Linking them to their smaller clan members was the fact all had one large curved claw on one of their front claws. Addressing them all Ozanus said, *"I am Ozanus, son of Kittal and Nejus of Keytel and defender of all dragons. Who speaks for you?"*

The one with the large frill lifted its head higher than the others and cleared its throat, *"I will speak for us. Why are you bothering us?"*

"I am sorry to disturb you, but we need your help."

"Help?"

"Temijin will be coming here and not just to set up a new

169

camp. I need every dragon capable of fighting to join us."
They all looked to one and another and then one of the blue
dragons spoke up, *"but we are so few."*

*"That is the other bit I need your help with. I need you to
communicate with the others that cannot speak as you do.
The more of you who can help the better our chances."*

"This is an issue for man and does not involve us." The
spokesdragon snarled.

"It does." Ozanus challenged back, *"Temijin will be
looking for weaknesses and your homes are a weakness
that he can take advantage of. A few boulders on those
cracked cliff faces to add to the bones at the bottom and he
can make himself a ramp to get on the big ledge and then
up the steps."*
Aryana and Miryama glanced at each other, surprised that
just by one fly pass and the visit that morning had been
enough for Ozanus to evaluate their home.

"There are enough of us to stop him." The dragon
retorted.

*"No there aren't. Most of you are not in a condition to
fight. They'll either be dead from the attack and rock fall or
can't fly well enough to. The youngsters will just leave as
their instinct will be to survive and that leaves you
seventeen plus any other capable adults and you'll be
attacking his main army."* Ozanus explained while wishing
Ozi and Joli were here to help him make these ignorant
dragons understand the seriousness of the situation. He
turned to the two women, "did you understand any of
that?"

"Some of it. You are clearly fluent in their language."

"Thank you. These are your dragons and your
responsibility, and they need to be made to see sense. Their
home is this mountain's biggest weakness."

"Can we do anything to make it less so?" Miryama asked.

"The only good thing is that the steps mean Temijin's

170

men can only come up single filed so they can be picked off one by one but they will still overwhelm you."

"What are you saying about us?" The dragon demanded. Ozanus turned back and sharply said, *"be prepared to all be ridden."*

There was grumbling amongst all of them. He turned back to Miryama, "I want to see your twenty-five best archers in the morning." And then stalked off.

Aryana looked at Miryama, "do you think he's right?" She didn't want to say it out loud so just nodded.

"What do the council think of him?"

Miryama didn't want to talk about it. To the dragons she bowed her head, *"thank you for coming."* And without waiting for a reply left. She had a lot to think about and work out how to deliver all the information to the council. The leadership decision was going to have to be paused while they prepared for Temijin's arrival with his army.

"He was rude."

"He was honest." Aryana calmly replied, used to the dragons' arrogant temperaments. She wondered if the dragons of Keytel were the same. One thing was certain, the Daughters' dragons needed new blood to be able to survive.

Twenty-One

Ozanus' body was protesting by the time he collapsed into his bed opposite Diego. For a few minutes he had lain there staring at Diego and remembering the image he had seen the previous night in his sleep. The only assurance he could take from it was that Diego would be awake in time for Temijin's siege but he may not survive it. He didn't want to think about that.

He slept longer than he had planned. His shoulders ached when he did finally wake and swore as he remembered what he had demanded of Miryama. He didn't know if they would still be waiting or not. Mada tried to convince him to eat as he pulled clothes and boots on, "I'm late, maybe later."

"You are still injured, you need to slow down, let your body heal."

He looked over at her, "I can't stop now."

The look he gave her told her that the new burdens and responsibilities were already weighing him down. She saw him glance over at Diego and realised that he already knew how much he relied on the older man and was struggling without him. Only time would tell. She tossed half a flatbread over to him, "take this at least to wherever you are going."

"Thank you." He gave her a tight smile as he caught it.

He glanced down at Diego again.

"I'll let you know if there are any changes. Now, go, the rest of us need you more at the moment even if they won't admit it yet."

"Have you seen Lylya?"

"She'll be around somewhere."

"If you see her, can you tell her I want to talk to her?"

"Of course."

"Thank you." He ducked out of the door, stretched his back and drew in a deep breath of clean air.

It was with relief that Miryama saw Ozanus marching towards the training ground. She was starting to think he wasn't going to show up and the twenty-five women were getting restless as most had other things to do and were also not impressed that they were at the training grounds at a man's demand. They stood as a group with arms crossed or hands on hips as Ozanus approached them, quivers of arrows at their hip and their short bows leaning up against their bodies. They were all dressed this time, knowing a man was present, but had pulled tight their clothes and wrapped leather straps round their wrist so the strings didn't catch on their sleeves. Miryama demanded "what took you so long? We do have other stuff to do."

"Let's get on with it. Have you a spare bow?"
A little flustered at his abrupt reply Miryama looked around, "yes of course."
She tried to hide her blushing as she handed the bow to him as he stripped off his tunic revealing his taut muscles again. Why did he have to take if off? Why was she letting herself be affected by him?   She had carefully sought out the bow with the best draw weight for him. He felt the weight of the bow and pulled back the string and grunted his satisfaction. She smiled with relief as her eye for draw weight was something she was proud of.

173

The older women scowled at him as he approached the group with Miryama behind him, holding her own bow. The younger ones were blushing and smiling nervously at him as if they had never seen a half naked man. He quickly glanced over them all before saying, "thank you for coming here today. I know you don't want me here but currently you need all the help you can get. I know dragons and I know how to fight from the sky."

Someone scoffed from the back. Ozanus looked to the back of the group and continued by asking to try and identify the scoffer, "has anyone ever fought from the back of a dragon? Have any of you ever drawn a bow while atop a dragon?"

"Yes." Miryama replied from behind him.

Ozanus turned and didn't quite hide his surprise. He would definitely have to find out more from her later, "and how is it?"

"Hard without practise."

He turned back to the group, "anyone else?"

"The same." The scoffer replied without revealing themselves.

"Thank you. I asked for the best archers as in the next two weeks you are going to be trained to be the advance force. Not all of you will make the cut but I need to see your archery skills before we match you with a dragon and then work with you as a team."

"For the moment we are all we have." Miryama added as she came to stand by his side. She gave him a nod and he nodded a thanks back.

He noted how they all looked at her with respect. Miryama went on, "let's get going then. Ozanus, as our guest would you like to go first?" She handed him an arrow from her quiver.

"Thank you." He took the arrow and went to where the ground was worn by the years of archers' feet standing in the same place.

As he notched the arrow to the bow string he glanced up at the butt ten metres away. His well trained eye quickly took in the distance and noted the rag blowing in the breeze. He adjusted his position to take in all the factors and then pulled the bow back. His shoulders protested so he knew his first flight wasn't going to be perfect. He concentrated on his breathing as he held the taut bowstring. He glanced at the rag again to check the wind direction before releasing the arrow with a hiss of breath. It hit left of the centre.

He ignored the women murmuring and held out a hand for another arrow. He rolled his shoulders in the hope of loosening the tension in the muscles. Again he notched the arrow and aimed it, taking note of the breeze. With his breath steady he released the arrow at the butt and with a satisfying thud it hit the red centre, the head burying itself into the tight packed straw. He smiled to himself. Turning he asked, "who's next?"

As he stepped away from the line five stepped forward to face the five butts set up and another went to retrieve his two arrows.

Miryama and Ozanus watched from the sidelines as the women and girls took it in turns to fire. Occasionally Ozanus would step in and nudge a hand or elbow or remind them about the effect of the wind. Miryama asked as he returned to her side again, "well?"

"They are all good. Do I get to see you?" A smile danced on his lips.

She gave him a small one back, "maybe later."

"Can we get a message to Aryana? I want to get them and the dragons together tomorrow. It will take a few days to get the right woman and dragon pairings."

"Of course."

"Do you have a dragon to ride?"

175

"I lost her to Temijin."

"You said you have fought while riding a dragon?"

"Not now." She wasn't ready to talk about it for it was when they had lost Esfir to Temijin. She took some of the responsibility for that on her own shoulders.

He studied her face and realised she was feeling the same as him though for different reasons.

As he was thinking it was time to stop for the day, he had seen enough of their skills and tomorrow would be more important, there was a shout and a young girl was running towards them. Everyone stopped to look, fearing the worst. She reached them and paused to catch her breath.

Miryama asked, "what's wrong? Is it Temijin?"

The girl shook her head, "dragon, a big dragon."

"Joli?" Ozanus asked.

She shrugged her shoulders as she had no idea who Joli was or what he looked like.

"How far away?" Miryama asked.

"I just got told to tell you."

"Take us to where he was seen from." Miryama ordered. To Ozanus she asked, "do you think I'ts yours?"

"I hope so as I'm going to need him."

Exhausted Joli crash landed in the fields, knocking a short tree over in the process; much to the annoyance of those working in them. Diego's saddle was starting to rub sores on his back where he hadn't been able to take it off and one saddlebag had been lost as he grabbed a bison to eat. He snapped at one woman as she approached with her hoe raised in anger and she backed off. They kept out of reach but glared at him until he spotted Ozanus hurrying over with a woman. He called out, *"Nejus!"*

"Joli, am I glad to see you!" Ozanus shouted with relief.

Reaching the blue dragon Ozanus smiled, *"I am glad to see you are well. I need you."*

176

"Where is Diego?" Joli asked with concern.

Ozanus frowned, *"what happened Joli? He is currently unconscious."*

"I'm sorry. I think I threw him off but he was tired." He had noticed that Diego hadn't been gripping him very hard, *"and I'm sorry I flew off, I just needed to...."*

Ozanus put his hand up to stop the dragon, *"you needed time to mourn but now I need you at your best."*

"Why?"

"You destroyed Temijin's camp so now he will be coming here with an army."

"Sorry."

"You were within your rights to extract your revenge." Ozanus tried to console the dragon, *"but now is not the time for remorse. I need that energy now. Let's get that saddle off, it looks like you are developing sores. Mada will probably have something for them."*

As Ozanus unbuckled the saddle Joli asked quietly as there was a growing crowd, *"how much do they understand of our language?"*

"It varies."

"I'm not staying with their dragons. I have some standards."

"I'm sure there is space near the village and we'll catch up properly later. I'll explain what I need from you then." Joli nodded, *"I'll make my way over to the village. I think I'll rest here for a little bit first."*

"Have a good nap old man." Ozanus teased as hc hefted Diego's saddle on to a shoulder.

Everyone else was sheltering from a cold wind that was blowing across the mountain top, cutting off the last of the day's thermals. Joli had found some shelter behind the smithy enclosure, close to the wall where the furnace was. His large body made a wind break in itself for the fire

177

Ozanus and Lylya sat beside wrapped in blankets from Mada's. During the afternoon Ozanus had oiled Diego's saddle and rubbed ointment into Joli's saddle sores.

Leaning against Joli Ozanus felt comforted by the rise and fall of the dragon's scaly chest. It wasn't Ozi but it was a dragon he knew and trusted and with Lylya there he could almost imagine he was home in the Valley on top of the cliffs.

"So, tell me then?" Lylya demanded, "what's going on? I've barely seen you these last two days."

"And you probably won't tomorrow either. We are gearing up for war but I have one problem we need to solve and only you two can help me."

"You should be taking it easy." Lylya pointed out, "you did bang your head."

"I'll be fine." He retorted, "now listen. There are two things to be done in Moronland. First we need to destroy Temijin's army which will do two things, save this lot from being wiped out and save Keytel from his ambitions. Secondly, I need to destroy that arena which I'm sure the women here will gleefully help me with. That can't be allowed to remain standing for someone else to use.

"What are you talking about?" Joli asked.

"I'll explain in a bit." Ozanus looked up at the dragon, *"Lylya and I need to work out the plan first."*

"Hmpfh."

"Ssh."

"How are we going to go about it?" Lylya asked with a frown.

"This is what I need to work out. They aren't going to survive with the forty dragons that are capable of fighting of which there is probably only twenty that can take a rider."

"That it?" She asked in amazement.

He nodded, "a poor show really. I need to get Keytel's

178

Suwars here to stand a chance of winning this fight."

"How are you going to do that?"

"Can you let me finish." He protested, "I need Joli for a couple of days to get the dragons and riders organised here and then he needs to get to Keytel to get the Suwars here, but I can't go." He looked at her then.

"What?! Me?" She exclaimed.

"Yes, you. You'll need to ride him. It will be safer with you away from here."

"I won't stay away, I'll come back with the Suwars." She protested.

"No, I want you safe, where Temijin can't touch you."

"He's underestimated me, and you underestimate me. This is where I belong." She retorted stubbornly.

"Now is not the time to discuss this Lylya. The important bit is that all of the Suwars are brought here. I can't get a message to them as it will take too long which is why you'll need to fly with Joli across the cataract and to the Valley to fetch them."

"Why don't you go?" She challenged; arms crossed. Ozanus sighed, why was she doing this now? "Lylya, I would go but getting this lot into some sense of fighting unit is more important."

"I think you underestimate them. You've seen their skills and I'm sure there are those who can lead them if given the chance. You do know women can lead as well, our aunt did and the Daughters of Scyth have survived for generations without male influence." Lylya stood, her voice getting louder. This was one of those times where Ozanus was irritating her. She didn't give Ozanus a chance to reply as she walked off, annoyed with her brother for forgetting women could be just as good as men.

Ozanus glared at the fire. Women?! Joli asked, *"what was that about?"*

"Lylya reminding me that women are just as good as

179

men."

"*Why do you think that the Nejus rides a female?*"

"*Something I am now lacking in.*" Ozanus muttered.

"*And me,*" Joli added sorrowfully, "*and Diego.*"

"*I'm missing Diego as well but I've got something to keep your mind off it.*"

"*You have?*" Joli asked with interest.

"*I need two things from you. Firstly, will you let me ride you? I need your help in training the Daughters of Scyth to ride and fight on dragon back then you'll either be flying me or Lylya back to the Valley as I need the Suwars.*"

"*Of course you can ride on me, you are my Nejus, but not with the saddle, my back is too sore for that. Do they not already fly?*"

"*Not much it seems for safety reasons and also they don't have a large number of dragons who can be ridden either. I need your help getting them to help. They didn't appreciate me talking to them yesterday.*"

"*How dare they ignore their Nejus.*" Joli growled, "*I'll put them straight.*"

"*Carefully please. Now,*" Ozanus stood and stretched, "*it's time for some sleep.*"

"*Do you think Diego will wake up soon?*" Joli asked with concern.

"*He will, I dreamt it.*" He didn't add he'd also been shown his friend's death by the blood hungry War Dragon, "*see you in the morning, it's going to be an interesting day.*"

Twenty-Two

There was a lot of snarling and growling as Joli tried to make it clear that he and Ozanus were now taking control and organising some discipline amongst them. If they wanted to save their homes and their keepers they were going to have to step up. There were chases into the sky as some protested with Joli flying over them, dominating them, and forcing them back to the ground. He didn't enjoy all of it as Ozi would have been better at it than him. She had had the domineering nature and would have quickly earnt their respect from being part of a long line of dragons who carried the Nejus. Now that era had ended and he took it out on the slowest, biting through its tail in frustration. Ozanus shouted, *"enough!"*

The dragons began to land and settle, breathing heavily, nursing scratches and the tail bite. Others glared at Ozanus and muttered under their breaths. Joli snarled, *"have more respect."*

The spokesdragon from the day before snapped at Joli, not happy with the new dragon.

"Enough! All of you!" Ozanus shouted, hands on hips, his gloves tucked into his belt and a headscarf wrapped round his neck. Behind him stood the women and Miryama staring in awe and shock at how Joli had got their dragons under control. He continued, *"yes you are noble dragons*

with minds of your own but now you need to be what you were brought here for all that time ago. You are meant to be ridden to enable the Daughters of Scyth to explore beyond Moronland and to defend yours and their home. All of you will have a rider by the end of the day. Normally that would be decided when you are both young so a lifelong bond can be made, and you work together as one."* He frowned briefly as he thought about Ozi. To distract himself he turned to look at the women to see if they understood anything he was saying, *"but this has been lax so there will be some trial and error."* He wasn't going to admit this was new to him as well and sent a silent pray up to the Dragon Lord for guidance. The healing hand had become a fist as a reminder to both himself and the God of what he had done to show he could be trusted.

He looked at the gathered women who wore an odd assortment of flying clothes dug out from storage chests. Elaheh stepped out of the group, "you don't know me, but I flew your sister here on my dragon, Calluna."

"Not yours." Calluna, a pale grey dragon snorted.

"My dragon sister, comrade then." Elaheh sighed, the long-suffering human in the woman-dragon partnership. Ozanus was surprised and asked, "are there any others?" The rest shook their heads. Miryama remarked, "Elaheh and Calluna are a rare thing these days."
Calluna puffed up her chest with pride.

"She was an orphan so my mother was asked to raise her with me." Elaheh explained. Miryama's mother and hers were close and Aryana had inherited the dragon keeper's role off her.

"Hmfph." Calluna snorted.

"Ssh Calluna." Elaheh exclaimed in frustration.

"This is good…?" Ozanus asked.

"Elaheh."

"Elaheh, you can help me."

Buoyed up she went on, "I'm not the only one, well, now I am. Miryama used to have her own dragon and so did our leader Esfir."

Ozanus raised an eyebrow at Miryama and she remarked, "later."

He nodded in understanding and then suggested, "Miryama, why don't you choose a dragon."

Miryama felt nervous and then glanced at the grumpy dragons, *"perhaps they should pick us?"*

"Excellent idea." The one with the large frill remarked though with little enthusiasm. She didn't want to be ridden by anyone, not even the supposed Nejus.

Ozanus closed his eyes and sighed, no one was making this easy and though he knew it wouldn't be and had been prepared for it, it was still frustrating. He took a deep breath and then started pointing at women and dragons to pair them up. Elaheh and Miryama helped get the padded cloths on dragons' backs and then their newly allocated rider. It took two attempts for Ozanus to get his own, borrowed from Mada, padded blanket on to Joli's back. The blue dragon helped the Nejus up with a forearm. Joli asked quietly, *"ready for this?"*

"No, but we might be surprised." He answered as he knew not everyone was made to be a dragon rider, before calling to everyone, "everyone up and keep above the clouds."

So as not to affect the smaller dragons Joli waited till they were in the air before pushing off himself. He flew up above the others so that Ozanus could observe the dragons below them.

Shifting on Joli's back the Nejus remarked, *"and they think this is better?"*

"Today yes, it feels lighter without that saddle, but not sure how comfortable it would be on a longer flight."

"So, what do you think of them?"

183

Pointing at the two blue dragons off to their left Joli remarked, *"those don't work. I think it's the riders, they are scared and the dragons aren't making it easy. Oi! You two, play fair! We are trying to ensure you have a home."*

It took most of the day to match up riders with dragons. Several of the women, once in the air, realised it wasn't right for them and retreated to the comfort of solid ground. Miryama, after a few tries found herself on a dark ochre coloured one with spikes down its tail. They flew off by themselves. Calluna and Elaheh got bored and went off to do other things as well, Elaheh having to drag Calluna away who was trying to make eyes at Joli.

With everyone in a pairing they were sort of happy, or at least comfortable with, Ozanus ended for the day. The new day would be to start practising firing arrows while on top of their dragons. He was going to have to persuade Joli to put on the saddle so he had the stability it had and wondered how the women did it. He wondered whether Miryama would be willing to give a demonstration. He was becoming more intrigued by her by the day and hoped she would talk with him.

The others had all gone by the time Miryama returned on her new dragon. She slid off his back and pulled off the padded blanket, *"see you tomorrow Spilla and it's been a pleasure getting to know you."*

"The same here. I hope we can be a good team to defeat Temijin." The dark earthy red dragon replied with a bow of its head.

She turned to see Ozanus waiting, "oh, you didn't have to wait for me."
She could feel his eyes taking her in, her red cheeks from the cold air, her bright eyes from the thrill of flying on the back of a dragon again, her hair escaping from her plaits. She found herself smiling shyly at him. He remarked, "you

don't belong here do you?"

"We've heard of the Keytel Suwars even if you've never heard of us. And we knew of your aunt. I wanted to be her." She covered her mouth, shocked she had revealed something so secret.

"I never knew her. She died while I was still a baby." He said thoughtfully, "but she was respected and loved and I heard she was a brilliant leader. It's nothing to be ashamed of, everyone has someone they aspire to be." But he certainly wasn't going to tell her his. Instead he added, "there is something to being in the air. The freedom."

"It's a privilege." She agreed as they began to walk towards the village.

"Considering how few of you can fly on a dragon, how come you do? If Spilla isn't your normal ride where is your dragon?"

"You know Aryana? We are sisters and our mother was also Keeper of the Dragons. I grew up with them. Fez and I played together and it went from there. Esfir and I…." She paused and looked to see how Ozanus was reacting. He wasn't revealing anything so tentatively she went on, "Esfir and I, we were lovers as well as comrades. We were always flying out together and then we saw some of Temijin's men battling with a captured wild dragon. She couldn't stop herself, we went down. She was captured and Fez was killed." She brushed tears off her face.

He hesitated in saying or doing anything. The only person he had ever consoled was Lylya.
Realising she had said too much she hurried on leaving Ozanus staring at her, one wounded soul to another. He knew where he needed to take her even if she didn't want to. To progress to where she wanted to be she needed the blessing of the Dragon Lord.

Ignoring Joli's grumbles he put the saddle on the

dragon. He wanted the stability it gave him for firing an arrow from the back of a flying dragon. Miryama was there as well throwing a padded blanket over Spilla. Looking over Ozanus asked, "are you going to be stable enough on that to fire a bow?"

"I will but I'm not sure about the others." She smiled across at him.

"Joli, you'd best be ready to catch some falling women." Ozanus warned him.

Joli rolled his eyes. Ozanus ignored it, "is the field with two butts ready?"

"One upright and one lying on the ground."

"Great. Do you think anyone will show up?"

"Woman or dragon?"

"Both."

"Calluna will, even if only to moan. That's all she ever does." Miryama chuckled, "she has always thought she was cut out for more than being a pack animal as she puts it. And here she comes now."

Calluna landed between Spilla and Joli and quickly sidled up to Joli and bowed her head trying to look meek, *"Joli."* Miryama and Ozanus glanced at each other and laughed. Joli growled at Calluna but she wasn't deterred.

"Leave him alone Calluna." Elaheh called out as she joined them.

Calluna reluctantly moved away from Joli. Elaheh greeted Miryama, "morning, there are others on the way."

"Miryama, would you like to lead this and Joli and I will just catch anyone who falls off?"

Her face lit up and he smiled as he pretended to be busy with a buckle on Joli.

It was an hour before all the women and dragons were in the sky circling the field with the two butts. Both Miryama and Ozanus demonstrated, neatly piercing the centre of the butts. Over the course of the day a crowd gathered at the edge of the field to cheer on the successes and to laugh at anyone who fell off their dragon. A few of the girls became arrow retrievers.

As the day came to an end everyone was talking with excitement, thrilled at what they had been doing. None of them had done anything like it before and put their archery skills truly to the test. They all thought that the twenty of them could easily defeat Temijin's army.

Ozanus and Miryama were the last to leave again. They walked back to the village side by side. He remarked over the top of Joli's saddle, "you are clearly respected, why are you not competing for leadership? You are the sort of person that is needed right now."

"It's complicated."

"Try me." He challenged.

"As I am the temporary leader due to Esfir being lost to the arena I cannot stand for leader. They have seen what I am capable of and that would be an unfair advantage."

"Are you really going to let an untried leader lead you through this critical time?"

"There is a council meeting to discuss that tonight, and before you ask, you are not invited." She ended sternly, "you have interfered enough already."

"You know my reasons though."

"I do and have accepted them but not everyone else has or will." She paused in her walking and looked at him. He didn't realise and carried on.

She thought about how he was. Today he had come alive with the dragons and people and training them in the skills they needed. And though he had said she was respected he had today earnt the stubborn women's respect as well. He was clearly an expert in the art of war and preparing for it.

She was drawn to him, even with that almost permanent frown on his face when he wasn't giving her a shy smile. Life had taken its toll on him already and he had greater responsibilities then she did.

Reaching Mada's roundhouse they both entered. Mada greeted them both, "Miryama, stay for dinner."

"Thank you Mada. I was hoping to talk to you before the meeting later." Miryama smiled.

"I'm glad one person wants my opinion. The others seem to think I'm a mad old lady."

"Because you ensure they get that impression." Miryama laughed and then asked, "how is our other guest?"

"We can only wait." She looked between Miryama, Ozanus and the comatose Diego and smiled to herself, whether they knew it or not she had a feeling the Gods were having a hand in everything. She could see the Nejus was learning to trust and believe in himself and Miryama was discovering the other side to being a leader. There was a glow around them and Mada realised they would make a formidable pair when they realised. She decided to give it a little nudge later.

After dinner Miryama made her excuses. She, Mada and Lylya had spent most of the meal discussing the planned meeting. It was decided that Lylya would go for her knowledge of the Suwars as it would be more readily accepted than if Ozanus spoke. Ozanus stepped out with her and then hesitated in what he wanted to say. She gave him an encouraging smile, "forgotten something?"

"I am going back to Keytel in a day or two, leaving you to carry on with the training. I have to get my Suwars here."

"Can Lylya not go?"
He looked in surprise at her and she looked just as surprised at what she had said.

"We discussed it, and I am the better to go now, she was the original plan. I think you can make sure they continue their training. You don't need me here for that."

188

"Thank you."

He took a deep breath before saying, "look, I know you don't believe in the Gods but will you come with me to the temple tomorrow?"

She frowned. She really wasn't interested in going down there with the obnoxious priest. He added, "it would be early in the day."

She didn't think she would say the right thing so just nodded. He smiled, "thank you."

Just inside the roundhouse Mada stood in the shadow of the door and chuckled to herself. Her assistant eyed her, "what are you up to?"

"You are too young to understand." Mada remarked as she stepped away so Ozanus didn't know she had been eavesdropping.

As he walked in, he started to ask, "have you...?"

"Have a look in the chests, there is all sorts of things in there." Mada smiled knowingly.

He frowned suspiciously at her before saying, "thank you."

"Lylya, are you coming?"

"Can I borrow her a minute?"

"Of course. You know where you are going don't you?" Lylya looked between them, "yes. Ozanus, what's going on?"

He waited till Mada left then guided her to his bed. He glanced across the room to check where Mada's assistant was before saying quietly, "I am taking Miryama to the temple tomorrow."

"Why?"

"She knows I've got to leave in a few days' time but I think it will help her. I know there is a council meeting tonight and Miryama is going to be offered the leadership during this next month or so."

"You don't know that." She hissed in protest.

"Be sensible, would they let someone else take over now

189

and watch all of them die? Who has the experience at the moment?"

"Alright, you are right. Why are you telling me this?"

"Though she doesn't know it she needs the blessing of the Gods, without it who knows what will happen."

"They've survived this long without it." She pointed out.

"Down there, there is an energy just waiting to be needed and used." He pointed aggressively at the floor, "it's not for me that power down there. We both need to be dressed right tomorrow, I'm not trusting that priest to be able to do it properly."

"Do you? You never cared to read the books with the ceremonies in them."

"I know enough, now please just listen." He grumped, "hopefully I'll find something in these chests. Can you help her get ready in the morning?"

She smiled then, having a suspicion then of how her brother was feeling about the temporary leader of the Daughters but held back on the teasing, "of course."

He sighed, "thank you. Now, you'd best get to that meeting before they talk themselves out of our support."

"Mada and Miryama won't let that happen. See you later." She gave him a kiss on the cheek, "and you'd best shave."

With Lylya gone Ozanus went to stand by Diego's bed, "do you think I am doing the right thing? The fact they haven't thrown me off the mountain yet would suggest I am." He chuckled to himself, "let's see what I can find to make her an official dragon knight? Can you even hear me?"

He started in the chests at the back, the ones covered in a thick layer of dust. Mada's assistant brought him over an oil lamp to help him see. Without a word to each other they began looking through the chests. He found a couple of old embroidered robes and put them to one side

190

for a closer look later.

In another chest he was surprised to find some dragonscale armour made of actual dragon scales but wasn't sure if it would fit Miryama. In there also was a leather breastplate with worn gilding on it. He put both to one side to polish. Lylya would get Miryama to wear the best fitting one. He also found several curved knives with carved dragon headed handles. With a bit of polish and sharpening one would be ideal as a gift for the end of the ceremony.

He spent an hour beating the dust out of the robes and the assistant sewed up the two holes found. Together they polished the two breastplates and he noted the 'S' carved across several scales and wondered who it had belonged to. The knives were cleaned before a whetstone was used to sharpen the blades. The young assistant couldn't help staring as he concentrated on a particular bit of dirt that wasn't coming off. She was in complete awe of him which is why she had been pretty much silent around him.

Carefully he worked on the gilding to not take any more off and it revealed an image of the flat topped mountain with a dragon with wings spread protectively above it. Ozanus chuckled when he realised that the representation of the Dragon Lord was female. He wondered how the God felt about that.

Twenty-Three

In daylight the age of the robes could be seen and the cut of the red one he had found was on the feminine side but not so much he couldn't fit in it. The gold and silver threads were worn and a dragon on its back could only just be discerned. For Miryama he picked the dark green one with a mountain scene painted on to it. He bundled both into a blanket along with the two knives and then went to wake Lylya.

He handed her the bundle with the two breastplates, "take these to Miryama and get her to wear one of them." Lylya rubbed sleep from her eyes, "what are these?"

"I found some breastplates. I've cleaned them up. Hopefully one of them will fit. Tell her to meet me on the ledge."

"It's barely dawn you know."

"I know but this is the right time for this."

"Are you sure about all of this?" She asked with worry as she pulled on clothes.

"This feels right. They aren't going to survive without the Gods on their side however much they don't want it. She's going to lead them through this time and then she will be remembered forever. Now, please go." He pushed her towards the door.

It was quiet, not even the birds were up. He hurried

to the pools, pulled off his clothes and dived in. Though Miryama should also purify herself he felt the Gods would let her off. He pulled his clothes on to his damp body and hurried across to the top of the crack and down the steps.

There was a rustling and chirps amongst the nesting dragons and thankfully the priest didn't emerge from his room. The apprentice's head peered round and Ozanus put a finger to his lips. The boy nodded in understanding and disappeared back into the room.

The sun slowly crept round until the whole crevice had a warm glow of morning light and Miryama showed up, not quite sure what to expect. Ozanus appraised her appearance and was satisfied. Her hair had been brushed and plaited into one long one apart from the strand that was beaded.

Lylya hadn't told her anything except to help her into clean clothes and the breastplate. She wore the dragonscale breastplate though it dug into her side. She gave Ozanus a tentative smile, "what's going on?"

"You'll see but first I need to blindfold you." He approached and borrowed the scarf she had wrapped round her neck as she thought she was going to be flying. Out of his bundle he drew out the green robe and guided her arms in.

"What am I wearing now? Why do I have to wear this ancient armour? Where did you even find it?"

"Ssh. I need you quiet now. Soon you'll understand." He left her standing helpless as he pulled on his own robe. His back straightened as he reminded himself that he was Nejus and a high priest about to bless a new dragon rider and give her the knife that would mark her out as a Suwar.

He took her hand and she didn't fight it. She found it felt right to be holding it in his larger one. Her long fingers intertwined with his instinctively.

This time there were no torches to lead the way

down the passage and he wouldn't have wanted them diluting the effect any way as they venture into the hallowed spot. The dawn light followed him down giving him just enough light to detect the end of the tunnel.

All of her senses apart from sight were heightened. She could hear water dripping and could smell the damp cold ancient air. The hair on her arms began to stand up on end though she wore long sleeves and a hum appeared in her mind. She wanted to put her hands to her head to try and get rid of it but she couldn't free her hand from Ozanus! In fact his grip felt tighter and then it was feeling more like a claw! Was Ozanus some sort of magician like his father?!

She let out a scream as the hum engulfed her whole mind and fell to her knees. She realised then that her hand was free. She ripped off the blindfold with a sob that caught in her throat, all the breath taken away. Ozanus commanded, "look up!"
She didn't think she could, she felt weighed down and her neck muscles couldn't hold her head up. Slowly she forced herself to lift her face and then open her eyes.

Was there a dragon behind Ozanus or was he the dragon?! She had to squint to let her eyes get use to the golden white glow. There was definitely a dragon shape around him. She was forced on to her hands as a voice said, *"so one of you have finally decided to visit, but are you worthy? My priest here seems to think so."*
She looked up again at Ozanus. He stood still, bathing in the glow, a small smile on his lips, so it clearly wasn't him speaking but there was still the look of the dragon to him. She opened her mouth but no words came out.
"Quiet!" The voice echoed round the cavern.
She closed her mouth.
"You wear the armour of a dragon rider. Do you think yourself worthy of wearing it? Do you deserve my

194

blessing? Are you equal to your lover?"
She tried to think if Esfir had ever mentioned visiting the temple. The energies swirled around the cavern, agitated. She looked deep within herself and knew this was what she wanted most in the world. She knelt up, her back straightened and she looked directly at Ozanus. Aloud she said, "I am worthy. I will lead this band of non-believers through the coming battle. I will ensure this temple and you are honoured once again."

"*Prove it.*" The voice demanded.

"How?"

"*Nejus, show her.*"

Ozanus came back to life and the dragon returned to the stalactite pillar it clutched. He stood there looking more regal than she expected him to, was it something about the robe that brought out another side of him?

She found she was able to stand. There was still the untapped energies but they weren't as oppressive any more. She realised she had wet cheeks and wondered when she had started crying. Now she could finally take in the cavern with its stalactites and stalagmites. She spotted the stone dais with the roughly hewn altar on it and the stone bowl on top.

She didn't realise how quiet it had been until Ozanus remarked, "now do you understand?"
She didn't think she could speak so nodded.

"Come, let me show you what you must do to complete the ceremony." He took her by the hand and guided her towards the altar.
Finding her voice she said, "he said I had to prove it."
He nodded in understanding.

"What do I have to do?" She asked with concern.

"You are about to become one of my Suwars and in doing so you pledge your life to me and the Dragon Lord."

"What?" She started to back away.

195

There was a growl and the energies in the cavern started to pulse a warning.

"I will not hold you to putting my life before your own but you must show the Dragon Lord that you mean everything you said to him."

"You heard?"

He nodded and added, "there are vows you must make but I need to find them. I don't know them myself as I never had to pledge myself to my father as would normally happen." For him it was assumed he was a Suwar as he was Nejus. He had heard them spoken but had never paid attention to them.

She had nowhere to go now. If she renegaded on her promise her life might end. She gulped and then said, "tell me."

He drew out the two knives he had sharpened and polished out from a sleeve of his robe and presented them to her in their sheaves on the palms of his hands for her to pick one. Gingerly she took one of the offered knives and he slipped the other into his belt. She realised what she was going to have to do, "can't I offer him some food or wine?"

"No. Your blood gives him life." He answered sternly, "now, cup your hand and slice across it. Let the blood pool before dropping it into the bowl as your offering."

Delaying it just a little longer she asked, "do I need to say anything?"

"Only if something comes to mind. Get on with it. He grows impatient."

"How do you know?"

"I just do." He could feel a growing tension beginning to pulse.

She turned to the altar and took a deep breath to calm herself as she needed a steady hand. She winced as she cut deep across the palm of her hand and felt the tears. He gently held her hand cupped and she was grateful for it.

196

He drew her up on to the dais and turned her hand over so the blood that had gathered fell into the bowl of milky water. It fizzed and then disappeared. He smiled at her, "it has been accepted."

"What does that mean now?" She asked cautiously.

"You must obey me as your overall leader but as you are the first here you will lead your own Suwars, even if you are not the leader of the Daughters."

"But I have none."

"When I come back from Keytel I will ensure you will with the help of mine. Now, it's time to head up."

"Here's the knife." She offered it back to him.

"That, along with the armour are yours to keep. That is your ceremonial armour."

"But it's dragonscales, ideal for a battle." She protested.

"Just remember where it has come from. The previous owner's dragon was so dedicated to its rider it pulled scales from its body to make it, a sacrifice in itself. What you wear is a rare thing."

"Oh." She looked down at it again, now knowing and felt great respect to the deep relationship a dragon and rider could have, "do you have some?"

"I have my father's but it is of leather as most are. Excuse me one moment." He turned back to the altar and gave it a deep bow, bending on one knee, *"thank you O Lord for blessing this woman."*

He felt a warm wind past him and down the corridor, taking some of the energy with it. He smiled as a realisation came to him and added, *"your humble servant will always be grateful for your benevolence."*

He stood and carefully stepped backwards before returning to Miryama's side. She asked, "what was that?"

"I think we will shortly find out." He grinned and then grabbed her by the uncut hand and began to pull her out of the cavern.

A person blocked the light and demanded, "what is going on here? How dare you disturb the sanctity of the temple?!"

As Ozanus and Miryama drew closer the priest realised, "oh, it's you. Have you been performing a ceremony without me?"

"Remember, I don't need you." Ozanis pointed out in annoyance.

Spotting the blood dripping through Miryama's fingers and the robes they were wearing the priest got angry, "this is not the place for women!"

"They are equal in the Dragon Lord's eyes. The blood that is offered in a promise, a vow." Ozanus pointed out, "now please excuse us, there is someone I need to see." He pushed past the open-mouthed priest.

Miryama asked, feeling like she had missed something, "there is?"

"In a moment." He smiled knowingly.

It was then that there was a shout, "Ozanus!"

He called back up, "yes?"

Lylya appeared, carefully making her way down the steps, "oh good, you are done."

"What is it?"

Lylya paused on the steps and gabbled, "I don't know how or why, you must have done something but Diego, he woke up."

Ozanus smiled and unprompted grabbed Miryama's face in both his hands and kissed her on the lips. He declared happily, "I knew it."

He ran up the steps and squeezed past his sister leaving the two women alone.

Miryama looked stunned, she certainly hadn't expected that and now she wanted more. Lylya laughed, "that's the happiest I've seen him in a long time. Oh, look at your hand." She stopped laughing and became

concerned, "why haven't you bandaged that?"
Miryama glanced down at her hand, in all the confusion she had forgotten about it.

The dignity of the last half hour had all but vanished as Ozanus ran with a woop towards the village with the robe trailing out behind him. He burst into Mada's roundhouse startling the three occupants. Diego was sat up, resting against Mada while being fed broth by her assistant. Though he was awake he looked ready to go back to sleep. Ozanus exclaimed, "I knew it."

  "Knew what?" Mada asked.
Diego wanted to speak and ask a lot of questions but he couldn't find his voice. Currently all he remembered was a voice ordering him to wake up, that it was time for him to open his eyes. Sensing his frustration Mada patted his arm, "give it a day or two, you are still weak. Now that you've had some proper food inside you rest again and maybe later you will feel stronger."
He closed his eyes with relief.

  She let Diego lie back down and he rolled on to his side. She pulled the blanket up as she said, "now what has been happening?"
Ozanus smiled at her but said nothing as it was not for him to tell at which point Lylya and Miryama showed up.

  Seeing Miryama's wrapped hand Mada demanded, "what have you been doing?"
She stopped in her tracks when she realised what the young woman was wearing. She wondered whether anyone knew the significance of the dragonscales. She thought it lost but clearly the armour of Scyth had re-appeared. She looked back at Ozanus who was taking off his borrowed robe and smiled, "you don't need to tell me anything. Let's get that hand sorted so you can go off training."

  "Ozanus?" Miryama said.

"Mmm." He was helping himself to a bowl of broth as he had realised he was hungry. He offered her a bowl, "want some?"

She shook her head and added, "can we talk?"

"Of course."

"Now."

"No, let me look at your hand first." Mada held firmly Miryama's arm and forced her to sit down on Ozanus' unmade bed.

"Let her, it will take longer to heal as it was your first time."

Mada heated a needle and Miryama gritted her teeth as the medicine woman stitched the deep cut closed. Mada wrapped a bandage round it, "there, now you can go." Miryama grabbed Ozanus' arm and dragged him out the door, "you've got some serious explaining to do."

Behind them Mada chuckled to herself.

She was so angry with him that she couldn't even wait till they were out of the village. What she wanted to say never came out of her mouth. What she said instead was, "what was all of that?"

"All of what?"

"The temple? The God, was he really speaking through you? The energy in there?"

"That," Ozanus smiled, "is the pent-up power of the Gods and it's been waiting."

"For me?"

"No, but soon." He had an idea of what, but it wasn't the right time. She first needed to get use to the idea of being a suwar.

"You tricked me." She protested.

"Perhaps, but it was the right thing."

"Uggh. You don't know everything."

"I know the Gods. And I have a duty to your dragons

200

however inbred they are but cannot do it alone." He replied firmly, rubbing his own healing scar, "if he didn't think you could be a suwar you wouldn't have felt anything in that cavern."

"I have never felt anything like that." She exclaimed in awe as she remembered how it had felt.

"And you may never again."

"What does this mean for me now?"

"Many things. You may never lead the Daughters of Scyth but you will be the first in living memory to become a suwar."

"But will that defeat Temijin?" She asked, feeling exasperated by Ozanus' cryptic answers. She preferred the outspoken man but maybe he was still somehow channelling the Dragon Lord.

"Your chances have definitely improved now you have acknowledged that the power of the Dragon Lord exists."

"You're clearly not going to give me a clear answer."

"I am." He protested, "I'm only telling you as much as I understand. The Gods never give us the whole story. My father was better at understanding." He looked down at his feet, why did it keep coming back to his father? He muttered, "I am not him and never will be."

"What did you say?" Something told her to take his hand and she gave it a squeeze. He looked at her and she saw pain in his eyes. She felt a pressure from behind forcing her towards him. Damn the Gods!

She wasn't sure who initiated the kiss but it felt good. His calloused hands cradled her face. Common sense then broke into her thoughts and she pushed him away, this was all wrong. He looked hurt but she ignored it as she said, "now is not the time. We are late, we must meet up with the others and carry on with their training. Get this damn breastplate off me." She shrugged off the robe and turned for Ozanus to undo the buckles.

Silently he undid the buckles and held the dragon scaled breastplate while she extracted herself from it. She didn't even thank him as she hurried off leaving Ozanus standing there feeling confused. As he picked up the robe he thought it was probably a good thing that he would be heading back to Keytel. He should go and saddle up Joli but wasn't in the mood. In fact he felt drained so returned to Mada's.

Twenty-Four

Diego and Ozanus sat outside Mada's roundhouse trying to ignore the rain. They had just enough shelter from the deep eaves but it was still dripping on their boots. Diego had been caught up on everything that had happened apart from the kiss. Also not mentioned was how the Gods had finally released Diego from his sleep. Sitting staring out at the rain Ozanus remarked, "I'm sorry to do this to you but I'm going to have to leave you in Mada's care and borrow Joli. I need to go back to Keytel. I will be back."

"I know." Diego studied his Nejus' profile and saw there was something new to it. There was still a fragility and aggression to it but there was also now a newfound strength of mind. Maybe he would finally be able to retire back to the village in the Valley.

"I'll go tomorrow. The sooner I'm gone the sooner I'll be back."

"Does Joli know?"

"Yes."

"I am sorry about Ozi."

"She was good. That's the end of her line now. I'll see if I can find another when home. It will take a few days once there to get everyone together."

"Are the Gods with us?" Diego asked with concern.

"For the moment, yes." Ozanus hoped that if everyone

went into the cavern the Suwars would become undefeatable.

Diego nodded thoughtfully and then remarked, "you'd best ensure the Gods are on your side to get across Moronland without being spotted."

Ozanus didn't answer, instead he stood, stretched and held out a hand to his old friend, "I've kept you up too long. I think it's time for bed."

"I think I'm sick of lying in a bed but you are right." Diego gratefully accepted his Nejus' hand.

She knew he was leaving in the morning but that didn't make sleep any easier. Thoughts kept circling in her mind. She feared he would leave and abandon them all to Temijin. Then others crept in, what would it be like lying beside him? Why was her stomach churning at the thought of him leaving? Why was she even caring considering she had led the Daughters of Scyth before he arrived and was now going to lead them into battle?

With a groan of frustration she gave up. She spotted the knife he had given her the previous day and actually took the time to study it in the light of the lamp she kept lit by her bed. She had never liked sleeping in the pitch black of night. He had cleaned and polished it with care and then she had dirtied it with her blood and not even cleaned it. The handled was of two dragons intertwined and wondered whether the Gods had had a hand in her picking it. She took it as a sign.

She realised she had never thanked him properly. She had been angry with him than more than anything else for tricking her but now she was starting to understand why he had done it that way. If she had gone in knowing she wouldn't have felt how she had.

Honouring the gods was another world for her and now she wouldn't be able to ignore it. She began to wonder what the Suwars of Keytel were like and whether they would teach her what she needed to know. She would never be like them, but Ozanus and the Gods had seen something. She looked down at her bandaged hand. She began to see it as a mark of unity and realised she needed to see Ozanus before he left.

She grabbed her clothes from the end of the bed and her waxed coat hanging, dripping from a hook in the eaves. She tucked her new knife into her belt and hurried out of the roundhouse, leaving her companions sleeping.

Something told her he would be at the temple. She slowly made her way down the steps by touch alone and being careful not to slip on the slick steps. She thought she was going so slowly she would meet Ozanus coming back up them. Then she started to wonder if it was another test by the Gods. It was with some relief that she reached the firm surface of the ledge.

She tried not to make a sound so as not to wake the idiot of a priest but the splashes of her footsteps sounded loud in her ears. A flickering torch marked the entrance of the passage and even from the ledge she could feel a pulsing energy, just a gentle wisp of it. Ahead was a white glow at the end of the passage.

Not sure how it would react to her entering she took a deep breath and stepped in. With steady steps she made her way down, hurrying as the light grew brighter and was relieved to hear no humming in her mind though her senses were still heightened. She stepped into the cavern.

Ozanus sat on the dais, his back against the altar wrapped in the red robe he had been wearing when she had become a suwar. His head was slumped forward as if he had fallen asleep. She called out, "Ozanus? I forgot to say…."
The head lifted and a pair of red eyes stared at her, deep into her soul. A hand, or was it a claw beckoned her

forward, *"Miryama, daughter of Cryana, heir of Scyth, I have been waiting for you."*

"You have?" She asked nervously, "Ozanus, is that you?" She took a few steps forward and her hand went to her knife.

"You think that you Daughters of Scyth are above us Gods, that we are not worthy of your devotions. But now you need us."

"Who are you?" Her voice squeaked and she made to step backwards and glanced behind to see how far away the passage was.

Ozanus' hand reached out and grabbed her and pulled her closer. His robe dropped open but it wasn't a human body under it. It was a dark copper scaled chest with deep scars where scales had been ripped off, *"you're mine now."*

The energy in the room grew darker and more threatening. Had Ozanus let his body be possessed by a God? She tried to pull away as he seemed to bath in the energy swirling around them menacingly. It laughed and threw her to the ground. She pulled out her knife as the possessed man stood over her. She slashed out with her knife, catching him on his bare leg and he hissed in anger. She used the brief seconds that were used for him to study his new wound as he exclaimed, *"bitch!"* to turn and made to get up and run but she was too slow.

He grabbed her by the collar of her coat and pulled her back. She slipped out of it but the God was too quick for her as it grabbed her hair and held tight to it, making her cry out in pain. She cried out, "please, no! Ozanus stop him!"

He took the knife from her and ripped through her trousers with it. He threw the knife behind him as he pressed her up against the altar and searched between her thighs with a clawed hand before thrusting into her with a laugh that echoed round the cavern, his eyes challenging the Dragon

Lord statue. She wept.

With a groan Ozanus slumped to the floor and she slipped from the altar and landed on her knees beside him. The God had one last thing to say before it abandoned the weak form of the man, *"watch for me. You have not seen the last of me. I know your inner thoughts, your darkest desires and they are the same as this man's. You are now his as much as mine. You have been joined in the time-honoured way and don't forget it."*
She didn't dare move as the energy within the cavern calmed. She pulled her ripped trousers up and turned to Ozanus. She didn't know how to react at the sight of him lying on the damp ground. Had he called the God up or had it taken possession of him? Who had the God been? And what had it meant they were now joined? Perhaps this was why the Daughters of Scyth had turned their backs on the Gods.

Tentatively she reached out to Ozanus as she found her voice, "Ozanus? Ozanus?"
If he hadn't moved she would have just run but he stirred and slowly sat up, a hand to his head. He looked around, dazed and then saw Miryama's tear streaked face. His eyes widened as it all came to him, "Miryama, I..."

"Why didn't you stop him?" She cried, fresh tears starting to fall.

"I couldn't, I wanted to but he was too strong. This wasn't the way I wanted it to be. You would have been warned beforehand." He cautiously reached out, not sure if she would let him touch her and added angrily, "my family has always been far too closely connected to the Gods. Sometimes I wish I could live as a normal person." More gently he went on, "come on, let's get out of here."
She held tight to his hand and like the morning before it felt right though she felt it shouldn't have after what had just happened. He picked up her knife and gave it to her as he

remarked, "this is my fault."

"Don't regret yesterday. I came here not sure if you would be here considering you've got a long journey ahead of you and to say thank you."

"Thank you?"

"I was harsh because I was surprised and hadn't expected it. I couldn't explain myself very well yesterday. It was indescribable what happened, who would have thought a God would honour me."

The situation then caught up with her. She stared down at the hand holding hers. She broke off the handhold as she realised the absurdity of the situation. She exclaimed, "I can't do this! This isn't a normal reaction. I..."

Tears began to roll down her face again as she had a flashback of moments earlier and as a throbbing pain emerged between her legs. She understood then why Scyth may have fled centuries before. She turned and ran from the cavern leaving Ozanus standing and confused. As it changed to anger at the Gods he turned and kicked at the wall and shouted, "damn!"

He ignored the pain in his foot as he stalked out of the cavern himself.

Only Lylya saw him and Joli off in the morning. He hadn't wanted to leave Miryama considering what had happened but had a feeling she wouldn't want him there. He would make it up to her somehow. Lylya tried to ask if something was wrong, but he ignored her probing. He didn't want to discuss it with her.

While Joli flew, Ozanus dozed in the saddle. Flashbacks of the night before kept coming back to him. He had gone to the temple in the hope that he could absorb some of the unused energy. Instead all he had got was a back seat view of Miryama being raped by the Dragon War

God using his body and no way to stop it happening. For that he hated himself and he hated what his family was. He knew he wasn't going to let that happen again and would somehow use War's patronage to his own advantage. He wasn't going to let the God control him again.

Twenty-Five

They were spotted by a group of children and a young dragon playing on the cliffs that encircled the Valley. Eager to pass on the news they ran and slipped down the path with the dragon flying a few metres ahead of them. Reaching the large lawn in front of the house they called out, "a dragon is coming, a dragon is coming! It's Joli."

The name caused the household to step on to the veranda not sure what to expect if it was just Joli. Ioan tried to hide the hopefully thought he was thinking.

It wasn't a graceful landing for Joli as he was too tired to land carefully. Arno ran across ready to help Diego and was surprised to find his Nejus, "sir? Where is Ozi and Diego?"

"Get the saddle off him so he can find a mud pool." Ozanus ordered and to Joli said, *"spread the word that I need a new dragon and I will see them in the morning. Go and rest first."*

"Yes Nejus." Joli bowed his head.

Ozanus strode across the lawn with intent, pulling off his gloves as he did and unwrapping his headscarf.

Ioan tried to hide his surprise, "brother, what are you doing here? Where's Ozi and Diego?"

"Later." Ozanus and then ordered, "I want to see Gaerwn

and the leathersmith in an hour."

"What?"

"Just do it." Ozanus snapped, "I'm going to have a wash, have something to eat and hopefully they will then both be here. Time is not on my side."

Ioan turned to the old secretary, "you heard him Rafferty."

"Sir."

Shuang tried to follow her older brother, "have you seen Lylya?"

"Not now. I want five minutes peace please Shuang. I need to gather my thoughts." Ozanus sighed as he could never be angry with his sisters. She stopped and let him go.

The hour went far too quickly even though he appreciated the massage given by one of the servants. He did wonder when the number of servants had increased briefly as in clean clothes that fitted he made for the study. His calm didn't last as he shuffled through all the maps on the large table. The leathersmith and Gaerwn glanced at each other and feared an outburst. In the end he grabbed a piece of paper and pencil and began sketching from memory the lay of the land of Moronland. They had no map of the country beyond the cataracts.

Finishing, he paused, nodded in satisfaction and then took a deep drink from the glass beside him. He looked up and finally acknowledged the two people standing, waiting for him, "thank you for coming. I know it's late but things need to happen first thing in the morning." He looked to the leathersmith and the man said "Jonoh sir."

"Jonoh, I need a new saddle."

"Where is Ozi sir? I would need her to get the fit right." Bluntly Ozanus replied, "she's dead. Tomorrow I will be selecting a new dragon. And I need that saddle in days not weeks as I will be leaving again as soon as its ready. You will be rewarded." He added at the end at the sight of the man's eyes going wide with horror.

Jonoh bowed his head, "I'll get started on the form now."

"Thank you. Now, Gaerwn, shall we sit, there is lots to talk about." He gestured to the two chairs on the veranda as he picked up his hand-drawn map and pencil.

"Certainly sir. What do you need from me?" Gaerwn asked as they walked over.

"I have been in Moronland."

"Is the Lady Lylya well?"

"She is now. While there I met a group called the Daughters of Scyth. Have you heard of them?"

"No sir. May I ask how Ozi died?" Gaerwn cautiously asked.

"She was killed by one of Temijin's war machines." Ozanus answered and managed to snap the pencil in his fist, "we are going to Moronland for revenge and a rescue mission."

"Is that wise?"

"The Daughters of Scyth live on a mountain top with a colony of dragons who now need to be saved. They cannot do it on their own. The women have the skills but most have never actually been in a battle. Only a handful can ride a dragon and even then they only have twenty who can be ridden. Most of the colony is too inbred to help but there will be some who can. I left them paired and practising being led by their interim leader." He paused and realised he had snapped his pencil. He threw the bottom out into the border below the veranda, "what I need to know is how many Suwars we have in a fit state after our first encounter with Temijin?"

"Two hundred and sixty, two hundred and fifty and some apprentices, but we still need to protect our borders."

"And if we leave a few at our pinch points, maybe get some of the Valley dragons to support them?"

Gaerwn shook his head, "still the same, maybe a few less to

212

protect the borders. Some of the Suwars have been grounded while trying to find a suitable pairing."

"How many?"

"Five. If you only want us, two hundred of us and some untested women and dragons aren't going to defeat Temijin." Gaerwn remarked with concern.

"The Gods are on our side and I have found something that will boost everyone."

Gaerwn was sceptical but didn't say anything. He was going to have to trust Ozanus as he had clearly found something and was that a flash of red in his eyes? Which God had taken an interest in his Nejus?

"So, with my team that will be just shy of three hundred again?"

"Think so Sir."

"Good. Get the messengers sent out first thing for them all to convene here and they are all going to need their ceremonial armour."

"Sir?"

"Wait and see." He smiled secretly and then back to business, "I'll talk to Lupe tomorrow about supporting the borders. Thank you Gaerwn." He studied his map and the numbers he had scribbled on the edge of it.

"Ozanus?"

Ozanus looked up, "yes?"

"I ask as a family member, not as your inferior. Are you alright?"

"Yes, yes, I'm fine." Ozanus answered dismissively.

"The Gods can screw with our heads."

"I know." Ozanus snapped, "now go!" He didn't want to talk about it and certainly not with a distant cousin.

The man stood, bowed and stiffly said, "Nejus."

Ozanus looked up from his map briefly and nodded acknowledgement before returning his attention to the paper, chewing the broken end of the pencil as he did. The

Suwar chieftain scowled once his back was turned. His leader was as obnoxious as ever then.

Ozanus sat for a while listening to the night sounds, an owl hooting its territorial warning, the crickets and somewhere frogs as well. From the cliffs a dragon's roar echoed out and he wondered who that had been. The wind blew through the bushes and grasses on the edge of the lawn and a night blooming flower's scent floated past. In the house he could hear chatter from Shuang and the table being cleared from the dinner he hadn't attended.

He rubbed a hand over his face and felt a tear slowly slipping down his cheek. He had never felt more alone in the world with no one to understand what had happened to him. He wondered whether the Dragon Lord had forsaken him for the dominance of the War God.

He heard footsteps and looked up to see Rafferty standing a couple of metres away. The old man tentative asked, "sir?"

"Yes Rafferty?"

"Can I help in anyway?"

"I'm not sure."

"I don't know if I can be as good as Diego but I can try." Ozanus smiled at that, "Diego is alive, don't worry."

"That is good to hear."

"There's one problem with being High Priest as when you need advice yourself you have no one to turn to apart from the Gods except that they are the problem."

"Your father struggled with that as well." Rafferty commented as he approached and perched on the chair next to his young Nejus, "he had your mother though and she helped. But there are also the books. You may have been too young to remember but when he brought the thunder God here he spent days pouring over books trying to find the answer as that's all he had."

"I don't think the books will have the answer to my

214

problem."

"There are diaries from your great grandfather, perhaps they might have something?" Rafferty suggested.

"Mmm, maybe."

"Shall I put them on the desk for you?"

"It won't do any harm and thank you."

Rafferty stood and gave the young man a squeeze of his shoulder, "everything happens for a reason."

"I rather it didn't." Ozanus sighed, "is there any food left?"

"I'll get you some, you must be starving and no one can think on an empty stomach. I'll find those books first for you."

"Thank you." Ozanus stood and followed the old man in. Rafferty found the four diaries and placed them on the desk and then went to find some food.

Ioan caught up with him in the corridor, and demanded, "what is going on Rafferty?"

"I don't know."

"He needs to talk to me if it's going to affect Keytel."

"Sir, I know he leaves you to do most of the administration but let him order his thoughts before he tells you."

"Not helpful Rafferty." Ioan complained, "you work for me remember."

"I work for the Nejus." Rafferty calmly replied, "he has more responsibilities than you have and clearly one of them is currently keeping him busy."

Ioan rolled his eyes, "he can't come and go as he pleases."

"Yes he can."

Annoyed Ioan turned and walked off. He needed to know what Ozanus was up to.

Ozanus needed to sleep but knew he wouldn't be able to until he had at least tried to solve his problems.

While picking at the plate of vegetables, cooked chicken and flat bread he began to scan through his great grandfather's diaries. He wondered why Rafferty thought these would be good to look at. He had read them long ago but couldn't remember what was in them. He struggled at times to read the scrawling handwriting in the lamplight.

It was in the second book he found a reference to the War God in a dream his great grandfather had had. Shortly after his great grandfather had gone to war with the God's blessing and he had had armour designed especially that induced fear in his opponent. He tried to think if he had ever seen it in the storeroom that held old equipment and armour pieces.

He took up the oil lamp and made his way through the now quiet corridors. His shadow stretched before him flickering like a flying dragon drawing him onwards.

The storage room was a long room with all the window shutters locked tight. The room was full of chests and racks of clothes, armour and weapons. A layer of dust covered everything. There was a musty smell of lavender from the bunches, old and new, hanging from a beam. It was the sort of room children would be banned from playing in, but they would creep quietly into anyway. No one had ever been told off when found in there.

As a child it was a place to play in on rainy days opening chests and trying on whatever they found, but now as an adult who hadn't ventured in for a long time the magnitude of history struck him. Here, in this dusty room was his whole family history. He walked the length of the room taking in the hanging armour and robes and wondered why certain pieces had been picked to be displayed while others hadn't.

He returned closer to the door where the newer items had been stored including his mother and father's clothes but didn't even open the chests. He had what he wanted of his father's already, or had had, it had gone up in smoke with Ozi. Shifting through another chest he found some of his great grandparents' belongings. He emptied it but found nothing of use. He pulled out another chest and found robes carefully folded up. He thought about his father's robe and realised he should stop trying to be him. He wasn't his father. He had to find something that represented himself and not his father.

He found a set of matching dark purple robes and knew this was more him. There were a pair of dragons facing up against each other on the back of one and the other, the female equivalent guarding her nest. Though she may not accept it he and Miryama were now permanently together so she would still need clothes to look the part.

He moved on to the arms. He had lost his sword and bow when Ozi had fallen to her death and there wasn't time to get new ones made. He tested the weight of a few of each and added them to the robes to be tried out in practice.

From there it was seeing if he could find this special breastplate and hope that it fitted. He wasn't even sure he knew what he was looking for. He shifted through a shelf of leather breastplates, mainly of imitation dragon scales and then on to a lidless box. He muttered to himself, "where would father have put it?"
It was not something his father would have worn so had to have been put away somewhere.

He stood up and surveyed the room and then spotted in a dark corner the glint of burnished copper. He crossed the room and wiped the dust from it and there before him engraved to look like the scarred chest of the War God was what he had been looking for. It rested on a T shaped rack hidden in clear sight. Resting on it was a helmet with a horsetail mane dyed ink black. This must have been how he had terrified his enemies, appearing to be the War God in human disguise. And with a good clean he could imagine why with it glinting in the sunlight. Ozanus grinned to himself, with this and Miryama at his side and the power of the Gods from the temple he and the Suwars would be undefeatable.

He had to make two trips and was relieved to fall into bed only for it to feel far too soon to be woken up by Arno. The young servant had already found the purple robe and had brushed it clean and mended a hole in the side seam. Laid out as well were clean clothes, "I guessed you would want to wear this sir?"

"Yes, thank you." Ozanus replied, pleasantly surprised as he sat up in bed. He looked around for the armour, "where's the breastplate gone?"

"I have it sir and the swords and bows. They are on my list to clean and sharpen today."

"No one can see the armour." Ozanus said sternly and then asked, "Ioan not need you?"

"No. He's put me at your disposal."

"Any word from Joli?"

"Yes sir. They are waiting at the arena for you." Arno replied as he handed his master the clean shirt.

"Have the weapons ready by this afternoon as I need to try them out."

"Yes sir."

Twenty-Six

He felt different in his great grandfather's robe, almost like he was more himself. It was going to need to be taken in as his ancestor was clearly a bigger man but it felt good. He didn't have the weight of his father's legacy on his shoulders. Joli noticed the difference as he walked, bare foot, into the dragons' arena and raised an eyebrow of curiosity. Ozanus scowled at him.

Four female dragons sat crouched on the dirt floor of the arena, just about fitting in. Around the raised dirt edge that encircled the four dragons, villagers and Suwars sat, stood and crouched, come to watch out of curiosity. There was no oral history of a Nejus having to choose a new dragon and start a new line. Suwars had had to work with new dragons but not the Nejus. Behind them were more dragons.

The chatter quietened as Ozanus slowly turned on the spot to see who had come. Directly in front of him was Lupe, still alive and not letting anyone challenge him for leadership. He realised the roar last night was probably from him as he learnt of Ozi's death. Into the quiet Ozanus said, *"as you may have heard Ozi is dead, killed by one of Temijin's machines. Do not fear she will be avenged but first I need a new dragon to ride and start a new line. Their daughter will be my son's dragon whenever he is born. The four of you have stepped up to be considered and that I am grateful for especially as I have known you all since your births. Waffen and Minta, I am afraid your natures are too gentle, you would not be able to cope with my temperament. I need a dragon who is fierier as Joli would be able to tell you."*

Waffen and Minta bowed their heads and lifted off to give more room to the other two. One was a rare dragon indeed with black scales edged in silver, some ancient recessive gene making its appearance while the other was a dusty yellow with a small frill of blunt spines and a longer body harking back to a desert ancestry. They would both be impressive dragons to ride. He didn't know either of them that well so the only way to work out who was best was to let them fight it out, *"Nimib and Savan I cannot choose between the two of you so I suggest a duel?"*

They looked at each other, neither were going to back down, so a duel it would be. Talking started up again, a female versus female duel was a rare thing indeed.

"I suggest we meet back here this afternoon to give yourselves time to prepare and decide if it is worth it. Lupe, can you stay, I need to speak with you."

With grumbles everyone dispersed except for Lupe. He joined Ozanus on the arena floor, *"how can I help you Nejus?"*

"I am shortly to go back to Moronland taking most of the Suwars with me. I need you to organise some dragons to support those left behind at our weak points and you will need to guard the Valley."

"I can do that. There will be those who will want to go with you."

"I ca not stop them but I'd rather they did not come."

"I will try to deter them."

"You know Nimib and Savan better than me. What are they like? Would either of them suit me?"

220

"Neither will equal Ozi, remember that. She grew up with you so your temperaments matched. You need to decide what you want. I know you said Waffen and Minta weren't right for you and I agree but do you want a dragon who challenges you for the sake of it or one who will challenge you in the right way?"

"You are wise my old friend."

"That's because I am old." Lupe chuckled and then became sober, *"I was going to request to see you once you had returned."*

"I am here now so what is on your mind?" Ozanus asked with concern. He had an inkling of what the old beast was going to say.

"It is time I stepped down. I have lived longer than my mate and now my daughter. It is time for some young blood to look after them so I may go to the stars in peace."

"Thank you." Ozanus gave the dragon a deep bow of respect, *"you have truly earnt that privilege and I accept your request. Once I have dealt with Temijin I will return and a new leader found."*

"Thank you Nejus." The dragon replied, pleasantly surprised by Ozanus' respect for him and his choice of words. He knew that Ozanus did not always want to be Nejus but clearly something had happened in Moronland to cause him to step into the role though for how long? He stretched out his wings and took off.

Over at the Suwars' encampment Ozanus organised some sparring partners to join him on the lawn for after Nimib and Savan's dual. Then he had a quick glance through the admin that Ioan liked so much and confirmed he still wasn't interested in it. Ioan tried to get him to discuss a couple of issues and make some decisions, but Ozanus refused, "you know what to do, you sort it." Lunch was a sullen affair with the brothers not talking to each other. Shuang tried to make up for it with mindless chatter but soon fell silent as Ozanus wouldn't answer any of her questions.

It was with relief he escaped the house and joined the dragons and Suwars back at the arena where he was more comfortable. He stood on the ledge dressed once again in his new robe and called out, *"has a decision been made?"*

"Neither of us desire to back down." Nimib, the dusty yellow dragon responded.

"Very well, let the fight begin and I will make judgement." He sat down on the edge as with a quick bow to each other the two females rose into the air.

They circled each other to begin with, seeking out any weaknesses. Savan attacked first, rising higher and then dropping down to grab at Nimib with her hind legs. Nimib hissed and defended herself with her tail. She turned and managed to draw blood with a claw. Savan roared out in pain and rose up quickly to headbutt Nimib in the body.

They broke apart and began circling again. On the ledge a group of villagers were sorting out bets. Not wanting to ignore their Nejus one cautiously asked, "would you like to place a bet Nejus?"

Nejus turned to look at them and looked disgusted, "this is not a time for betting. This is not for your amusement." The group shuffled further around feeling a little guilty.

Up above them the two females were clashing again. Using her tail Nimib swiped at Savan and the other snapped angrily at her opponent, narrowly missing the spiked frill and injuring herself.

Ozanus, as he watched, couldn't help comparing them to Ozi and watched with a frown of concentration, heeding Lupe's words from earlier. As the dragons parted again, blood dripping on to the ground he stood and shouted, *"enough!"*

Everyone turned to look at him.

"I have made my decision."

Nimib and Savan landed in the arena. With pent up energy still to be released Savan snapped at Nimib, drawing blood down the side of her opponent's neck.

"I said enough! Savan you cannot control yourself. I have chosen Nimib."

"I am truly honoured." Nimib panted with a bow of her head.

"We'll go for a flight tomorrow."

"Thank you sir."

He briefly contemplated reprimanding the betting villagers but knew, unlike Temijin's arena, this sort of fight didn't happen often, let them have a little fun for soon they would be watching over the valley for him.

Now it was his turn to fight but only in a sparring match. Arno met him at the edge of the lawn and took the robe and shirt Ozanus took off, "I have laid them out on a table sir."

"Thank you Arno."

Closer to the house five Suwars stood waiting for him, his sparring partners for the afternoon also bare chested, their shirts in a tidy pile and knives tucked into sashes and swords at their sides. He greeted them, "thank you for coming, shall we begin."

"Which one are you going to try first? They all look impressive." One of them remarked as Ozanus approached the table. Ozanus picked one up that had a grip that had been charred at some point in its life and balanced it loosely in his hand. It didn't feel the same as the previous night so put it to one side.

The next had a longer blade with a curved edge to a point that started halfway down it, "let's try with this one first."

The five Suwars formed a rough wide circle and pulled out

223

their swords with Ozanus at its centre, giving him space to flex the sword to get a feel for how it moved. He frowned but decided to keep going with it for the moment.

He turned to a knight and beckoned him forward and the bearded man advanced. Their swords quickly clashed. The man felt the weight of the attack through his arms and knew his Nejus would soon put the sword to one side. They broke apart, Ozanus' hands firmly on the hilt and he went in for a side swipe but didn't like the feel of the thick blade as it moved through the air. He stopped, "enough, not this one."

The men stayed where they were while Ozanus picked up the third sword from his selection. Looking down its length in the light of day he discovered it had a bend in it where it must have hit something very hard, harder than human bone.

Now he was down to two. The next, the grip was worn but the leather could be replaced and the guard was in the shape of a dragon biting its own tail. It was shorter than the second but still had a curve to it. There was a streak of copper running through it that he hadn't seen the previous night. It felt comfortable in his hand. Whoever had made it had been a very talented swordsmith. That made him think, if he was to make twenty new Suwars out of the Daughters of Scyth he needed twenty knives to give to them to complete their pledges along with the apprentices.

Gripping it tight he returned to the circle and with a confident smile he beckoned two of his sparring partners forward. They grinned for they always liked a challenge, and these were men hardened to fighting unlike the women he had sparred with on their mountain home. They charged at Ozanus with a shout and he put up his sword and deflected both of them at the same time. He grinned at them and with a grunt pushed them away forcing them to the ground.

He swung round as he heard a footstep behind him and then side stepped as the bearded knight ran forward, sword pointed directly at his Nejus. Ozanus swiped at the man and caught him on his back with the face of his sword, "you're out."

"Damn. Good move." And the man bowed out.

The two that had fallen had got back on their feet. With a hand gesture they got the other two involved and they all came in together from the four compass points. They made their Nejus work hard and no one got away without a few cuts. They had an adrenalin rush living dangerously by sparring with their sharp swords. Why play safe with a blunt one as you might let an attack through that if it had been sharp you wouldn't have.

It was one of the Suwars who finally admitted defeat, throwing his sword on the floor, "I'm done and I'm going to need stitches." He pressed his hand over a cut on his arm where blood was running from it."
Ozanus, breathing heavily, remarked as everyone paused to see how he would react, "Arno certainly did a good job sharpening this blade. He ran a finger over it and immediately it sliced through the skin. He gave it a suck as blood beaded out, "thanks lads, you've definitely given me a workout."

"Come with us to clean up and have food." The bearded one suggested, "you seriously bruised my arse, it's still sore."
Ozanus laughed, "That sounds like a good idea."
He felt good for having had the hard work out and being around men with the same attitudes to life as him. He placed the sword on the table and as a group they headed off to the encampment.

For a few hours he forgot all his troubles and was just one of the 'lads', eating and drinking a little too much.

225

It was good not to be sat with the resentful glare of Ioan. There were dirty looks from some of the older Suwars when they made too much noise, but no one cared. As darkness started to fall they began to sober up, helped by a few buckets of water thrown over their heads by some of the women.

They sat by the fire talking of lost comrades and dragons, talking of the past, talking of the Gods. And then Ozanus spoke of where he had been and what he had seen but not of Miryama and the War God and the temple. Then they understood why messengers had been sent out earlier and no one protested at the thought of encountering Temijin and his army again. This time they would know what to expect. This time they would not be defeated. This time Ozanus would stand his ground. Cups were raised in silence as the children were now asleep.

Before everyone went to bed plans were made for an archery competition so Ozanus could test the bows he found. They were all going to have hangovers so everyone would be on an equal footing, and they would sort out prizes as well.

Twenty-Seven

The Suwars were gathered outside the Valley waiting for Ozanus to show up. Not all of the Valley dragons had heeded Lupe's talk, and some were coming along for the adventure. No one knew what to expect. Rumours abounded already of a mountain top of virgins both human and dragon waiting to fall into their arms. Would they even all fit on the mountain top? None of them fancied camping at the bottom and becoming easy prey to Temijin's advance party if he had one. Then there was the rumour that Ozanus had ordered twenty-five dragon handled knives to be made; were the ranks of the Suwars about to increase?

With such a big encampment of Suwars; a rare thing these days, half of Linyee had turned up to feed, entertain and supply them. In living memory none of them had ever heard of the Suwars invading another country.

Up on the clifftops the dragons staying behind were waiting for Ozanus' arrival. There was a shout from the impatient youngsters, *"he's coming! He's coming!"* It was clear the Gods were in favour of this venture as the sun glowed red like blood turning Nimib a deep pink and Ozanus in his new armour red. Some even thought he was a god.

Ioan had been horrified as he had watched Ozanus

dressed in the armour and new flying clothes to match Nimib's colouring, "who do you think you are?! No suwar ever wears metal."

Ozanus paused on the top step and turned to his brother on the veranda, a gloved hand going for his knife, "now someone does."

His eyes flashed red and Ioan realised there was more going on than his brother would ever reveal to him and the Gods were very much involved, and possibly the wrong God. He knew enough of the family history to know his great grandfather acted like a warlord and now it looked like his brother was going the same way. He had read his great grandfather's diaries long before Ozanus had and knew the armour to be his. Jealousy bubbled up inside him then. Why did the Gods favour his brother when he wasn't a responsible Nejus? Why did he have to stay in the Valley and never go anywhere? A voice inside his head growled, *"it's your choice."*

Ioan scowled to himself and returned indoors. Ozanus was already strolling with intent across the lawn towards Nimib.

Nimib and Joli roared and the dragons below all roared too. Some of the Suwars had horns and blew those. They weren't going to let their departure be a solemn affair. This would go down through history as an event to remember. As one they rose into the air and everyone from Linyee had to cover their faces from the dust and wind from the dragons' wings.

Ozanus on Nimib and Joli led the convoy of dragons and riders with Gaerwn and his second in command behind them leading the Suwars. Swooping around the mass of Suwars were the riderless dragons. Each carried a pack of bedding and clothes with their ceremonial breastplates wrapped in them as ordered by Ozanus. They also carried their bows with full quivers of arrows and belted to their waists were their swords and as always their dragon knives were tucked into sashes and belts.

They stopped for the day at the bottom of the cataract and would make the flight over the mountains in the morning. Ozanus and Gaerwn gathered round a fire, sheltered by the curious Nimib, with a couple of Gaerwn's lieutenants. Ozanus had scaled up the map of Moronland with more detail after discussing it with Joli though there were still gaps of unknowns. They studied it together, Ozanus talking through it all.

It was decided a small group would go off towards Duntorn to see where Temijin and his army were, following the road if needed till they caught up with them. The chosen lieutenant took her own sketch of the map before departing to organise a group. Another group were to go ahead and scout the lay of the land to identify areas that would be good for ambushes or a full out attack. Another map was quickly drawn up and the other two lieutenants headed out to organise themselves for the morning.

Once over the mountain the groups broke away from the main mass. Friends waved goodbye and sent up a quick pray to the Gods in the hope they would be reunited. Ozanus and Gaerwn were saluted before they headed off on their missions. Nimib asked, *"is this wise? They will be warned of us."*

"They don't know how many of us there are. Once we are sighted it will still take a day or two to hear and by then we'll be on the mountain."

"It sounds like a curious place from what Joli has told me."

"Oh it is, it is." Ozanus remarked thoughtfully. He had tried not to think about Miryama but she had cropped up occasionally over the last couple of days. He didn't know whether it was guilt or whether it was attraction for her. He had no idea how she was going to react to his return, or

whether she would even accept his peace offerings.

"What are we going to do once there?"

"Plenty."

"Go on?"

"No." He debated with himself whether he trusted Nimib enough to explain some things but decided it was too early in their relationship.

Before they knew it the mountain with its blackened tree ring around it came into view. The cloud was up high, forced up by the up-draft. He spotted a couple of observation platforms he hadn't seen before. He turned in his saddle and shouted, *"let's make it a grand entrance, lets circle it! We are here to save them!"*

The dragons roared approval.

Twenty-Eight

Miryama had curled up in a ball in her bed after she and Ozanus had parted company. She was in too much pain, mentally and physically, after the violation to think straight. She didn't want to see anyone and sent everyone away who came to her.

Lylya came by, "I thought you would have seen Ozanus off. You should have as you are now a suwar aren't you?"

"So what, go away." Miryama pulled the blanket further over her head.

Lylya sat down uninvited on Miryama's bed, "there are things you are going to have to learn about being a suwar. It's not just a title. You need to show respect to the Nejus and to the Gods."

"Well, they should respect me as well." Miryama retorted from under her blanket.

Lylya frowned, "what has happened?"

"Just go away."

"Who's training the dragons and riders?"

"They can have a day off. They don't need me to supervise them practising."

Lylya left feeling confused and wondering what had happened between Miryama and her brother.

Her companions who shared the roundhouse

couldn't persuade her to eat or drink and discussed getting Mada. She heard and said, "no! Just leave me alone."

"We could have warned you men are no good and look at you now." They retorted from the fire, "you are meant to be leading us through this man-made crisis. You brought this on yourself."

"Go away."

The three women tutted and decided to ignore her for the rest of the night.

She was violently sick the following morning though she had an empty stomach. Feeling wretched she forced herself over to Mada's to seek help. Mada quickly sat her on Ozanus' bed when she saw how pale and feverish she was. Diego stared across from by the fire. He had yet to meet Miryama and wondered if this was she based on Ozanus' description. Mada sat beside Miryama and rested two fingers on the woman's wrist and felt the racing pulse and the very faint beginnings of two more. She asked, "what's wrong?"

"Everything. Ugh…."Miryama wrenched but had nothing but air and stomach acid.

"Diego, could you bring me a cup of water and then leave for a bit." Mada turned to the man.

"Of course."

He didn't go far. He had a feeling this concerned Ozanus so quietly sat on the bench by the door. Physically he wouldn't have made it much further anyway.

Inside Mada turned Miryama round to face her and asked in a tone that suggested there was no point hiding anything, "now, tell me what is going on? Are you lovesick for a certain man?"

"No." Miryama replied with a weak attempt at anger, "until he came, we were good weren't we?"

"You are skirting the question. What has happened?" Mada asked sternly.

"Ozanus… No, a God… No… Oh it's all so confusing."
Miryama buried her head in her hands.

"One thought at a time." Mada gently guided.

"I couldn't sleep, not after everything that has been
happening." She waved her bandaged hand at Mada, "and
knowing he was going. What if Temijin gets here before he
comes with his Suwars? What if he doesn't come back? I
feel sick to my stomach."

"He is the Nejus of Keytel and one of his titles is
defender of <u>all</u> dragons. He will return. He has left his sister
and his friend here and will have to come back for them.
Have you slept with him? Though it should be too early."
She murmured to herself at the end.

Miryama had only been half listening, "what did you say?"

"Nothing. You mentioned a God earlier?" Mada
prompted.

The tears started to run down her face, sticking her hair to
her face even more. She let out a sob.

Seeing she wasn't going to get a straight answer out
of Miryama Mada changed tack. She took hold of the
younger woman's face in both of hers and turned it to face
her. She wiped the tears away and brushed the damp hair
off her face, "you need to realise that you have been
honoured by the Gods because of him."

Miryama looked disgusted and broke away. She stood as
she spat, "honoured?! How can you say I have been
honoured? You don't know what happened."

"You don't believe me but take a closer look at the
breastplate you were wearing, and I suggest you get Catlin
to look at it and get it to fit you properly." Mada suggested.

"Mada, what are you talking about?" Miryama stared
down at the old woman, confused by the change in
direction the conversation was going.

Mada pulled her back down to the bed, "his father was the
last to hold all the power of the Gods and each of his

children will have received something of it even if they never realise or make use of it. As for you, you have been blessed as well. Scyth's breastplate was thought to have been lost but he found it with no idea of its significance."

"Scyth's?! Why didn't you just say that?" Miryama exclaimed.

"Where's the fun in telling you directly?" Mada smiled.

"What does this mean?"

"Mean for who?"

"For me? For us?"

"Great things." Mada smiled, "though we may have forsaken the Gods a long time ago they clearly have not. Why else would they have brought Ozanus here and then have him find Scyth's breastplate."

"Mada," Miryama sighed, "this has nothing to do with the Gods. We brought Lylya here so of course Ozanus came to find her and found us."

"Oh it does and I know." Mada's smile suggested a secret.

"How can you know?" Miryama challenged.

"This must never be repeated, but I am also of his father's blood."

"What?!" Miryama exclaimed in a voice that came out as a whisper.

"He visited here once, a long time ago and he got my mother pregnant. Some of their power must have transferred to me through his seed. I can sometimes see things that have yet to happen, and I can sense things occasionally too. And whether you like it or not you have been blessed as well."

"Nothing is a blessing, it's all a huge curse." Miryama protested.

Mada sighed, "I think you need to tell me a bit more. Did the Dragon Lord do something to you?"

"No." Miryama responded bitterly and then her face

creased with pain as she couldn't not tell any longer, "I went to the temple before Ozanus left as I thought he might be there, I don't know why." She shrugged but went on, "he was there but he wasn't. There was a form over him, like the previous morning, but not the Dragon Lord this time…." She hesitated.

"The Gods have decided to use him as a vessel?" Mada frowned and feared, somehow, Ozanus had attracted the attention of the wrong God. "What did it look like?"

"Old copper scales and there were scars as well. There was blood dried on it." She grimaced at the memory.

"The War God."

"He… It… Oh Mada," Miryama started to cry again. She didn't want to be this weak person she was currently being. She considered herself a strong and capable person, "let's say both of them, they, it… raped me." She whispered the last bit feeling shame as no Daughter of Scyth had been raped in living history in their mountain home, "and then he said he could see into my soul, that I was like him and that I was now joined to Ozanus and him and mustn't ever forget that."

"To those close to the Dragon Gods there is a lot of savagery that has not yet to passed into history. Sadly, you have experienced one of those ceremonies."

"What do you mean?" Miryama asked with fear.

"You are now married to Ozanus whether either of you wish to be or not. They follow the dragons' mating rituals."

"But it wasn't Ozanus. He saw it but couldn't stop it." Miryama protested, "and afterwards," she laughed then at the absurdity of it all, "we made polite conversation. I can't be his mate, his wife."

"You have no choice now. And another thing," there was no point holding back now, Mada thought.

"What?"

"You know I said I can sense things, well…. You are

235

carrying the next Nejus and….” She hesitated, “and his sibling.”

“No I’m not. No chance!”

“Do you think I would really make that up?” Mada looked sternly at the younger woman.

“Get them out! I don’t want them!” Miryama exclaimed.

“Ssh. Calm down. This is what the War God is wanting.” Miryama decided she had heard enough. There was no way Mada could tell she was pregnant with twins when she’d only been penetrated by a God using Ozanus’ body two days previous. She stood and hissed, “don’t you dare tell him if he comes back.”

“It’s not my place to tell but he will find out one way or another. The Gods won’t let a secret like this stay so.”

“What about your secret?” She challenged.

Mada laughed, “I am nothing to them, just an unfortunate mistake who will die as peacefully as I lived. Whereas you, they probably had your eye on you the moment you challenged Ozanus. Now you are a suwar and his wife, so you’ll never escape their attention now. And he, well he was born to interact with the Gods and will have done so all his life even if he wasn’t always aware of it and now at a critical point he has become so.” Her voice had deepened and become gravelly like it was a dragon trying to speak the human tongue.

Miryama froze. She felt pressure on the cut on her hand and knew the Dragon Lord was speaking to her.

“Together you will be a force of reckoning. Make of that as you will.” Mada said and then blinked and looked as if she wasn’t aware of what she had just said. Instead in her bright voice, “when you are ready to accept your situation, I can give you something for the sickness.”

Numbly Miryama nodded and staggered out of the roundhouse. She didn’t notice Diego on the bench.

236

Diego couldn't believe what he had heard though he hadn't heard it all. In respect to the woman who was caring for him he would not be revealing her secret to anyone though he was surprised. Kittal had never told him of a trip into Moronland. It was clearly a youthful transgression he had forgotten all about. He smiled to himself, so Kittal had had a brief moment of being a wild child; and Ozanus had never left it although there had been something different about him when he had come round. And clearly something had gone on between the Miryama woman and Ozanus but no one was talking which was a bad sign and Lylya would be excited if it had been good. He decided to wait it out and see what happened.

Twenty-Nine

Miryama decided the only thing to do was to ignore the pain and ignore the potential dragon spawn growing in her belly. She took Mada's offer on something to quell the nausea though she still had barely any appetite. She had to keep busy, prepare for the arrival of an unknown number of dragons, men and women; anything to wear herself out so she could sleep at night rather than revisit what she was trying to forget. She wanted warning of their arrival or even Temijin's when the cloud was high enough to see the surrounding land. A palisade was put up to divide the training grounds from the rest of the village to keep any prowling men away from the women. She had a duty to the Daughters of Scyth first.

She spoke with Diego and Lylya trying to get a sense of what would hopefully be coming and even a sense of Ozanus. In regards to Ozanus she felt even more confused. He seemed to have several sides to him that she hadn't yet to meet, the caring brother, the arrogant leader, the mercenary and the bored young man.

Then there was the decision on how to talk to Ozanus if and when he returned. She certainly wasn't going to run into his arms. Would she even let him see her?

It was with trepidation and a sinking feeling in her stomach that she heard that a large thunder of dragons were heading towards them. Soon they had reached the mountain and it was an impressive sight to behold. Every woman and child stopped what they were doing and had to cover their ears as the mass of dragons roared together and it could be heard for several miles around. They hoped that it would make Temijin afraid. The mountain's dragons rose up to greet the larger dragons and the small ones chirped and flitted around them all.

The dragons landed in phases, seeking places to land and it was soon cramp but there was nothing to be done and it wouldn't be forever. The women hung back, wary of so many men and dragons. Ozanus was the last to land with Gaerwn. He found a spot close to the village. He was out to make an impression and remained on Nimid until he saw the council approaching. He smiled as he saw Lylya holding back her excitement as she helped Diego hobble along behind the council.

He saw Miryama standing at the centre of the council with the other members fanned out either side. They stared at each other, unsure how to react or who should speak first until Mada gave a little cough.

Miryama blinked and remembered who she was. She stood straighter and ignored the wave of nausea that was coming, formally calling out, "welcome back Nejus. We have made as much space as we could for you and your Suwars with guidance from your sister and advisor. We ask that all single men stay behind the palisade and couples to the fields camp, but any single women are welcome to mingle with us." She said nothing of the dragons as they were their own entity.

"Gaerwn." Ozanus glanced at the Suwars' Chieftain.

"Sir." The man saluted, fist to his chest and then slipped off his dragon, "is there someone who can show me round?"

239

"Elaheh." Miryama instructed and the young woman stepped out of the gathered women.

"This way." Elaheh pointed through the village.

"Thank you for welcoming us and I hope we can work together to destroy Temijin." Ozanus remarked from Nimib, "there are more to come and hopefully with useful information."

The seriousness of the greetings were ruined by Lylya who could contain herself no longer and called out, "Ozanus, stop being pompous, it doesn't suit you and get down from there."

Ozanus glared at her but a smile danced at the corner of his mouth. He slipped out of his saddle and let Nimib lower him to the ground with a forearm. Lylya ran towards her brother, "I'm glad to see you back." She stopped, "what are you wearing?"

"Lylya, we'll talk later." He replied but his eyes weren't looking at her. She followed his gaze and saw they looked at Miryama who was looking everywhere but at him.

"Oh, of course."

"I'll be behind the palisade."

"You don't have to do that." Mada protested, "you are a guest still."

A few of the councillors grumbled.

"I am a single man and so will respect your wishes, but I think Diego needs to remain with you."

Mada bowed her head, "he is certainly welcome to stay."

"Thank you for respecting our wishes." One of the council remarked.

Miryama was relieved that the others had taken over the talking. She was trying not to stare at Ozanus but kept giving him glances. She wondered if he had gone mad or was trying to offend her dressed in the burnished copper breastplate. She was getting flashbacks she really didn't need right then. She fought the urge to run and carefully

240

turned and walked away as everyone else talked. She nearly bumped into Diego who tried to grab her arm.

She shrugged it off before it reached her and kept walking all the way to her home where she was promptly violently sick into a bucket. All of her fear and misgivings came pouring out as she hugged the stinking bucket. She should send them all away, tell them they weren't needed. Let the Daughters die by Temijin's hand, no one would miss them.

Aryana burst in, "have you seen the size of their dragons?! Imagine if all of our females had an egg from each of them, we'd soon start becoming a healthy colony again and then we would become as well known as the Suwars." She stopped and realised her sister was sat on the floor looking thoroughly miserable, "what's wrong with you? You should be thrilled at all these people and dragons come to help us."

Miryama looked up, "I know but…." she took in a deep breath and sat back against her bed.

"I thought you were getting on with Ozanus even if he is a little dominating." Aryana remarked and sat down beside her sister, "have you foolishly slept with him?"

"You could say that."

"Idiot! He didn't force himself?" She asked with concern especially as it was quite early for morning sickness to be happening.

"Not really." Miryama lied.

"You should tell him."

"No. Now is not the right time, there are more important things to worry about."

"If you are sure?" Aryana studied her sister's face, trying to work out what was going on in her mind.

"Yes I'm sure. There is time for celebrations once Temijin and his arena are destroyed."

"You are right." Aryana stood and held out a hand to help

241

Miryama up, "I think we need to go help with preparing for tonight's welcome feast. There's a lot of us to feed. We're a bit crowded up here now. Let's hope the mountain doesn't crumble." She joked in an attempt to lighten the mood, "I think they are going to set up a camp at the bottom of the mountain so there is a guard for all the dragons that are going to have to rest down there." Thankfully it raised a small smile.

A tent had been set up at the edge of the palisade for Ozanus with some basic furniture. Behind him his new armour was hung up but covered with a blanket as he didn't want War's influence staring at him. His new robe was currently lying on the bed waiting for the feast to begin. The women wouldn't care but his Suwars would if he didn't present himself properly amongst company. Around the table where he stood at the head of it was also Gaerwn, the lieutenants who had returned from their re-con missions and Miryama with Elaheh who had been co-opted as her deputy. Diego sat on a stool studying a piece of paper.

Maps were spread across the table and Ozanus was making notes on a scrap of paper. More of his own map was now filled in with the wide road Temijin would be taking to get most of the way before likely setting up on a ridge no one had been aware of. And he was certainly on the move for at spotting the group of dragons they were fired upon and though none of the arrows had reached them.

In his hurry to get to the Daughters of Scyth men had been coerced into helping pull and push his dragon killing machines along. The group reported back of half dismantled catapults and ballista that shot the same arrows that killed Ozi. Several carts being pulled along had nets so he could capture the smaller dragons. Ozanus asked, "you've seen the route, how long before he would be here?"

"Another week. He's pushing them." The blonde haired lieutenant remarked as he rubbed his tired eyes, dry from all the flying in the cold air.

"Thank you. Go and have a wash, there will be plenty of food and drink shortly." Gaerwn replied.

The man bowed and left.

Gaerwn turned to Ozanus and said, "we should attack now."

"Not yet. Our dragons have flown hard for two days and need a rest."

"He knows we are here now."

"No he doesn't. He knows there is a small group." Ozanus replied calmly, "a lot of this land is wooded and won't suit an all-out attack from us. Did you find anywhere clear enough for us to be able to take out his army? We'll have to attack in waves."

"Only one spot Nejus but we might have to make it wider by taking down some of the trees." The lieutenant dressed in brown flying clothes remarked, trying not to play with her plait from nervousness.

"There's one problem." Her companion interjected, "it is farmland."

"Hmm. Something to think about."

"How good are the riders here?" Gaerwn asked, trying to work out how to incorporate them into his cohort and whether they would accept his command.

"They still need work." Miryama admitted and as if she had read his mind she added, "and I will be leading them." She glanced over at Ozanus and he gave her a smile. She turned her head away.

"Fine." Gaerwn replied, not feeling confident. He really didn't need a weak spot amongst his Suwars especially when up against an army. He wanted to attack sooner rather than later, before Temijin could set up his war machines.

He and Ozanus would have to argue it out in the morning, away from ears that didn't need to hear. He looked at Diego to see if he could work out what the old man was thinking.

"Thank you everyone, plenty to think about but now's not the time. The Daughters of Scyth have organised a feast so we'd best all get ready for that but remind everyone that we are guests so they all need to behave. Ladies, thank you for coming." Ozanus bowed his head towards Miryama and Elaheh.

Everyone left apart from Diego. He was frowning at his piece of paper and finally remarked, "this feels too easy."
Ozanus leant on the table, "I know. I feel we have missed something."

"He's bullish and will do anything to win. There aren't enough war machines."

"Is there another direction he could be coming from?" Ozanus frowned at the map and said to himself, "War wouldn't be taking an interest unless something big was going to happen."

"Ozanus, I know you try hard to hide things from me but I know when there is something amiss. I saw what you were wearing when you flew in and," Diego gestured at the bed, "and where did that purple robe come from? I thought you liked the red."

Ozanus studied his advisor and friend, impressed by his attention to detail as always. For the moment he ignored his friend's observations while he thought about the other issue at hand. He studied the map and pointed at the blank space, "the only direction he could be coming in is this one, where we know nothing about the land. We should send someone out there and see what is found."

"Mmm…. Ozanus?"

"Fine." Ozanus sighed and pulled up a chair, "the War God has been haunting my dreams, like my great

244

grandfather." He paused, fighting the two sides of himself in regard to Miryama, "he took possession of my body, used me to his will and I couldn't stop him. I've come to realise I should stop trying to be my father."

"How long has that taken you?!" Diego chuckled.

"Alright, alright." Ozanus replied with a hint of a smile.

"Where did the breastplate come from?"

"The storeroom. I read of it in his diaries when he went to war and had War supporting him. He decided to take full advantage rather than fear it."

"Good, sounds like the right thing. And you and Miryama?"

"Who knows. War has destroyed what we were starting to discover. He forced marriage on her." Ozanus couldn't look at his friend, "we are now a couple though I don't know if we will be one."

"Oh." Diego didn't know what to say to that hearing it from Ozanus though he already knew. No advice from him was likely to help the situation for the moment.

Pulling himself out of his worries Ozanus said with forced brightness, "come on, let's get ready. Food, drink and sleep will bring a new day and hopefully some new thoughts on everything. Somehow I've got to get seventeen reluctant women into the temple along with everyone else. The Dragon Lord has a blessing to impart on all and we should not look a gift horse in the mouth."

"I think you know who you need to speak to there?"

"Yes I know." Ozanus sighed as he pulled on the robe and the responsibilities with wearing it started to weigh on him again.

Rules were forgotten over the course of the evening as new friendships over food and drink were made especially among the younger people. Fuelled on the thrill of a huge adventure some of them slipped away into the darkness. Music and singing happened and a smaller Valley dragon was coerced into supporting with some acrobatics, helping the young Suwars somersault and flip over it. The oldest stayed sat by the fire comparing stories and aches and pains. Lylya was on the giddy side and filled the gaping silence between Miryama and Ozanus with incessant chatter till Ozanus snapped, "enough!"

"What has happened between you?" She protested. She looked at Miryama picking at her plate of food.

"Stop trying to play matchmaker."

"But you were starting to get on so well." Lylya exclaimed.

"I said enough!" He slammed his fist on the table as he stood. He moved round to leave as he felt a headache coming.

In almost a whisper Miryama said, "we should talk."

He spun round to stare at her. His face fell but he recovered and snapped, "now is not the right time."

With a deep breath he turned away from her scared face. He needed air and it was too smoky and noisy. He needed the darkness to dwell in and wondered whether it was War encouraging him towards the blackness of death. He had evaded what was clearly death in disguise in the Valley when he was six and now what challenge was he being tested with.

The night grew darker and the stars disappeared and the smell of the bonfire became more acidic and of burning homes and flesh. Then the light of fires leapt into view. He heard a voice, *"do you want this?"*

"What do you want from me?"

"Your rage, your anger, your blood." It hissed, *"I want to feel it. I know it simmers inside you. I see you found that armour, stunning, isn't it? He thought he could defeat me by being me but no chance, what he felt drove him mad and look what it did to your father? Scarred him for life."*

246

Ozanus spun on the spot and saw a flash of glistening copper amongst the burning buildings. His anger certainly was increasing. He shouted, *"I am not them! You do not control me!"*

The scene disappeared in the blink of an eye and the stars re-appeared but there was a cackle lingering in the air.

He knew what War was trying to do. He was trying to push him so he made a mistake which would turn the coming battle into a bloodbath. He wasn't going to let that happen. He was good at planning and he wouldn't start anything until the enigma of the area north of the mountain was solved. He knew that was the weak side where the dragons lived. As he returned to his tent he debated whether he should just head out himself first thing. In the end he decided it would be better to send some of Miryama's women out with the Suwars for the experience.

And then his thoughts turned to Miryama again….

Thirty

There were plenty of sore heads in the morning and reluctance to head east for reconnaissance duties and with novices that they saw the Daughers as. Miryama and Ozanus saw them off and she asked, "will they be alright?"

"They know how to use a bow and I'm sure if there is any trouble they know not to take the risk and return home. My Suwars won't let them do anything foolish."

"Are you up for talking?" She studied his profile as she tried to work out his reaction to the question.

He continued to stare out though the clouds hung too low to reveal anything. His fingers twisted the signet ring, "here?"

"No."

"Where?"

She took his hand and though she didn't want it to be it still felt right. She led him away from the edge and towards a grove of short trees, stunted by the winds. She sat down on a fallen tree while he remained standing.

She wanted to slap him but refused to let War win. Why was she the only angry one? She decided now was not the time to tell him how she felt. She said, "we need to be united."

"And we are but you need to also understand this is a serious situation of which the majority of your support is from me and I have the knowledge and skills."

This wasn't the way she wanted the conversation to go especially as he wasn't really looking at her. He didn't seem to be in the conversation, "how can you be so calm?"

"This is what I was born to do. I have known nothing else."

"Why aren't you angry?"

"About what?"

"What was done to me?" She tried to remain calm but there was bitter tone to her voice.

His eyes widened and he turned to look at her properly, "angry? Angry? Want to really know why? Because I'm not going to let Him win. Being possessed so a God can taste human pleasures is the least of my worries. Out there," he gestured behind him, "out there is an arsehole who is cleverer than you give him credit for. Those machines of his, he created them, every single one of them, I've seen the plans. And he's coming here to wipe you out. He invaded my country and I had to sell my sister to him to save it and that tears me apart. And now I'm here to protect your inbred insignificant dragons so that they can carry on interbreeding till it's pointless even laying an egg and why you ask? Because that is my role, that was my father's role, his grandfather's and on and on. He cannot be allowed to enter Keytel again." He spat at the end, "you want us to be united, I gave you a gift which so far has been scorned and I am going to bestow that same gift on the others so you can support in saving your miserable blinkered home. You are nothing to me, nothing." He panted, "happy now?"

Her lips were pressed in a tight line as she fought to keep the tears at bay. She whispered, "so, afterwards, you were just being polite?"

He shrugged, "who knows. We were both in shock. Now, if you'll excuse me I have things to work on."

He walked away, hating himself but it was the truth,

249

most of it. He had the sense that she had wanted to talk about them, just the two of them. Could he have handled it if they had? He swore under his breath at the Gods for messing with him and Miryama. Seriously, he thought, he could fuck any woman he wanted. Why then did he care so much about this one?

Miryama stared after him and realised the God had won the round. At least she had seen a truer side of him and perhaps it was best he didn't know about the pregnancy. But a part of her still craved his hand holding hers, wanted to feel his touch like back when he had made her a suwar, so gentle.

They should have been back by evening but the Suwars weren't too worried. They must have flown further than planned and were camping out but the Daughters of Scyth were worried and were up early the next day scanning the horizon as soon as the clouds lifted. It wasn't long before Suwars began to join them as well. Gaerwn visited Ozanus, "this doesn't feel right Nejus. If this was Keytel I wouldn't be worried, but anything could be out there. Should we send out others?"

"Maybe they've got lost." Diego remarked from the table.

"That is ridiculous!" Gaerwn exclaimed, "I'm going to send another group out."

"No." Ozanus up from the table of papers and the map, "tomorrow morning you can if they haven't arrived by then."

Reluctantly Gaerwen left but was planning for the worst.

It was two hours later when there was a shout of a sighting. Everyone ran to the east side of the mountain straining to see who was coming back safe, even Ozanus. The delay of their return had them all thinking anything could have happened to them. Six had headed out the previous day but there were only two returning. The two large dragons scrabbled to make traction on the mountain top from exhaustion. One of the Suwars leapt off, unwrapping his scarf and exclaimed, "those bitches! Those idiots!"

"Not here." Ozanus ordered, "back to my tent."
The suwar looked around and realised there was a very large crowd, some of them now frowning at the insults.

Miryama pushed through, "where are they? Where are Yasmin and Roxana?"

"It was disaster." One of the dragons remarked, *"my rider needs some help, he was injured."*

"Miryama, can you find Mada?" Ozanus asked as several Suwars ran forward to help their comrade down who was holding an arm in a rough sling with a bloody bandage wrapped round it. They turned to their Nejus and replied, "we'll look after him sir."

"Back to the tent for a debrief, now." Ozanus ordered. He turned and walked away.

"Wait for me." Miryama called out.

"This isn't going to be good." Ozanus pointed out as she caught up with him.

"I can see that."

The suwar was given a warm drink and stool to sit on. All eyes were on him. Ozanus ordered, "tell us what happened."

"You were right to be worried sir." The man said, "Temijin is about two days away, east of here. There is clearly a quicker route from Duntorn that way." He glanced over at Miryama and Elaheh before going on, *"the bitches! They took it upon themselves to attack."*
Miryama inwardly winced.

"Watch your tone." Ozanus warned.

"Sorry sir." The young man blushed. This had been his first chance to prove himself and it had ended in failure. "It happened so fast. One minute they were with us and then next they were attacking Temijin's convoy. I will admit they took a few men out, but they got too close. They had a huge arrow thing with them, and it took out Fleur. She flew into the smaller ones and they all fell to the ground. Temijin's men jumped on all of them."

"And Cordelia?" Gaerwn asked.

"She got too low trying to rescue them and got caught in a net that pulled her and Kinla down to the ground. She got out of the net and started to fight her way clear so we could rescue her but they took her out and Dominic got injured as well as he went down to try and get her."

"Thank you. Now I need the facts." Ozanus said firmly.

"Dominic has the map."

Diego turned to a Suwar standing at the entrance of the tent, "go fetch Dominic or at least the map."

The young woman slipped out and ran off. He continued, "if Temijin is only two days away then we need to check on the other half of his army. Gaerwn send some riders out, experienced ones and ensure they stay high."

Gaerwn clicked his fingers at another of the Suwars by the entrance, positioned there for such purposes, "you heard, go."

The scarred man saluted and left to organise a group to get into the air.

"Good. Now Willim I need numbers." Ozanus demanded, leaning on the table.

"Yes of course. There were about five hundred men and apart from the already made-up arrow thing there were what looked like five half built and another five that were like the ones that threw the nets back in Keytel. There were several carts loaded with stones as well."

Ozanus, Diego and Gaerwen looked at each other, what they had feared was coming true. Ozanus looked next to Miryama. She nodded, however much everyone would want their two sisters rescued that would not be happening.

And Ozanus had been right, Temijin knew the weaknesses of the mountain and Joli had given him the advantage he had been waiting for. She asked, "what do we do now?"

"We prepare." Diego remarked grimly.

"We have to destroy all of it." Gaerwn exclaimed, "if any of those stones land on here no one is safe."

"Everyone leave, I need to think." Ozanus said sternly, "but I still want that map."

It was good to have some peace. He glanced over at the hidden armour and murmured, "you'll get your blood soon."

He returned his attention to the map and finished filling in a rough idea of the landscape from Dominic's sketch. He twisted the ring on his finger as he considered his options.

There was no point sending everyone but he needed to send a large amount of them. Could he even trust the Daughters of Scyth to obey any instructions now? Was it going to be wise giving them all that waiting power hidden in the temple?

As if she knew he had been thinking about her she appeared at the tent entrance, wearing her breastplate, which had now been adjusted to fit her chest. She took a deep breath in to calm her nerves before saying, "I've come as the soul Suwar here on this mountain to pledge my allegiance to my Nejus."

He beckoned her in, "thank you, but what about the rest of them? You heard what happened? I can't have them doing their own thing if I take half of my Suwars to face Temijin. Can I be able to trust them?"

"I don't know." She admitted.

"You are their leader you need to make it happen. I am about to give them the ability to destroy Temijin's army but I need to be able to trust them."

"I can talk to them." She offered already knowing it

wasn't a good enough answer.

"I have one day at most to get them to work with my Suwars and after today not many of them are going to trust your fifteen women." He pointed out sternly.

"I'll talk to them." She repeated.

He gestured to a stool at the table as he said more calmly, "the other day, you wanted to talk to me, but I don't think we actually discussed what was on your mind. What do you want from me?"

She declined to sit down, "I don't know."

"We are stuck together because of that damn God and you need to be the one deciding. I was willing to put my faith in you and made you a Suwar. You don't have to like me or be with me but you will have to obey me." He declared.

"Is that the lot of a Nejus' wife then?" She challenged, "I deserve more than that. Do you know what I wear? I am wearing the breastplate of Scyth. That must mean something in your world of Gods and destiny? I bet you don't have any armour made of actual dragon scales?"

"No." He stared at her, taken aback by her outburst. Then he smiled before saying in a softer tone of voice, "as Nejusana you can have any sort of relationship you want, but as a suwar I expect loyalty." He tried to recall his family's history if there was ever a couple who had both been Suwars and what that had meant to Keytel but couldn't think of one.

She had no answer to that and turned as if to leave.

Thinking she was leaving Ozanus went back to his planning, trying to work out the best way to split who he had to keep fatalities down. He heard a cough and looked up and was surprised to find Miryama standing next to him. She bent down and whispered, "this is what I wanted to do that morning." She kissed him hard. Breaking off she was panting a little, "let's start again."

He nodded as he pulled her on to his lap and held her head to kiss her again.

Their sexual frustrations poured out then. He carried her to his bed which creaked under the weight. He unbuckled the breastplate and pulled off her shirt and buried his face in her breasts. He closed his eyes as he breathed deep her feminine smell. He could smell the wood smoke from the roundhouses mingling with a slight musty smell that was not unattractive.

Carefully, with glances up at her face, he undid her trousers and pushed them down while lying alongside her. They kissed again as she pulled his shirt off and they lay down with him holding her close. His hand ran down her side to her buttocks and gave it a squeeze before heading between her thighs. She tensed and then relaxed, letting his fingers explore as she turned her head so they could awkwardly kiss. She could feel his erection through his trousers pressing against her thigh but wasn't ready to have that penetrating her again.

She whimpered as he found a sensitive spot and he smiled as they kissed. He continued to rub it with his thumb as he pressed a finger inside her. Her body responded naturally to it even though her mind hadn't wanted it to. She felt herself getting wetter and tightened as he pressed a second finger in. She panted and clung to the arm round her leg as with a shudder and a long moan she came and pressed her thighs together to stop him. He tried hard not to think of the erection tight in his own trousers.

She began crying. He got up, uncomfortable with the tears and got her a drink. He pulled on his shirt and robe against the chill of the evening and silently went back to his planning. The crying subsided and glancing over in the lamplight he saw she had fallen asleep. He pulled the bedding up over her naked body before making up a bed on the ground for himself with a spare blanket.

At some point during the night she woke up, her eyes feeling puffy. She looked at Ozanus curled up on the floor, wrapped in the blanket and felt emotional all over again. He hadn't forced her to do anything she didn't want to. Somewhere behind his emotionless exterior was a gentleman. She slipped out of the bed, reached for her clothes, carefully crept round Ozanus and walked out into the night.

There was resentment on both sides when Ozanus gathered the Daughters of Scyth and the leaders of the Suwars together. Each were blaming the other. All the goodwill from the feast had vanished. There were several metres distance between them as they stood before Ozanus and Miryama. Others had gathered on the sidelines out of curiosity and some of the Suwars were making a circle between hand and thumb to protect themselves from bad luck. Ozanus chose to ignore it, "we have one day at most to organise ourselves into a fighting force to be reckoned with, including our newest fighters."
Depending upon how they did today would determine whether he would hold off on using the temple's energies or not, "I want at least one Daughter of Scyth in every group and I want to see you including her in your training. Miryama, anything?"
"No." She shook her head. He had made it all pretty clear. She would inform him later that if he flew out then so would she.
"Good, now get to work." Ozanus ordered while starting to think about when the group he sent off the previous afternoon would get back with hopefully no mishaps. He said to Gaerwn, "any sightings of our trackers, let me know and I want them in my tent as soon as they land."
"Yes sir."
Ozanus walked away.

Miryama crossed to her women to ensure they understood. One remarked, "he has a nerve and did you see what some of them were doing?"

"Enough Magnalia. They didn't have to come."

"His dragon didn't have to burn down the camp and infuriate Temijin." Magnalia retorted.

"And we didn't have to bring Lylya here."

"She needed rescuing from him. He's a brute."

"I understand why Yasmin and Roxana did what they did. We all want a piece of Temijin for what he did to our dragons and to us and Esfir. But they shouldn't have attacked, they were not ready and they endangered the whole group unnecessarily. You now need to all win back the trust. And as for what some of them were doing, I don't particularly care as once this is over they will be gone with only a few pregnancies to remember them by."

A couple of them blushed.

"Until this is over we will have to listen and obey. They know what they are doing as they have grown up with it and trained for this and used their skills unlike us."

"We've trained hard as well." Another pointed out with her arms crossed.

"And have we ever put it to use?" Miryama challenged back with a raised eyebrow.

The woman backed down, "no."

"Let's use this time to learn and next time we are attacked we will be able to do it without outside help."

There were nods then as they realised that.

"Now, you'd all best get going. Let's show our guests how good we can be, remember how we showed their Nejus."

With a few mutters they left and Miryama sighed with relief and then ran to find a bucket.

Thirty-One

Word began to spread that something important was going to happen that night and everyone was to dress in their ceremonial armour and ensure they were clean and presentable. There was no time for fasting and abstinence which would normally be required. No one knew what was going to happen, but it was a result of new information that Temijin's other half of his army were now making good time. Where they had first been spotted had been swamp land and now back on a hard surface, they had picked up speed, not what Ozanus had wanted to hear but he had already been planning it.

To add to the sense of mystery the clouds descended over the mountain so no one could see more than a metre ahead of themselves. They gathered in groups suddenly nervous and wary of what their Nejus and the Gods were planning.

Soon the time came for them to descend the mountainside on steps they hadn't known about, torches smouldering in the damp air and barely giving them enough light to walk by. Their senses heightened as with the dark and fog they were going by feel alone, feet seeking out the edge of each step before stepping down. There was relief at the sight of a fire on the ledge. Torches lit the entrance to the rock carved passage and the priest was shut away in his rock carved room with his apprentice.

At Ozanus' arrival earlier he had sworn at the man for bothering him and his temple again. He wanted full involvement in whatever the younger man was doing. Ozanus had fought the urge to kick the fat man off the ledge and see what the dragons would do to him. Sternly he told the man, "this is between me and my people alone. You do not need to know nor involve yourself. As a High Priest to the Gods I have every right to be here and use this temple for my purposes."

"The Gods won't approve." The priest tried to protest.

"The Gods do approve." Ozanus' eyes flashed gold. The priest retreated to his room and barricaded himself inside out of fear.

With the priest dealt with Ozanus had entered alone and stood on the dais at the centre of the cavern, eyes closed, arms out, savouring the power swirling around him. Under his newly adopted purple robe he wore his new breastplate. He moved his hand to rest on the handle of his knife and the energies pulsed. A small part of him wanted all the power for himself and go off on his own and challenge Temijin directly but that was not the Gods will. Like the rest he would get a piece of it and would have to wait. He took his hand from his knife. In an hour he could offer his blood up in exchange for his portion.

And now it was time. With only the barest of flickering torchlight the Suwars filed in, each pausing and staring round at what they were seeing and feeling. Was this what the temples of old use to be like compared to the ruinous one in their Valley home? Never had they seen the like and they all knew they would never again after this night. None had even known of untapped power like this had even existed. They all thought that the last of such powers bestowed on man had gone with Kittal when even he hadn't been able to save his wife from the demands of the Gods. Hands went to knives as they all knew instinctively what would be expected of them.

Before them, as they entered, they could see their Nejus standing silent and still in his purple robe. Their heightened senses in the flickering light of the four fire bowls kept throwing dragon shapes around him especially as his robe hung open revealing the unique breastplate that shimmered in the light. Laid on the altar were the knives to be handed out.

Of even more significance for the Suwars was that five of their apprentices would be given their knives. They had also heard a rumour that sixteen Daughters of Scyth would also be joining their esteemed group.

A hush descended as Gaerwn led the Suwars' five apprentices in blindfolded. They were pressed down on to their knees. Now they waited for the Daughters.

Apart from telling her when and what they all needed to wear Ozanus was relying on Miryama to ensure they all came. She had had some protests considering it involved the Gods until she told them of her experience down in the temple. She didn't know what convinced them more, the idea of a once in a lifetime experience or being given an opportunity to take Temijin out for definite. She didn't want to let Ozanus down and could only hope they would meet her at the top of the steps.

Waiting at the top of the steps in the green robe Ozanus had given her she was relieved as out of the fog her new riders started to appear looking a little uncomfortable in the breastplates that had been searched for throughout old chests. A few frowned at her appearance, thinking she was stepping too far into a role she only had temporarily.

She led them down the steps and then blindfolded

260

them at the entrance of the passage and as the most nervous protested she soothed, "trust me, you'll thank me once this is all over."

They held on to each other as Miryama led them down the corridor. She could sense the bodies in the temple pressing out the energies, causing it to bulge out into the passageway. The first, coming up against it, paused and started to step backwards. Miryama whispered, "don't resist, step through, embrace it."

"It's in my head." The young woman complained.

"It will go. See it like when you are training muscles to do something they've never done before. The Gods are reminding us how strong they are and how we have ignored them."

The girl took a deep breath and stepped forward.

A couple of Suwars came forward and guided the women to their knees so there were three rows facing the altar. Ozanus lifted his arms, "welcome everyone. Here in this hidden temple there is a once in a lifetime event about to happen. We welcome not just the five apprentices to our ranks but also the Daughters of Scyth."

His words echoed around and swelled in the air.

"Here, in this holy place we are to be honoured by the Dragon Lord with what we need to defeat Temijin."

There was a roar from the Suwars that was deafening. Over the top, as the men and women's came to an end, was a deeper one. They looked round trying to identify where it came from.

Ozanus held up a hand and the cavern went silent, "let us begin the ceremony. Bring the first one up."

Gaerwn pulled the first apprentice to his feet and ripped off the blindfold. The young man blinked, adjusting to the flickering light. He dropped to his knees in terror thinking Ozanus was a God, bubbling, *"please don't hurt me."*

"Arise apprentice."

Shaking the young man stood.

"Do you pledge to honour and obey the Gods and your Nejus. Do you pledge to defend the lives of all dragons?" The young suwar straightened his back and firmly said, "I do."

"Prove it." Ozanus gestured behind him to the altar where the knives lay out for each new suwar to select one for themselves.

With trepidation the apprentice approached the altar and selected a knife. He drew out the blade and sliced the palm of his left hand, allowing the blood to pool before letting it drip into the stone dish of water. He flinched when the water fizzed but when nothing else happened he turned and realised his Nejus hadn't been a God. Ozanus gave him a smile, "go and join your comrades."

The young man quickly went to where his parents stood and slipped in to stand beside them when they didn't embrace him as he thought they would. Discreetly his mother squeezed his hand.

The apprentices were quickly done. All were in awe of the magnitude of the event. Never again would they have witnesses to their vows of nearly all of the Suwars and in such an awe inspiring setting.

Next came the Daughters of Scyth. Directed by Gaerwn, Miryama stepped up to the first, pulled her to her feet and removed the blindfold. There were looks of disapproval as she promptly screamed and ran from the cavern. Sternly Ozanus remarked, "she will not ride again." The rest of the women were shaken as apart from the words being spoken they had no idea what was happening.

Next was Elaheh. She looked defiantly towards Ozanus as her blindfold was removed. His only reaction was a raised eyebrow and a twitch of a smile, "welcome Daughter of Scyth. Will you be the second to earn the title of Suwar?"

"Yes." She answered firmly. She had no desire to let this opportunity pass her by.

"Do you pledge to honour and obey the Gods and the Nejus of Keytel when it is called upon? Do you pledge to protect all dragons?"

"I do." Her back straight with pride, "and I will protect the Daughters of Scyth."

His only acknowledgement with the addition was a slow blink of his eyes. "Then prove it. Pick a knife which will mark you as a suwar and offer up your life blood to the Gods."

Elaheh looked to Miryama for guidance.

Miryama held up her bandaged hand and her friend nodded a thanks and stepped up to the altar. Selecting a knife she drew it out of its sheath and took a deep breath before slicing across the palm of her hand, biting back the pain as the blood dripped straight into the bowl. It fizzed and was then still.

"Join your new comrades." Ozanus ordered.

Elaheh glanced to Miryama who gave her a smile and nod. With her new knife held tight in her hand she stepped down and joined the Suwars. One kindly gave her shoulder a pat.

Some were bold and some were nervous as each one was un-blindfolded and spoken to by Ozanus. Most were in awe especially with the dragon looking over his shoulder which they couldn't work out whether it was alive or not.

Finally the last Daughter of Scyth had made their vow and stepped away. Ozanus took the last knife and broke the blade and left it as an offering on the altar. He paused then and took a few deep breaths to steady himself. He looked to the Dragon Lord statue for forgiveness before standing on the altar so everyone could clearly see him. There were gasps as no one defiled an altar by standing on it.

He knew what he had to do, a wild madness guiding him. He shrugged off his robe revealing that he was dressed as a suwar like everyone else except he had rolled one sleeve up. He called out, *"can you feel the energy? The power of the Gods is in this room!"* He held up his hand as he wanted to only hear his voice, *"we have been given this great responsibility by the Dragon Lord and in return he is bestowing some of his power on us all."*

He pulled out his knife and the metal reflected the fire in the fire bowls. Spontaneously they grew brighter as the energy in the room began to pulse. Behind him the Dragon Lord statue began to glow at the same pace as the pulse. Ozanus went on, "we must open our hearts, our minds and our bodies to the almighty Dragon Lord. Feed him and in return he will feed us."

As if hypnotised everyone pulled out their knives. The new Suwars squeezed their hands to open up the cuts they already had. Everyone else sliced open their scarred palms and let the blood drip to the stone ground. They felt the energies of the room begin to deplete as each person received their gift from the God.

Up on the altar Ozanus had gone one step further. He stood over the bowl and as high priest and Nejus he had sliced down his arm, blood pouring into the now pink milky water. He roared as he felt his own share of the Gods' power enter his body. They all roared in reply, feeling as if their dragons they rode and cared for had become part of them. Their reptilian strength was now part of them.

Suddenly the energy was gone. The air smelt cold and musty like a normal cave would with the oily smoke from the fire bowls. Ozanus remained standing, ignoring the pain in his arm letting the Gods have their full of him. He could feel a pressure on his self-inflicted wound as if something was sucking on it. He said loud enough for everyone to hear, "normally we would now feast but as we are to go into battle, rest, let those hands heal for I need everything you can give to defeat this bastard."

Everyone looking at him couldn't help but notice the long copper scaled body of the scarred War God wrapping itself around the altar and Ozanus and then seemed to slip into the man's body via the self-inflicted wound. Fear mingled with exhaustion and the anticipation of the fight ahead.

They began to leave, a few conversations happening in hushed tones. Ozanus waited until the last backs were turned and leaving before slowly lowering himself to sit on the altar, clutching his arm. Miryama and Diego ran over.

Diego was surprised that she had stayed behind. He couldn't help but think that his Nejus and her had a strange relationship and hoped it would sort itself out soon. He exclaimed at his friend, "are you insane?!"

"Possibly." Ozanus tried to smile and then more weakly added, "I think I need Mada."

"Why Ozanus?" Miryama demanded.

"He needed more from me to know I am His."

"Who? Which one? You have two vying for you."

"Does it matter?"

"The Gods demand too much of your family. Your father had to pretty much bleed out to be able to absorb all of the ancient powers." Diego remarked with a frown.

Behind them there was an ominous rumble. They all turned to look. Diego remarked, "I think it's time we got out of here. I think this cave has done its duty and with all that energy gone it's not going to stay up much longer."

"It can't cave in." Miryama protested as she quickly wrapped Ozanus' arm up, "that will be half this mountain gone. We can't have a huge hole in the middle of it."

"Maybe take it as a hint to move somewhere else." Diego

suggested as he pulled his Nejus to his feet.

"Where though?"

"That's something your council will have to decide. Come on, I don't want to get buried in here."

"They won't let that happen." Ozanus remarked as he began to shiver.

Miryama grabbed his robe and wrapped it round him and said, "keep that arm up. We can't have you bleeding out on us."

"Don't worry, He won't let me die."

They reached the end of the passage and with a large crack and rumble the passage collapsed in on itself and a cloud of dust swept around their legs. The fat priest ran out from hiding and exclaimed, "what have you done?!"

"It had finally done its duty." Ozanus remarked calmly.

"Duty? It's a temple." The man protested in disbelief, "did you do this?!" He turned to Miryama, "you lot have never taken this place seriously."

"Enough." Ozanus exclaimed. His eyes flashed gold and the man grabbed his chest and his eyes were wide. Weakly he asked, "what are you doing to me?"

"You are no longer needed. You served me poorly."
The last thing the priest saw was his Dragon Lord looking at him with disgust from Ozanus' face. He collapsed to his knees and then fell forward.

The little apprentice peered out and stared at his dead master and then at the three adults and back again. Diego said, "it's alright, he can't hurt you anymore. Come with me and we'll find you a new trade." He beckoned the boy out of the doorway, "it's not safe down here now. Come on, I need to get my friend looked at. Can you hold a torch for me? Light the way up the steps?"

The boy nodded. He took up a lamp from the priest's room and skirted round his master's body.

Thirty-Two

Reaching the top, the clouds had lifted, and a full moon shone down. Ozanus murmured with little idea of what he said, "a healing moon. My father was a healer, but he couldn't heal himself."

Diego and Miryama glanced at each other with concern, had Ozanus lost too much blood? Ignoring their own pain from their hands they hurried across the village to Mada's roundhouse. They burst in expecting to find her asleep, but it looked like she had been waiting for them. They dropped Ozanus heavily on the bed as Diego asked, "can you fix him?"

"I can but try. Let's see." She unwrapped the bandage as Diego kept his young master sitting up. Mada tutted, "what you all put yourselves through for the Gods is crazy."

"They ask it of us." Ozanus remarked coherently.

As she tied a piece of rope tight above his elbow to slow the bleeding Mada replied, "if that is what you want to believe. I don't know if I can stop the bleeding, but I can slow it. I'll have to do a few stitches inside as it looks like he cut a blood vessel. What was he doing?"

"What we all do to appease the Gods." Diego held up his own hand, "but, apparently, they wanted him to go one step further."

"Lie him down and hold his arm firmly as this is going to

hurt." Mada instructed.

Whether from pain or light-headedness Ozanus fainted and Mada took advantage. She quickly cleaned up the cut to see where she needed to stitch and then threaded a heated curved needle. With the internal ones done she did some more through his skin, into the muscle. She placed a poultice on the top and wrapped a bandage round it, "the poultice will cool it and hopefully let it knit back together. How are you my dear?" She studied Miryama.

"Slowly." Miryama responded with a tight smile. Changing the subject away from herself she remarked, "he mentioned a healing moon, would that help him?" Mada looked thoughtful for a moment before answering, "it's worth a try. He needs to bathe in some moon water."

"Moon water?"

"Anything that has had the moon reflecting on it can be considered the moon's while she is out but only if it's a full moon and all of her can be seen in the reflection so a bucket of water, no...."

"What about one of the pools?" Miryama suggested.

"Possibly, can't guarantee it."

"It's worth a try don't you think Diego?" She turned to the older man, "we're going to need him in a fit state."

"Can't do any harm I suppose." He shrugged his shoulders. He had never heard of the healing Moon himself. He pulled Ozanus to his feet, "come on sir."

"Just want to sleep now." He murmured, "need to be ready for today."

"I think it will be tomorrow, everyone will be sleeping today and you can soon but let's see if the moon pool can help."

"It won't, it will just bring trouble. It showed that God he was one and then he destroyed my family." Ozanus moaned.

Diego rolled his eyes, "you brought this on yourself so you

are coming." He pulled the young man to his feet.

Mada led the way to the pools above the waterfall. A breeze rippled the surface but the whole moon could be seen reflected in the bathing pool. They carefully stripped Ozanus and undid the bandage. Miryama led him down the steps.

Behind them Diego let out a long hiss of concern. The dragon tattoo he knew so well as he had tried to deter the young man from having it done had changed. When had it filled in with an ochre colouring. Mada put a hand on his arm to calm the fist she could see. He murmured, "the Gods…"

She nodded in understanding.

"What does this mean? Why do they do this?"

She didn't get a chance to answer as with a splash Miryama had pushed Ozanus in.

Ozanus came up spluttering, "what do you think you are doing?!"

His audience looked shocked as they hadn't expected that reaction. They had been preparing to save him from drowning, but the cold water had woken him from his daze. With relief they laughed. Ozanus staggered up the steps and held out his hand for his clothes. He glared at them, "what are you laughing about? Come on, we should all be getting some sleep." He walked off across the grass only to drop to his knees a minute later.

Mada remarked, "you'd best get him to bed. As long as he doesn't develop a fever he should be fine. One of you should watch over him though. I'll visit later to check on that wound."

Between the two of them they got him back to his tent and into bed. Miryama remarked, "I'll stay if you want."

"Are you sure? I think you need just as much if not more rest than me?" He raised an eyebrow.

She frowned.

"I'm afraid I overheard your conversation with Mada."

"So you know? Have you told Ozanus?" She asked with fear.

He shook his head, "we all have our secrets, including him." He nodded his head to the sleeping Ozanus, "are you going to tell him?"

"I don't know yet." She admitted, "what do you think?"

"That's your decision to make. But now you are very much involved with the Gods and like him you won't be able to escape though he tried to ignore them till a few months ago when they demanded his attention. Now, we both need to get some sleep. I'll stay, it's part of my duties." He pushed her towards the tent's entrance. With reluctance and relief she left.

Apart of him wanted to sleep the sleep of oblivion. The ceremony had taken it out of him and then the surprise cold dip but he wasn't going to get the empty sleep he needed. He felt a cool calloused hand on his forehead and his bandaged arm and he thought of his father. He moaned in his sleep and beside him Diego stirred as there was only the one bed.

Ozanus carefully opened his eyes not sure if he would find he was dreaming. His father stood beside his bed, bending over to check on him. He was dressed as if he had just come back from flying with Kite. Looking down at himself he was his six year old self before his heart was sealed away. His father gently said, "be careful Ozanus, you are playing with fire with the Gods and being reckless."

"I am under control."

"Don't let them drive you mad like my grandfather. I know you have his robe and his breastplate. It was that madness that did this to me, that killed my father." The ghost of Kittal commented mournfully, "why do you think I locked all of that power away for as long as I could. That's why I became a healer. I'm sorry I wasn't there to help you grow up and be a better man."

"I'm fine." Ozanus protested.

"But you are not at peace."

"Go away! You don't have the right to tell me what to do. You gave up that right when you left me when I was six!" Ozanus exclaimed, "you chose mother over your own children who still needed you!" He screwed his eyes tight shut.

The next time he woke daylight streamed in. His head ached, his shoulders where his tattoo was ached and his arm ached. He frowned as he tried to work out whether his father's visitation was a dream or a vision. He looked down at his bandaged arm and the night came back to him. He unwrapped the bandage to study his handiwork. It looked like it had healed more than it should have done in a matter hours, the skin had started to knit itself back together.

Diego and Mada walked in and Ozanus asked, "what is the hour?"

"Quite late. Everyone is starting to prepare themselves for tomorrow. Do you want something to eat and drink?"

"Yes." Ozanus carefully stood and walked over to the table, "how is everyone feeling after last night?"

"Keen."

"Fetch Gaerwn in a bit as we need to finalise the plans."

"Of course."

"Not until you have eaten." Mada remarked, "and I've looked at that injury of yours. What were you thinking?"

"I don't need mothering." Ozanus retorted, "I am no orphan who needs to be fussed over."

Mada raised an eyebrow in surprise as she crossed

to the table with lips pressed together in her disapproval at how he had spoken to her.

He ignored her as he was not in the mood for small talk. The conversation he had had with his father was eating at him. Was he slowly going mad? Was he too weak to handle the Gods now that they were making demands of him. But last night he was sure he had been in control until he had sliced his arm open. He had sensed the War God curling round the altar and his feet and then…. He shook his head, he must have imaged the God winding up his body and entering through his self-inflicted wound. He did feel different though but that could be the power from the cave.

Out on the rest of the mountain the Suwars were waking and preparing for the next day. There were those that were meditating, calming hyped minds so they would be able to concentrate with the new day. Others wrote letters to loved ones who were back in the Valley. Couples fucked either with urgency or slowly, gently, to remember the other by. One thing they all agreed on was Temijin would see them at their best and worst. There would be no running away this time, only complete destruction of one side or the other and it definitely wouldn't be them being destroyed.

The Daughters of Scyth ignored the pain and practised. Mada prepared with the other medicine women. They made pain draughts, poultices and bandages with no idea how many would return injured.

Diego, Gaerwn and Ozanus finalised plans. Gaerwn would go with a third of the Suwars and take on the army coming from the west. Ozanus would lead the majority east and confront Temijin.

Thirty-Three

The excitement of the forthcoming battle meant it was a restless night's sleep. Hearing the tent flap open he sat up and called out, "who's there?"

Miryama, in a loose nightgown appeared in the low lamplight, a blanket wrapped round her shoulders and her hair in a plait down her back. The lamplight made her glow.

"What are you doing here? You should be abed getting a good sleep ready for tomorrow. This coming battle might last all day." He said, surprised to see her.

"I cannot sleep because of you." She protested.

"Me?"

"Yes, you." He was an addiction she didn't want to feed, but she craved him as much as she wanted to hate him.

She climbed into his lap and pressed him down on to his bed and followed. She kissed him hard on the mouth and felt the gratification she knew she would get from it. She ran her hands over his bare chest and felt the toned muscles as his breathing grew more rapid. He gasped, "Miryama, we..."

She bent down and kissed him to silence him. She murmured in his ear, "let me, I need this."

She pulled her nightgown off and he stared up at her naked form glowing gold in the low light. He licked his dry lips and gasped as she reached beneath her and gripped his growing erection. He reached up and put his hands to her waist and held them there feeling her warm smooth skin. He watched her raise and then sit on his erection. She clawed at his chest, drawing red lines down it, as she slowly rode him. He had no control over the situation. He could only stare up into her face where her eyes were closed as she took pleasure from him. Her head rolled back and she moaned as she felt him come inside her closely followed by herself.

She slipped off him and curled up on his bed. Carefully he sat up, staring at her. He pulled the blankets over them both while feeling confused over what had just happened. He was used to being the taker of pleasure and here he was the one being used.

The one result was he slept more fitfully until Diego came to wake him in the morning. Diego raised an eyebrow of question as he saw Miryama in Ozanus' bed. Ozanus shrugged as he pulled on dusty yellow trousers and his boots, "how's it going out there?"

"Everyone is getting ready and your bed companion should be doing so as well if she is to fly."

"Miryama?" Ozanus called over his shoulder. Back to Diego he said, "can you get us both breakfast? And send someone across to get Miryama her clothes."

"Of course."

Turning to the bed Ozanus said, "you were awake already weren't you?"

She smiled beneath the blanket, "I was admiring your fine buttocks." She wondered whether to be afraid of the change in his tattoo and whether she should mention it to him.

"You are going to have to get up you know. I'm not going to be late because of you." He gruffly said as he pulled on his shirt.

Everyone was up in the air or nearly so when Ozanus walked to the centre of the village where Nimib waited for him already saddled and his bow and full quiver of arrows buckled on to it. His old team barely recognised him as he strolled with purpose towards Nimib. He wore his new flying clothes and the polished copper breastplate of engraved dragons. His sword was buckled at his side. As customary his dragon headed knife was tucked into his belts and he was pulling on his thick leather gloves as he walked. There was an aura about him, a hazy copper glow. This was a man who walked with purpose and intent to do some serious damage.

As Nimib helped him up into his saddle Ozanus asked of his new dragon, *"ready for this?"*

"They all are Nejus."

"Excellent, lead the way."

"It will be an honour." Nimib lifted into the air with a graceful flap of her wings and curved around the group of Suwars waiting. He could feel her gearing up for a roar and ordered, *"not a sound. We don't want him to know we are coming."*

He felt her deflate and in silence come to the head of the thunder of dragons where a rider with a horn waited so Ozanus could communicate.

At the front were the ones with no riders then behind them were the Suwars though once flying they would fly at different heights. Somewhere in amongst them was Miryama but he put thoughts of her away. He felt sure there would be plenty of time later to work out what their relationship would be.

The plan was for surprise as Temijin didn't know how many there were however it was them getting surprised as a huge boulder came flying in their direction, over to the left. It missed the solo dragons but slammed into

275

a suwar and the dragon-man pairing went tumbling down towards the ground. Ozanus shouted, "fly higher! Higher!" Everyone went up, just in time for another boulder to come flying past. Ozanus couldn't work out what Temijin was aiming at. It was too short to hit the mountain and didn't seem to be aimed at them. He looked ahead and spotted the catapult surrounded by men pulling it down and loading another stone. He raised his hand and held up all five fingers so his aide could pass on the message and then pointed forward with a flat sided hand.

The Suwat beside him did five short blasts and five Suwars split off, readying their bows and selecting an arrow. They dived down towards the catapult. Most of the men scattered, dodging or falling to the arrows. One stayed firm till the last and pulled the lever just as a small solo dragon descended, hind claws out ready to try and destroy the catapult by pulling it up if it could. Instead it received the full force of the boulder and went falling backwards with it. The man was quickly pinned to the ground by five arrows.

They had a quick scout around for the fleeing men while one of the Valley dragons pulled the catapult up and let it crash back to the ground, damaging it as it had only been pulled up by ten metres or so as it was too heavy to get any higher. They then returned to the rest of the Suwars, joining up at the back of the group.

Ozanus felt uneasy. He felt as if he had been purposely baited with the catapult and told Nimib to fly up higher. He stood up in his saddle and looked around. He spotted Temijin's army off to the right and shouted down, *"go right."*

They all turned in a gentle curve to adjust their direction. He unwrapped his scarf and shouted down to his aide, "one long blast!"

His aide blew long and hard on his horn and others within the crowd did as well so all knew they could attack.

In small groups they began to descend, excited but wary as they knew Temijin could be out to ambush them as they had heard he had his war machines ready even as he travelled.

Half of Ozanus' team from Linyee rose up to join him. Together they would be seeking out Temijin himself and either by arrow or sword Ozanus planned to take him down. One shouted out, "where to sir?"

"To the back. I think he likes to hang back and direct the show. We are going to stay high but take it in turns to dip down and don't take risks, we know how tricky he is. Look out for something that looks like a command post."

"Yes sir."

He hung back, still feeling suspicious and looked behind to check he hadn't missed anything. He couldn't see anything amiss. He wondered how Gaerwn was getting on.

Down below the fighting had begun. Though prepared for Temijin's war machines they were still surprised as without warning three huge arrows were flying through the air, taking two dragons out in their flight paths. They roared their pain and anger as one, taken in the wing, plummeted to the ground just shy of Temijin's front line of archers. The other dropped low enough for his rider to leap off and start fighting before flying away to either nurse his wound or die.

A large group decided it would be wiser to attack from the ground. Although renown for their skills from the air they were also extremely proficient fighters on the ground as well. With their two accompanying Daughters of Scyth their dragons flew them a safe distance away so they could jump off and run through the thorny dry scrub to Temijin's encampment. They hoped to take out some of the war machines before they took out too many dragons and riders.

They charged in from the right and instantly clashed with a group of soldiers guarding a catapult loaded with a net. Soon they were doing what they did best and trained for, fighting and even the two Daughters of Scyth were impressing them when any had a second to catch their breaths. The two women had discovered a taste for it and didn't even notice the blood being splattered across their bodies. They attacked like they were undefeatable, the swirling energy given to them in the cavern making them stronger, bolder. Dragons swooped down to try and pull apart the war machines.

Over to the left another group had landed and were coming in from behind the back of the front line only to find more than they were anticipating. The group that had flown over the other day hadn't see the second army following a day behind the men accompanying the war machines.   They had kept low, hidden under leaf covered nets. Their leader kept them there till they were almost being stepped on before shouting, "now!"
They sprung out of their hiding places and overwhelmed the small group of Suwars on foot. They kept fighting longer than normal thanks to the power of the Dragon Lord but slowly, one by one, they were defeated.

A group of Suwars flew over and with roars from their dragons they flew down low and grabbed men with their hind claws before letting them drop. Others were taken out by arrows from the Suwars. Any arrows that were fired up just pinged off the dragon's scales.

Another group of Temijin's men leapt into view and threw hooks attached to ropes to try and catch a dragon and pull it to the ground. They managed to catch one and began to pull it down but then one of the ropes snapped and the three men still holding on to the other two rose into the air with screams of terror.

Standing on a cart Temijin laughed as he watched his men dangling on their rope. He was loving all of the violence and destruction. He remarked to the men around him, "they seriously think that they can destroy me. They turned tail only a few months ago and I bet the Daughters aren't any help at all. More fool them. Have we any other surprises? I wonder whether he sent his full force this way because of me?"
No one answered as they knew the Nejus would be on his way.

Thirty-Four

Wary of the Suwars and going with them the majority of the Daughters sought Miryama out. They all wore helmets and chest plates raided from chests. They didn't have the confidence of the Suwars who didn't think they needed armour. Miryama wore the adjusted dragonscale breastplate and felt the weight of its past weighing on her. She had to do it's history justice.

They all had one intent in mind, seek Temijin out and kill him. They hovered back and one called out, "what do we do?"

"We fly around till we spot him. He's arrogant enough that we'll see him." Miryama remarked.

There were nods of agreement.

"Let's go."

Their dragons hadn't been trained for war and grew more skittish the further into the fighting they got. They flinched as arrows flew past even though they knew they wouldn't be hurt. Distracted by something below one was taken out by one of Temijin's large arrows. With a scream rider and dragon fell and the rider was instantly jumped on. One of the women cried out, "we've been given this supposed power and it's killing us. What a waste of time!" Miryama wasn't going to admit it, but she wondered what it had done to everyone as well. She didn't feel any different apart from the current lack of sickness. Observing those fighting they didn't appear to be any stronger and as she didn't know everyone's skill levels she couldn't tell if they were any better.

With one of them gone the dragons decided they had had enough and all apart from Spilla and Calluna turned and fled. Elaheh shouted, "this is not good!"

"Let's get out of the sky. I'll feel happier on the ground."

"Me too. Where should we go?"

"Spilla, there's a space over there, get us close and we'll jump off."

"Is that wise?" Spilla asked, eyeing up the fighting below, *"perhaps you should team up with Ozanus."*

"We don't need him." Miryama retorted and she couldn't see him anyway, *"just do it Spilla."*

On the ground she and Elaheh pulled out their swords. Elaheh asked, "where to?"

"He's got to be leading this from somewhere. Ozanus said he was at the back of the fighting in Keytel so let's head to the back. Take care."

"You too and we'll kill the bastard."

"Yes we will." Miryama grinned with the thought of plunging her sword into his heart to avenge Esfir's death.

"Let's get going before we are spotted." Elaheh ran forward and quickly encountered her first soldier as above them some of the Daughters had got their dragons under control and were now arriving as reinforcements, dropping to the ground ready to participate.

Temijin was getting impatient. The only person he would fight today was up in the air amongst all of his Suwars. Once he realised he had been deceived he had set out with his army, splitting it in two so that he could hit the two weak spots at the same time. He was not happy that Ozanus had not expressed love for his arena but what did

281

he expect from a filthy dragon lover. Then his sister had mysteriously disappeared and he had fallen for Ozanus' trap to go get her back. He was sure the man had lied about having no knowledge of the bitches that called themselves the Daughters of Scyth and who was Scyth anyway?! He felt his anger growing and he shouted, "where is he?! It can't be that hard to spot?!"

There was a whisper in his ear, "look." He spun round but there was no one there. He glared down at the men standing around the cart he stood on, the horses tied up nearby so they couldn't suddenly run off in fear. Their ears were pressed back and their eyes were white and they would bolt if they could. There was the whisper again, "look."

He could feel a breath tickling his ear and then out of the corner of his eye he saw a copper scaled snout. He turned again but there was nothing there. There was a chuckle, "you don't get to see all of me non-believer but I will fuel your rage. Now look."

A copper claw pointed out into the battlefield, one clawed toe ripped off.

Temijin looked along its length but he quickly turned his head to try and see who was guiding him. The limb disappeared and it snarled, "what did I just say?! Now look again. Down there is Esfir's lover and now she is Ozanus' and his wife and carries his unborn children. How's that for good fortune? Have her and you'll get him." A smile was forming on Temijin's face which turned into a grin. He shouted down, "Edgar, Cerdic, get up here."

"You bellowed sir." Edgar said, heaving his bulk up on to the cart.

"Over there, see the group of women, they are the so called Daughters of Scyth, the thorn in our side. I want them here."

"All of them?"

"You'll be guided to the right one."

Edgar frowned in confusion.

"Have faith." Temijin smirked, "now get going. This will mean that traitor will come and I will kill him myself, watch him bleed to death at my feet begging for mercy pompous arrogant prick." He chuckled to himself and rubbed his hands together.

Edgar and Cerdic rounded up a few men and they moved with intent through the fighting, slicing at a clawed foot that got too close and not getting engaged in any one-on-one fighting where possible. Considering the Suwars were the smaller force they were controlling the fighting and though some fell many seemed to have endless amounts of stamina and just kept going and going.

They came upon the Daughters of Scyth and surrounded the group. As each killed their opponent one of the Temijin's men stepped in with a grin and quickly disarmed the majority. Miryama and Elaheh kept fighting, leading the group further and further into the battle like a leaf in a stream with the fighting flowing around them. The first two men to try and disarm them lost their lives. Cerdic stepped in and found himself facing up against Elaheh. He gave her a smirk, "you are feisty, aren't you?"

"Come and get it you bastard." She beckoned him towards her, daring him. With two hands on her sword she swung it at him and he defended it with his bigger blade. She felt the vibrations up her arms and he pushed her backwards with the weight of his arms. She stumbled over a body and fell to the ground, dropping her sword. Her eyes grew wide and she scrambled for a weapon as he came bearing down on her with a grin, "not so confident now."

He froze and his body shuddered as he felt an arrow in his back and turned his head. At a steep angle was an arrow buried in his back clearly having come from above. With a roar of frustration he grabbed a spear sticking out of a nearby body and threw it upwards, hoping to strike anything, he didn't care what.

Elaheh was hauled to her feet and arms twisted behind her back. She fought to free herself but stopped when there was a hissed warning, "stop or you'll get a knife across your beautiful throat. Hurry up and get the last one Harrin. Which one did Temijin want?"

"You want this one." A voice said and a claw grabbed Miryama by the ankle. She looked down and saw it. She exclaimed, *"no you don't!"*
She tried to shake it off but with her attention distracted Harrin stepped in and twisted her sword out of her hand. She quickly grabbed her knife from her belt and slashed him across the face. He shouted in shock and let her go. She kicked with her free foot at the God's claw and began to run, stumbling over bodies as she went.

She could hear the man panting behind her after he had ordered for the others to be killed. She was starting to think she was in some nightmare she would shortly wake up from. They had been doing so well till the War God had decided to make mischief. She still didn't know what he wanted with her and Ozanus.

The man behind her shouted, "get her! I need her alive!"
Men turned and one large man, holding a sword, stepped into her path. She slammed into him and started to fall backwards but he grabbed her and pulled her hard to him.

She still had her knife and she stabbed her captor in the side with it. He stepped back and released his hold on her as he hissed, "bitch!"
She turned and glared at him, "no one is taking me. I will die by my hand if necessary."
She turned and ran, her determination to kill Temijin renewed. He was her problem not Ozanus' and she would deal with it. The Gods or Scyth clearly thought she was

284

capable of doing it.

She spotted a sword and grabbed it from the ground as she continued through the fighting, occasionally having to fight someone off. Before she was prepared she stumbled out of the fighting, ducking as a dragon flew low overhead. She paused for breath as she looked ahead, through the scrub. She saw Temijin standing on a cart.

She took a deep breath, refocused, and marched forward before Temijin spotted her. She adjusted her hold on the stolen sword and unconsciously checked her knife was at her side.

She emerged from the bushes and shouted, "Temijin, I am here seeking revenge."
He turned and fought back surprise. He put his hands on his hips, "well, well, I've underestimated you, but I don't care about you."

"You are mine, not Ozanus'." She shouted, standing her ground.

"I'll use you as a warmup then." Temijin jumped down from the cart.

As he headed towards Miryama he pulled his longsword out of its scabbard. He raised it so it pointed diagonally up, ready to swing it at Miryama. It looked heavy and slow but once it was being swung it could cut a man in half. He thought, one swing of it and she would be dealt with and perhaps with the head cut from the body the Daughters of Scyth would be no more.

Miryama ducked under the sword and as he twisted with momentum she sliced through the back of his padded jacket. She stepped back to keep away from his huge sword. He was realising the sword was too big against her nimble feet. He stabbed it into the ground as he roared, "get me a smaller sword."
One of his lieutenants threw him one in a scabbard. He drew it out and instantly went on the attack.

She was pushed back and back, defending herself all the time, her sword up and tiring her arms. She stumbled and found herself on the ground with Temijin standing over her laughing, "you fool. I'll just have to kill you now."

Thirty-Five

Up in the air Ozanus and his team of Linyee Suwars were still circling. Temijin had been identified but Ozanus wanted to ensure the battle was going in their favour before confronting Temijin. Some of his Suwars had gone to fetch help when they spotted some of their comrades in difficulties. Miryama and a group of her women had also been spotted and as they were handling themselves well Ozanus had left them to it.

Having done a few circles of the battlefield and satisfied there were no more active war machines he turned first to check where Miryama was but couldn't see her. Then he saw War flying alongside him, dripping blood and grinning maniacally. Ozanus exclaimed, *"have you not had enough yet?!"*

"Oh, I get very thirsty. Keep it up and I might be satisfied. Your men are doing an excellent job." It laughed at Ozanus.

"What do you want?"

"Ooo, straight to the point, I like you. Your great grandfather always wanted to try and talk his way out of it. You've accepted me. Take a look Nejus, can you see what I can see?"

"It's not like I can get rid of you." Ozanus retorted bitterly, *"all I can see is a ferocious battle."*

"All that anger, it was far too tempting." The God

drooled, savouring the controlled rage radiating off the man flying beside him.

"Look more closely, she carries our children."

Ozanus stared at the God, *"our children?"*

"Has she not told you?" The God asked in mock shock.

Ozanus snarled, *"no."*

"Oops. Well, we are getting off track. Have you seen your wife recently?"

"Why?"

"Look ahead."

Ozanus looked and saw Miryama stumbling and falling with Temijin leaning over, ready to stab her with his sword. She kicked out at him but it didn't do much apart from anger him. He exclaimed, *"you bastard!"*

The God disappeared with a chuckle, *"she has that same fire inside her."*

Ozanus ordered, *"Nimib, get me down there fast!"* He reached for an arrow but found his quiver empty and realised he would have to clear his own path. He climbed out of his saddle and on to Nimib's upper arm and then swung himself down so he hung from the dragon's forearm.

Nimib got as low as he could, with Kenene and his dragon following behind, but Ozanus was already dropping down, landing on a soldier and slicing him through the throat with his knife. Another approached thinking he was an easy target until Ozanus swung round with a snarl and slashed at the man with his sword.

That bubbling anger that simmered inside him started to boil and overflow as he moved through the fighting. Anyone looking at him would have seen the shimmering form of a scarred copper dragon around him. He was angry at his parents, the Gods, himself and Miryama. All of that rage was now being used to kill and maim a path through to Temijin who was gloating at the back of the battlefield thinking he was safe. He didn't care who he took out and even lashed out at any of his own men and women who didn't move fast enough out of his way.

He stepped out of the fighting and roared, "Temijin! It's you and me, let her go."

Everyone froze and the battlefield went silent. It hadn't been a man they had heard shouting. Blood ran cold and some found their bowels loosening. Miryama's stomach lurched as if was going to miscarry, but the embryos clung to the wall of her womb.

Temijin turned away from Miryama and stared at Ozanus. He had to blink and rubbed his eyes to check he what he was seeing. In a blink of an eye the burnished copper dragon form was gone but a sense of it lingered in the air, watching, waiting.

Time unfroze and everyone returned to their personal fights. Temijin stepped over Miryama and swung the pommel of his sword at her head knocking her out. He sneered, "coming to rescue your used whore? Carries your bastards you know."

Ozanus, face set in a grim expression took a few steps forward and re-gripped the hilt of his sword and put away his knife, unfazed by Temijin's taunts.

Temijin started circling Ozanus with mock jabs of his sword, hoping to lure his opponent into spinning on the spot and getting dizzy. Ozanus kept an eye on it but wasn't tempted. Instead on the turn of his heel he swung at Temijin as he came to Ozanus' right. Temijin's reflects were quick enough to defend himself. Neither moved for a moment, testing each other's strength.

Ozanus stepped back as he felt Temijin retry pushing all of his strength into his sword, unbalancing his opponent and with a flick of his wrists sliced across Temijin's arm. Temijin roared out his pain and frustration and lashed out. Ozanus dodged again, completely composed and slashed Temijin's back, his sleeve riding up to reveal his bandage.

Temijin's eyes glinted at the weakness and wondered how long before Ozanus' arm would start to tire. He decided to keep pushing him on that side and if he could get a few hits all the better. He stretched his back to test what muscles had been cut by Miryama and then Ozanus and was satisfied his padded jacket had protected him from the worst of Ozanus' sharp blade. He retreated a few steps to compose himself as recognised he was making mistakes and he knew he couldn't continue doing so with his skilled opponent.

He adjusted his hold on his sword before swinging it at Ozanus. They clashed again and for a minute they went through the rhythms of defending and attacking until Temijin managed it, hard with the flat of his blade he hit Ozanus' bandaged arm. Ozanus gritted his teeth to keep the shout of pain locked inside him. He couldn't stop himself from hugging it to his chest for just a second while fighting back tears.

Ozanus knew he was weakened but he looked into himself and found his inner strength and that power from the cavern he had absorbed. He went in for the attack again but was distracted and he only realised when he felt his arm being sliced into that he was. He refocused his mind while still watching Temijin and concentrated on the swing of his sword and where it was going. It jarred through his arms and he felt Temijin pushing him and his body letting it.

Breathing heavily he found himself on one knee. Temijin laughed and looked around to see whether anyone was watching. He was too slow in turning back as with a grunt he was thrust forward. He coughed and felt blood rising up his throat. He felt a hand come round and his throat was slashed. He dropped like a stone to the ground when he was let go off.

290

While Temijin had been starting to gloat, thinking one last swing of his sword would be enough to kill Ozanus, Ozanus had pushed himself up with his sword. He was tired of playing Temijin's game now and thrust his sword in and up Temijin's back till he felt sure it was about to come out the other side. He pulled it back out and let it fall to the ground as he pulled out his knife. For good measure he grabbed the bigger man hair, pulled the head back and slashed Temijin's throat from ear to ear as he whispered, "never turn your back on an angry animal." He closed his eyes with relief as the dead man slumped to the ground.

He opened them and Temijin's men were hesitating around him. Some were contemplating fleeing, others had itchy hands over their swords, trying to find the courage to attack the man who had just killed their lord. Eyes flickered upwards as dragons approached and made their decisions for them. Some turned and fled. The rest took a step back and held their ground, wary but curious.

He felt the wind from flapping wings and looked up as three of his men swung down from their dragons. They had been circling, ready to kill Temijin if their Nejus had been killed. They were in a celebratory mood as they ran towards Ozanus but he held up a tired hand and they came to a halt in front of him and waited for their orders, "it's not time to celebrate yet. Kenene, we need men to go after his men before they can rally the troops. Homer go check on Miryama." He was too tired to move, "Charin, get the horn-bearer to blow the signal that we have won and find Nia. She needs to fly to Gaerwen and tell them it's over and Nimib."

They all saluted and ran off as Ozanus slowly crossed to the cart where Homer knelt at Miryama's side and helping her to her feet. More Suwars arrived and made it clear that no one was welcome. There were clashes between

Temijin's lingering men and Ozanus' warriors. Ozanus was oblivious to the scraps happening around him as he approached Miryama.

He stumbled backwards as Miryama flung herself at him. She reproached, "how could you?! I was meant to kill him."

"He had you on the ground!" He protested angrily. Then he sighed, "let me sit down, just for a moment." He made his way to the abandoned cart and sat on the edge of it feeling drained, not helped by the blood he had lost already. She carefully approached and with a softer tone observed, "you are hurt."

"I'll survive. What about you?" He spotted a cut on her head. For himself time would tell if he would be able to hold a heavy bow. Where he had cut himself it was feeling weak, not helped by Temijin hitting it and ruining anything the Moon or his father had done to help it heal. He brushed some loose strands of hair from her cut, "we need to talk."

"About what?"

"Nejus, I am here." Nimib called down.

"Later." Ozanus remarked sternly as he became leader again. He climbed on to the cart and pulled himself up on to his dragon and back into his saddle. Above them a horn was blown twice, two long blasts. The battle slowed and cheering and roaring was heard.

Up in the air Ozanus surveyed the scene. He remarked to Nimib, *"we are going to have to burn the bodies."*

"Sir, I cannot as yet." She remarked. Though she was now considered an Alpha dragon having become the Nejus' she had yet to develop the heat in her belly to breath fire. That took time.

"Don't worry, I'll use Joli and we'll need to find the injured first. Can you fly a little lower, I need to speak to them all."

292

"Of course sir."

She dropped down and Ozanus shouted, "attention men of Moronland! Temijin is dead! Killed by my hand. Leave this place now and if I hear of any dragons being harmed then you will face my wrath. Go now, take your injured for this place will burn by this evening."

Everyone was staring up as Nimib soared low over them all.

Ozanus' attention was called away as a dragon called out, *"Nejus!"*

The dragon came from the direction of the mountain. It's rider shouted, "sir! We need help. Temijin's catapults were aimed at the waterfall and they drained the pools and now there's a hole in the middle of the mountain where the temple was. We need more Suwars to help defeat his men. Also, to the northeast of here there are boulders coming from somewhere hitting the dragon nesting area."

Ozanus swore before saying, "I've just sent a messenger, Temijin is dead."

"Congratulations sir."

"Nimib, we need to get Miryama and then head back to the mountain." He glanced behind and saw Kenene behind him on his dragon and called out, "Kenene, take some Suwars and head northeast of here. There are some catapults we didn't know about, destroy them. Don't underestimate them."

"Yes sir." Kenene called back and urged his dragon to circle so he could gather up some Suwars.

"Yes sir." Nimib turned and headed back to the rear of the battlefield.

Ozanus swung down on to Nimib's forearm as he called down, "Miryama, grab hold and I'll swing you up." He held out a hand and she reached for it. He winced as her weight pulled at her injured arm. With a grunt and Nimib's help Miryama clambered on to his saddle.

She felt small sat on the back of Nimib even with Ozanus' arm round her waist. She asked, "where are we going?"

"Back to your home, there's trouble." He answered stiffly.

"What about the injured? And you talked of burning."

"My Suwars will look after their own and I'll burn the dead, there will be too many to bury or make individual pyres for."

"What's happening at the village?" She asked with worry.

"Apparently you no longer have a waterfall and the cavern has collapsed in on itself."

"Oh no. *Nimib, please hurry.*" She said to the dragon.

They circled the mountain, taking in the damage. The waterfall had gone. Boulders filled the bottom pool and there was only a dribble of water filtering through the rocks where the spring used to be. They narrowly missed a boulder aimed at the dragon nesting site which was crumbling as well, huge boulders now lying at its foot and ledges missing pieces. The dragons were up in the air, frightened. Close to the centre of the village was now a sinkhole where the roof of the cavern had collapsed in on itself. The wreckage of the smithy could be seen in it. Ozanus remarked softly, "I'm sorry Miryama. It looks like you are going to need a new home for all of you."

"But where?! We've known nowhere else."

"You'll come up with something. At least Temijin is dealt with and I'll ensure he doesn't have anyone to continue it on."

She nodded.

"Take us down." He said sombrely.

Thirty-Six

He left her to find out what was happening to seek out Lylya and Diego. He was ready for sleep but he needed to check they were safe. Lylya flung herself at him, tears on her cheeks, "Oh Ozanus, I'm relieved you are alive. Are you hurt?"

He shook his head, lying, as she hadn't seen his wound. To distract her he asked, "I need to ask you something but first can you tell me where Diego is?"

Lylya stepped back and brushed the tears away, "I don't want to tell you this, but he's dead."

"Dead?!" He wasn't liking hearing that word associated with Diego's name even if he had foreseen it.

"The hole in the village, he was talking with the smiths. They all went with him."

He didn't know how to react. Cautiously he asked, "have we a body?" At most his friend and advisor deserved the best burial possible.

Lylya shook her head, "no and I don't think we will get his body either. Ozanus, I'm so sorry." She went to touch his arm but he pushed her away, he needed to think. He changed the subject, "Lylya, I need to know who Temijin's top men are. Who was planning to succeed him or oust him if they wanted to?" He started walking towards his tent.

"What?" She had to trot to keep up with him, "Ozanus,

you need to stop and mourn."

"I don't have time."

"Time?!" She exclaimed, "you've just killed Temijin, haven't you? I'm guessing, considering you are here. You've earnt a day off now." She grabbed hold of his bandaged arm outside the tent and he gritted his teeth as her nails dug into it, "Ozanus, stop!" She pulled him round, "you haven't stopped for the last few days."

"Not yet Lylya. I need to find Joli and burn the dead and then need to start planning the next moves. I've just won a country. I need to go to Duntorn and ensure they know I now own them."

"I don't think anything will be happening in Duntorn yet, it will take them a few days to get there and the dead can wait. I'll write that list if you rest. And, what have you done to your arm? I know you too well not to notice you are hiding something."

She pushed up his sleeve and stared at the blood-stained bandage, "I think I need to look at this. What have you been doing to yourself?"

"Everything and more." He knew he wasn't going to win against his sister and gave in. With a groan he collapsed on to the bed and was asleep before he knew it.

He hadn't planned to fall asleep as he had far too much to think about. He needed to decide who would run Moronland now that it was technically his; whether there were any supporters of Temijin's that he would need to ferret out, hidden in the countryside and towns. And for the sake of his ego, after Temijin's strike he wanted to check he could still draw and hold a bow steady. He didn't know whether he had foolishly damaged some nerves and the muscles he had cut needed to heal. Then there was that God given power that hadn't risen in him and he wondered what had become of it.

Like a female dragon guarding her egg Lylya

wasn't for letting anyone disturb her brother. With tears running down her face she wrote the list Ozanus wanted as she also mourned Diego's passing. Both Gaerwn and Kenene were sent away. She looked up as the tent flap moved again and shouted, "get out."

Miryama froze at the entrance and asked, "is Ozanus here? I haven't seen him for a while."

"Go, you've caused enough trouble."

Miryama looked confused, "what do you mean?"

"If it wasn't for you, he wouldn't have injured yourself or be exhausted." Lylya's voice was growing louder.

"Enough sister." Ozanus called from the bed as he slowly sat up trying to undo his breastplate. He frowned at his torn sleeve and freshly bandaged wounds and wondered what that had happened, "what time is it?"

"Time for doing your duties sir." Gaerwn remarked as he stepping in, hoping to find his Nejus awake this time, "thanks for your support, we finally wore them down, though this mountain doesn't look like it's going to stay habitable."

"I've got stuff to discuss with you Gaerwn but can you find Joli first? I've delayed the burning of the dead." Ozanus asked as he stood and searched for a clean shirt.

"You need to eat first Ozanus." Lylya said with concern as Gaerwen left the tent.

"Later." He waved a hand at her, "have you written that list?"

"Yes." She answered sullenly.

He finally registered Miryama was still there, "how is your village? Are the injured being taken care of? How's the head?"

"We are having a meeting in the morning to discuss what to do about our home. Do you have to go?" She tentatively asked.

"Nejus duties call me." And he headed out of the tent.

They heard the roar of the dragon for several miles around and everyone fit enough to be on their feet stood at the edge of the mountain saw the silhouette of the dragon in the dusk light and then saw the hot flames begin to burn. They closed their eyes as they remembered their fallen comrades.

As one large group they moved to the waterfall side and watched as Joli lit the ground of bodies with his flames. They smelt the rancid smell of burning flesh and pitch used to grease the war machines and could feel the heat. They stood for a long time but slowly one by one and in small groups they returned to their camps to get drunk as they mourned. The Daughters of Scyth sang their laments, an eerie sound for what should have also been a night of celebrating but no one was in the mood for that.

By midnight the only light still glowing on the mountain top was in Ozanus' tent where he and Gaerwn were discussing the Suwars' return to Keytel via Duntorn and the arena. He had his sister's list so knew who he needed to capture but that still left the power vacuum that would need to be filled.

They decided a few days of rest would do no harm to anyone and then they could also advise the Daughters of Scyth of anywhere suitable they could move to. It was only then that Ozanus went to bed, still thinking but he let sleep absorb him.

He dreamt of flying towards Duntorn, the sun on his skin. He felt a heat beside him and there flew the Dragon Lord. They flew in a companionable silence. Finally the God spoke, *"you have done well so far."*

"Thank you sir." He answered warily.

"It is true that your wife bears your children but one must be killed."

Ozanus tried to hide his emotions. He was surprised but

also not at the same time. He wondered why Miryama had yet to tell him but maybe she didn't know yet.

"One is not as it seems and must be killed at birth otherwise great destruction will occur across the land and many will die."

"Why should I believe you?" Ozanus challenged.

"Do you disbelieve me?"

"Why do you keep testing me?"

"Because you need to see the Nejus you can be." The God replied calmly and in the blink of any eye disappeared leaving Ozanus feeling frustrated that nothing was simple.

Miryama had kept her distance as she hadn't wanted to tempt fate. Lylya also seemed to be protective of her brother and she wasn't sure why she had turned against her. What did she know that Miryama didn't?

Admittedly she was busy with the council. The fight was over and now they had to find a new leader. Apart of her was relieved that she couldn't stand considering the pregnancy and her mixed emotions in regard to Ozanus. She wanted him gone so she could clear her mind of him but a part of her wondered what life would be with him.

Before she knew it the eve of his departure came and it felt too soon. She knew he was heading to Duntorn and then more than likely back to Keytel and as was traditional with the Daughters of Scyth he would never know she was pregnant unless she birthed a son, but this would be a special son for he would be heir to Keytel.

She hesitated outside the tent, trying to hear if there were any voices within but it was quiet. She slipped in and found him gently cleaning his stitched wound. He glanced up as he began to wind the bandage back round it, "Miryama, how are you?"

"How are your wounds?"

"Oh, they'll heal and be added to my collection." He

answered dismissively. Wary, as he didn't know what she wanted and the last times she had come visiting late they had ended up in bed, he asked, "what can I do for you?"

"I..." She found herself lost for words. It wasn't what she really wanted to say but she said, "thank you." It was like the Gods had her tongue if she even thought of telling him she was pregnant.

"Not a problem." He said gruffly. He glanced up again and saw her frowning in her frustration at herself, or was it him? He stood to head to bed as he wanted a clear head for the morning as he didn't know what he was going to find in Duntorn.

He hesitated in telling her to leave. They stood staring at each other, neither daring to say a word or make the move that needed to happen. What might have happened was slipping away because neither wanted to reveal what they knew to the other. He turned away from her and headed to bed. She called out, "Ozanus?"
He looked back but she couldn't speak as she realised it was over for them, the spark hadn't been properly fed. She added reluctantly, "good luck."
He grunted and returned to getting ready for bed. She left, maybe it was a good thing the fire had gone out if this is what he would be like. And anyway, she was a Daughter of Scyth and was a strong independent woman.

Thirty-Seven

Wounded Suwars were out to see their Nejus and the group heading out with him. A few more days and the less seriously wounded would head back to Keytel with tales to tell. The majority of the Suwars had left the previous day.

Before climbing into his saddle he approached the council, "thank you for your hospitality and allowing those too injured to return home to remain until they are well enough to."

"It is the most we can do for coming here and ridding us of Temijin. We wouldn't have been able to do it by ourselves." Mada answered for the council, "and thank you for sharing with us possible places we could make a new home." She glanced over to Miryama who was looking at her feet and wondered what had happened between her and Ozanus considering how promising it had been. She watched Ozanus as he bowed his head and then wrapped his headscarf round his face. She caught the barest of glances in Miryama's direction and hid the smile- ha! He would be back.

He was glad to be in the air since it had become tense between him and Miryama. He still didn't understand what had been going on between them and now he was flying away he could forget all about it. He had more important things to worry about then some silly woman who couldn't decide what she wanted. But she wasn't a silly woman. She fascinated him. She was a skilled fighter, brave and could clearly lead. What more did a Nejus need in a wife?

He shook his head, he really didn't need to be thinking about her. He had Duntorn to deal with.

Soon Duntorn was in sight. It was not a place Ozanus liked, too money and man orientated. The group slowed down and circled the stretching suburbs and the original walled town with its tower. They couldn't see any suspicious activity. They continued with the plan and landed by the fishponds. The dragons rose back into the air with Nimib heading to the tower to perch ominously on top of it, the stonework cracking under her weight.

With bows at the ready and swords loose at their hips they headed up the road towards the double arch of open gates in the wall of the original town. No one seemed to be around, scared inside by the arrival of the dragons, even the guards at the gates had hidden away, peering through a hole in the shutters of their guardroom. Ozanus was wary of the quiet, fearing an ambush in retaliation to the fact he had killed their ruler.

They moved cautiously up the wide road and into the town. The roads and lanes were empty. Citizens peered curiously through their windows but no one attacked. They had heard of the God man from the few soldiers who had already made it back to Duntorn and now he marched through their streets dressed for a fight.

They reached the tower and found the doors open. Ozanus and Kenene looked to each other with raised eyebrows in question. Kenene looked behind and said, "take care with every step."

They nodded their heads, slung their bows and unsheathed

their swords. It was suspiciously quiet as they entered as if everyone had fled, clearly Temijin's deputies were cowards unless they were recruiting in the countryside to prepare for a reprisal.

Temijin's hall was empty with the tables and benches set out for dinner. Ozanus ordered, "stay here, I've got a room to check."

"Take Homer with you at least." Kenene said with concern, "and be careful."
Ozanus nodded and beckoned the man forward so they could team up and head up the stairs together. He knew where he was going, Temijin's study where all his maps and notes were. He smelt smoke and ran down the corridor and swung the door open to find everything burnt. Homer appeared in the doorway, "why have they abandoned this place? They so could have held out here."

"I think we need to be prepared for a regrouping and a possible attack. Let's go back down and get everyone in the courtyard." Ozanus kicked at a pile of half burnt books in his frustration.

"Yes sir." Homer ran down the stairs.
Ozanus crossed to the window and threw open the shutters. The view out of the window was of the arena in the distance. He gripped the windowsill in his frustration. He would have liked a fight to finish it off and then install a caretaker while he worked out what to do with the country. He knew the Daughters of Scyth wouldn't want the responsibility.

Returning downstairs someone had already fetched his saddlebags. He pulled on his purple robe as Kenene said, "the town leaders are gathered in the courtyard sir."

"Excellent, let's go."

Hush descended on the courtyard as Ozanus stepped out of the tower. He quickly surveyed the courtyard. His Suwars were standing around the edge, hands on hilts, keeping an eye out for trouble. The townsfolk were glancing warily at the armed Suwars and at Ozanus. With their attention on him Ozanus spoke loudly, for all to hear, "Temijin is dead. I killed him myself. I am Nejus of Keytel and defender of **all** dragons. I now rule this country and the arena will be destroyed. No dragons are to be harmed ever again. If I hear that any of you plan revolt or learn of it and don't inform me then there will be consequences. Now, where is everyone that resides here."

A councilman of the city stepped out of the crowd, "sir, they have fled but I can't tell you where."

Another man, stepped out of the crowd, red haired Sigwear, "sir, I hope I can help you."

Ozanus recognised the man and beckoned him forward as he said to everyone else, "if anyone hears anything I want to know straight away."

He turned and returned to the hall with Sigwear and Kenene following him. Outside the crowd talked amongst themselves.

Inside, Kenene asked, "what do we do now?"

"I need someone to fetch Lylya."

"Lylya?"

"Yes, Lylya." He answered sternly, he wasn't going to explain himself. Then to Sigwear he said, "I need to know what side you are on?"

Sigwear hesitated at the tone of his new overlord's voice, "sir... I serve whoever needs it."

Ozanus scoffed.

"I am no fighter sir but I know this country. I can share my knowledge with you and help whoever you chose to govern this country."

Ozanus now knew why Diego had liked the man. He was a kindred spirit. He remarked as he gestured to a table and they both sat down, "she will definitely need your help but first I need it. What happened here?"

"Some of his cronies, yes I use that word willingly, got here, told us he was dead and then headed to his study."

"A lot of the paperwork has been burnt."

"They won't have wanted you to know what they know."

"How likely are they to actually try to fight back. I have a list here Lylya made me of everyone who would probably be a threat and you are also on it? How much can I trust you?" He pulled the list out and showed it Sigwear.

The man glanced over it, "only about two on that list could pose a real threat. All the rest were hangers on, enjoying the power from being by Temijin's side while it lasted. Some of them were talking of Gods and monsters when they got back here. His mistress hasn't any children by him so none of them will rally round her to put a child on the chair and rule through them."

"Good. Would they attack here or just be a thorn in my side?"

"That I cannot say. They are their own men." Sigwear shrugged. He had managed to stay employed in the tower through the fact he kept quiet and watched and listened, much to Temijin's glee. Temijin had liked his knowledge and the fact he dealt with all the boring complaints that came in from the people of Moronland.

Lylya was not happy to be back in Duntorn even if Ozanus was encamped there. It held too many ugly memories. She entered the town and found Ozanus sat on the dais working on paperwork with Sigwear close by while listening to a complaining resident. She was surprised to see him doing something so mundane as that was what Ioan did.

He looked up as he heard her footsteps on the stone floor as he had had the reed flooring removed. He waved the townswoman away and stood as she approached, "am I glad to see you."

"Why am I here Ozanus?"

"I have a proposal for you."

"A proposal or an order?" She asked suspiciously.

"Let's walk in the garden." He stepped down off the dais.

In the little walled garden they were the only ones in it. She couldn't wait any longer and demanded, "what's going on brother?"

"I need you here, here in Duntorn." He answered sternly.

"Why? One of the Suwars could stay. What about Ioan? He's always wanted to rule in his own right?" She objected, "what about the Daughters?"

"I have thought about this alot and you are the best fit. Any rebels will recognise you as Temijin's wife and I won't leave you here alone. You will have some of my Suwars and you've got the Daughters of Scyth who I'm sure will gladly support you as they owe me. As for them leading I don't think it will be an option for them at the moment."

"I think Miryama would be more than capable." She offered.

"No." He sharply retorted making her take a step back with fear. More calmly he went on, "as for Ioan, I need him in Keytel however much he might moan." And he didn't trust Ioan to not take advantage and suddenly become a new enemy and claim Moronland and Keytel. He would see if Kenene wanted to stay here in Duntorn for the moment to support his sister.

"And if I was to say no?"

"There is no choice." He sighed, "I can't stay here." He rubbed his forehead as if a headache was forming, "I am not going to argue with you Lylya."

"All you are going to go back to is playing at soldiers." She protested.

"And be Nejus of Keytel. I thought you would be happy to be doing something other than living in the Valley. You deserve more than floating round the house looking pretty, use that mind of yours. You'll have Sigwear to help you." She walked away, without agreeing to anything.

With that issue half dealt with, for he felt sure his sister would come around to the idea, he had a horse saddled and went to the arena. He needed to free any dragons still there. Without the crowds creating the atmosphere it felt like a sad place and he could smell the fear and death that the dragons had spoken of when they had first flown into Moronland.

He walked around the outside and then found his way into the basement. The lions and dogs were back in their cages. A few criminals looked hopeful as he walked past before sinking back on to the floor. He found three dead dragons, flies humming around the wounds that had killed them.

There was a roar overhead and they looked up to see the surviving riders of the Daughters of Scyth flying over the city. Lylya frowned, "what are they doing here?" Ozanus smiled, "the last piece of revenge. Let's head to the roof and watch." He headed into the tower at a quick pace.

Lylya had to run to keep up with Ozanus who was running. Up on the roof in the shadow of Nimib who was perched there they saw the Daughters circling the arena. Nimib asked, *"can I go too?"*

"Wait, let them have their revenge first." Ozanus put a hand on the dragon's claw and patted it.

Nimib huffed with frustration above him.

Across the city over at the arena the Daughters of Scyth on their dragons were taking it in turns to fly down and break parts of the wooden seating off with their claws and throwing it to the ground. Miryama, on Spilla, watched

307

on. She should have felt joyful at the destruction of the arena but she felt angry. It should have been the finale to her triumph but instead she would be stepping down to whoever was elected and a cursory thanks given to her. She wondered whether she should defy their traditions and just claim the leadership. She knew she would have Ozanus' support; she felt sure of it, and didn't he now rule Moronland?

She began wondering then if she should go to Duntorn and speak with him about a multitude of things. She glanced towards the city wistfully. Would he see her? She wanted to scream her frustration out but controlled herself though her hands were fists. Spilla could feel the tension, *"want to talk?"*

"No." She responded sharply.

The dragon turned its head to eye his rider, *"you sure."*

"It's human matters." She replied sternly.

"Do you know, this would make a good home for the dragons? Let's take ownership of this place, this country."

She paid more attention to the arena and the surrounding area. Spilla was right, the dragons could use the arena as artificial cliffs to nest on and they weren't so many that there wouldn't be room to grow, and she was sure there would be some new blood coming if any dragons had mated. There was plenty of flat land around it for the Daughters of Scyth to create a new village. This was a perfect opportunity for the Daughters of Scyth to finally wield the power! She would take Moronland for them if she had too. She heard a familiar chuckle but instead of being afraid of it she smiled. She called out, *"enough!"*

The dragons and riders turned to look at her and she went on, *"this will be our new home."*

"Are you crazy? The place recks of death." A dragon protested.

"Temijin is dead and now it's our turn to rule this land."

308

The riders glanced at each other wondering if this was Ozanus' influence.

"It's time we stopped hiding. We are perfectly capable of ruling." Miryama added, "the arena is a good alternative to natural cliffs. We should give it a try at least."

"No harm in that." One of the riders replied with a shrug. "We probably should find a new home before we elect our new leader. This can be temporary, can't it?" She looked to the others to see if they were in agreement, and they nodded.

"Well let's go pass on the good news." Miryama carefully smiled, careful not to reveal her secret thoughts and ambitions.

Epilogue

The fortress of Linyee definitely emptier without Diego's presence. The men and women were more sober but were bored so more squabbling was happening especially without Kenene there to control them. Apart from one venture back over the mountains to support Kenene, Lylya and the Daughters against a small uprising little was happening. The borders were currently safe since word had got round of the God Nejus' defeat of Temijin.

In the quiet of dawn he would work on his archery but there was a shake in his hand however much he tried to ignore it. He was Nejus and no one needed to know he now had a new weakness.

He took to standing at the battlements of his tallest tower looking out at Keytel and the distance mountains. Occasionally he thought about Miryama but would push the thoughts away. He didn't need images of her distracting him from he didn't know what. He realised he should probably find himself a wife and make an heir….

"The time is upon you."
He really didn't want a visitation from the Dragon Lord. He thought he had done everything requested of him so why was he bothering his sleep now. Ozanus demanded impatiently, *"what now?"*

"Your children are soon to be born and one must die. Kill it, burn it, destroy it so nothing of it remains."

"Why do you do this to my family? What happens if I refuse? I cannot kill an innocent just because you demand it."

"Then you will suffer the consequences." The Dragon Lord vanished.

Ozanus called out, *"and what would they be? Screw you, screw all you Gods. I've had enough of all of this."*

He flew to the Valley the next morning after telling his company of Suwars it was over. He strode into the house surprising everyone. He found Ioan still abed with his mistress. Ozanus rolled his eyes and remarked, "just make her your wife."

"Ozanus?! What are you doing here?" Ioan sat up in surprise, "it's early."

"It's all yours."

"What's all mine?"

"Get out of bed and come to the temple." Ozanus ordered and stomped out of the room. He didn't want to waste any more time tha,n necessary now the decision was made. He would turn nomadic with just himself and Nimib to look after.

Ioan and Shuang came to the Valley's ruined temple and found Ozanus before the altar dressed in his purple robe. To one side crouched Nimib watching on out of curiosity. Their brother turned to look at them and frowned briefly at seeing his younger sister with Ioan, "thank you for coming."

Ioan sighed, "what do you really want Ozanus?"

"You are to become Nejus." Ozanus grinned at him.

"What?!" Ioan looked shocked.

"Well, you always wanted it and now you can have it."

"It's not that easy Ozanus." Ioan protested.

"I think we can make it as easy as we want." Ozanus smirked, "and I, as Nejus, am telling you that I am stepping down and you can be Nejus."

311

"But no one will respect me, I don't have a dragon."

"Ioan the Dragonless has a good ring don't you think and you have the Suwars. Just remember to look after the dragons and the Gods won't bother you." Ozanus replied cheerfully.

"Is everything alright with you brother? Where will you go?" Shuang asked with a frown. Ioan was up himself enough as it was, and she really didn't want to live in the Valley if he became Nejus. Maybe she would go to Moronland and stay with Lylya.

Ozanus shrugged, "not sure yet, where the winds take Nimib. Now Ioan, you want this or not?"

"Of course I do. I still think this is far harder than you are making it out to be."

Ozanus shrugged, "you can do what you want when I'm gone. Now come here. You need to offer up your blood so the Gods know."

"They will know already." Ioan protested, not liking the idea of purposely cutting himself. Also he felt sure the Gods would not approve of all of this. Even if he was Nejus his brother would still be high priest and Defender of all dragons. And he didn't like the rumour people were calling him a God from the stories that had been coming back from Moronland. Unlike Ozanus, who seemed to have become impulsive, he had researched it all as he had in the past debated wresting the title from his older brother.

"Oh don't be a wimp." Ozanus grabbed his younger brother and dragged him across to the altar, "open your damn hand."

"I'm sure they don't need my blood."

"They live off it so show them you are willing to be Nejus."

"What about all the other parts of the ceremony?" Ioan protested remembering the two days of preparation when Ozanus had come of age to accept the title in its fullest

responsibilities. He tried to pull his hand out of Ozanus'
tight grip.

"What, the purification process? I don't think you can
survive two days without eating or a week without sex so
as high priest I say don't worry."

"You've always wanted this Ioan, just get on with it.
Ozanus is giving his blessing rather than you having to do
everything for him. You'll be making the decisions in your
own right." Shuang pointed out.

"Fine." Ioan reluctantly said, "and you aren't going to
change your mind?"

"Ha, no chance. You've always wanted it more than me
anyway." Ozanus laughed as he drew out his knife.
Ioan noticed the slight shake in his brother's hand but said
nothing. That would be something to store away and
exploit another day.

Ioan gave in and held his hand out. Ozanus kept
hold of it as he turned to the altar, *"oh Great Lord I am not
worthy to be Nejus of Keytel. I pass that responsibility on to
my brother, Ioan."* He sliced open Ioan's palm and let the
blood drip into the bowl on the altar.

There was a rumble of thunder. Ioan frowned, sure
that was a sign of disapproval, but the Gods would get used
to it. Ozanus glanced up as well and shouted, *"tough!"*
He let go of his brother's hand, shrugged off his great
grandfather's robe and laid it on the altar. To his brother he
said, "good luck."
And with apparently no care in the world to hold him down
he crossed to Nimib and climbed into his saddle.

"Where do we go sir?"

"Moronland first. I need to see Miryama. Let's go." Even
if he didn't kill the child as the Dragon Lord demanded he
was curious to see how Miryama would react at seeing him.
He felt sure there was unfinished business between them.
Nimib stretched out her wings and with one flap of them

313

rose into the air.

Most of the Daughters of Scyth had moved to set up a fort on the edge of Duntorn that they could live in and continue their traditions and also act as Lylya's guard of honour. What few dragons had stayed with them had taken up new homes in the ruins of the arena. The rest had been abandoned to their own devices as the battle had shown them not worthy to be ridden. The only people left on the mountaintop was Mada and her assistant and Miryama.

For the moment Miryama was going to let someone else look after the Daughters until she was ready to return and claim the leadership she was convinced was rightfully hers. She hadn't decided yet if she would take Moronland as well. She wondered if Lylya would be willing to be sister rulers.

Miryama felt sure she had to stay though she couldn't explain why to either herself or Mada. Her pregnancy advanced and she grew bigger and towards the end struggled to go further than a bucket for yet another wee as her bladder was squashed by the twins. She had never been pregnant before but even she knew there something different about it, not helped by War having been involved. The two babes shifted inside her again and she felt sure they were fighting with each other again especially as a breath was forced out of her.

She tried to be strong but with her body feeling bruised from the inside all she wanted to do was cry. There had been flickering contractions all day so she knew they would be coming. A part of her wanted Ozanus there in the hope he would know what to do. She sat on the bench under Mada's eaves dressed in a plain high waisted wrap dress to allow space for her bump. As it was a cool day she wore a light robe over the top left behind by Lylya on a short visit. She wondered how she was getting on as ruler

314

of Moronland. She heard a shout from her dragon, *"a dragon approaches."*

She kept her eyes closed. Since Temijin was gone the dragons on the mountain had grown more daring and a few, from unknown places, had passed through.

The two babes went still and she suddenly felt all of her muscles around her womb contract. It nearly took her breath away from relief as well as pain. She called out, "Mada."

"Yes?" The old woman appeared with a frown.

"I think it's time." She gasped as another contraction happened.

"Are they in a hurry?"

"I don't know but this is better than them fighting." She laughed as she let Mada pull her to her swollen feet and lead her into the roundhouse.

Softly Mada said, "kneel against this." And helped Miryama kneel against a high-backed birthing stool and pulled the skirt of the dress out of the way. Miryama groaned as another contraction happened.

Both women looked up as they heard a shout, "hello? Anyone here?"

"No one but the others know we are here." Miryama remarked with a frown.

"No one can get up here without a dragon and that is not a woman's voice." Mada pointed out.

They looked at each other with fear. Mada found a rusty spear and handed it to her assistant, "guard the door."

Her assistant was wide eyed but did as she was told. She glanced back to Miryama as the pregnant woman let out another long moan.

Miryama felt as if she was going to split open as the twins inside her started one final fight for seniority. With a winner decided she felt it squeezing through her. She called out, "Mada!" Blood pooled on the floor.

"Careful Miryama, you need to control it. Take a deep breath and then push." Mada said calmly as all first mothers were the same, panicking from what was happening.

"It's going to kill me!" Miryama cried out with fear, "if that God ever wants to rape me again he will lose that cock of his!"

Mada laughed.

"Hello?" A voice called out in concern.

The assistant peered out the door and exclaimed in excitement, "it's the Nejus!" She ran outside calling, "in here!"

He was a little taken aback to have Mada's assistant running over to him and grabbing him by the hand. She dragged him towards the roundhouse, "Miryama is soon to birth."

He stopped, "I don't think it wise for me to enter."

A voice from within shouted, "don't let him in! He doesn't need to know."

"Who is here?" Ozanus demanded.

"Only the three of us, Miryama, Mada and myself." The assistant answered.

From inside the roundhouse came a long low moan followed by silence and then the cry of a newborn infant. He realised then that Miryama had been made pregnant by either himself or the War God.

Inside Miryama peered round to look at the child Mada had caught as it slipped out. She cautiously asked, "is it human?"

"Of course it is." Mada said as she wiped the filth of birth from its skin.

"So the second will be a beast then." She exclaimed.

"Don't be foolish." Mada scolded, "now rest for we don't know how fast the second will come."

The answer came within half an hour. She felt as if

316

her insides were being clawed as it moved down out of its hiding place for eight and a half months. She wept now as Mada knelt on old knees to catch the second and grimaced at the sight of it.

It was an ugly deformed thing with an arched back where the spine showed through the skin like the back of a dragon. The fingers were definitely claws and the face was drawn back in a grimace showing sharp teeth. Mada knew Miryama should not see it and hoped Ozanus would know what to do. She quickly wrapped it up in an old blanket and took it outside before it revealed its arrival. She thrust it at Ozanus, "get rid of it."

"I cannot."

"I think you will if you care to look." She retorted, "and I must get back to the mother."

He was wary of doing so but still he opened up the bundle expecting to find a perfectly formed baby that he would have to kill. He heard a cackle over his shoulder, *"that one's mine."*
Ozanus stared straight ahead as he hid the child from the God's sight, *"but you won't have it. It will die tonight."*
Slowly he walked towards the hole in the centre of the mountain. He knelt down and unwrapped it. It withered on the blanket and then looked up and stared directly in his eye, daring him.

He pulled his knife from his belt and knelt down trying not to stare at the monstrosity Miryama had just birthed. If it had looked like a normal child he probably would not have obeyed the Dragon Lord's command but this was easier to do. He wasn't sure how he was going to react to Miryama though since she was the one who had birthed it. One thing for certain though was their other child must never know.

He stabbed down into the fragile chest where he could see the heart frantically beating away. It squealed a protest as the knife slipped easily into its heart and deflated as the last breath was drawn. He quickly wrapped the 'thing' (he couldn't call it a baby) and the defiled knife into the blanket and threw it into the hole, having forgotten what the Dragon Lord had told him to do.

There was a rumble and a piece of the edge of the hole went tumbling to bury the evidence. He returned to Nimib and grabbed his great grandfather's armour. He didn't need this anymore either. As he got it out, he said to the dragon, *"find Spilla and then find a farm nearby, this place isn't going to survive much longer, we need to get off it."*

"Of course Ozanus." She lifted up into the air as he crossed back to the hole. He threw the armour in shouting, *"have this back as well! I am no longer Nejus, I am just a man."*

He knew his new knife would have a plain handle; he didn't want to be recognised as a suwar even if he did fly a dragon.

More rock began to fall and he felt the whole mountain shake. He ran back to the roundhouse and called out, "we have no more than an hour before this whole mountain goes."

Mada appeared frowning, "we can't go anywhere. She has just given birth."

"I'm sorry, but the Gods are done here, the final act is done and now it will collapse in on itself as one hides what needs to be hidden and forgotten and another rages. I've sent Nimib to find Spilla and a nearby farm. Grab what you all need and be ready." He snapped.

"Let him in." Miryama called from inside, "everything we need is in here."

Ducking through the door the stench of blood and sweat swamped his senses and he felt War in him take in a big gulp of bloody air. As his eyes adjusted to the gloom he

318

spotted Miryama sitting on the birthing stool, tired but awake. She held tight to their son. She gave him a tense smile and then frowned, "where is the other?"

"Stillborn." He lied.

She seemed to accept it.

"I know it's not ideal but we need to leave."

"I understand, I felt the shaking. What are you doing here?"

He shrugged, "I was passing through. I have given my brother the title, he is better at ruling Keytel than me anyway and Lylya is doing a good job of ruling Moronland. I am going to travel like my father did, explore new countries."

Her eyes widened in surprise of Ozanus' confession while Mada moved around them packing things into bags. She helped Miryama wrap the baby close to her chest and said softly, "we'll get him feeding once we are away from here."

Nimib and Spilla returned as the women and Ozanus came out of the roundhouse, *"we found a farm near here."*

"Excellent, let's hope they will be friendly." Ozanus answered, *"Nimib, can you carry Mada and her assistant and Spilla you'll have Miryama with me."*

"I can't carry both of you." Spilla protested.

"It is only a short distance." Ozanus replied sternly. Nimib snapped at Spilla to put him in his place. Sulkily Spilla answered, *"fine."*

"Thank you."

They were soon in the air. Mada and her assistant clung tight to Nimib's saddle. Her assistant's face was buried in Mada's back with her eyes tight closed. Beside them on Spilla Ozanus had an arm wrapped round Miryama's waist. One of her hands cradled her son and the other held Ozanus' hand. She leant back, ready for sleep.

He murmured, though he didn't know if she heard it, "it won't be long."

Behind them with rumbling, crashing and splashing and exclamations of shock from the inbred dragons that couldn't leave, the mountain carved itself in half. For a few days after there were still rockfalls happening.

Author's Note:

As an independent author I would like to thank you for purchasing this book and I hope you have enjoyed it. With no support from a big publishing house every purchase and review mean something to me so please spread the word and write a review. You can find me on Instagram as @f_garstang_author and let me know personally what you thought. You'll also see what I am working on and what will be coming out.

I am a multi genre author and I also have the below out:

Historical: The Crusade's Secrets
Historical Fantasy: Kukulcan's Messenger
Fantasy Series: The Defenders of the Valley
                    The Lost God
Romance: Biker Leather and Woolly Sheep.

Thank you

Made in the USA
Middletown, DE
29 August 2023

37438852R00179